MW00618999

Dare It All for Love

The Daring Daughters Book 5

By Emma V. Leech

Published by Emma V. Leech.

Copyright (c) Emma V. Leech 2021

Editing Services Magpie Literary Services

Cover Art: Victoria Cooper

ASIN No: B094WC9MDK

ISBN No: 978-2-492133-31-2

Other Works by Emma V. Leech

Daring Daughters

Daring Daughters Series

Girls Who Dare

Girls Who Dare Series

Rogues & Gentlemen

Rogues & Gentlemen Series

The Regency Romance Mysteries

The Regency Romance Mysteries Series

The French Vampire Legend

The French Vampire Legend Series

The French Fae Legend

The French Fae Legend Series

standalone

The Book Lover (a paranormal novella)

The Girl is Not for Christmas (Regency Romance)

Audio Books

Don't have time to read but still need your romance fix? The wait is over…

By popular demand, get many of your favourite Emma V Leech Regency Romance books on audio as performed by the incomparable Philip Battley and Gerard Marzilli. Several titles available and more added each month!

Find them at your favourite audiobook retailer!

Acknowledgements

Thanks, of course, to my wonderful editor Kezia Cole with Magpie Literary Services

To Victoria Cooper for all your hard work, amazing artwork and above all your unending patience!!! Thank you so much. You are amazing!

To my BFF, PA, personal cheerleader and bringer of chocolate, Varsi Appel, for moral support, confidence boosting and for reading my work more times than I have. I love you loads!

A huge thank you to all of Emma's Book Club members! You guys are the best!

I'm always so happy to hear from you so do email or message me :)

emmavleech@orange.fr

To my husband Pat and my family ... For always being proud of me.

Table of Contents

Family Trees

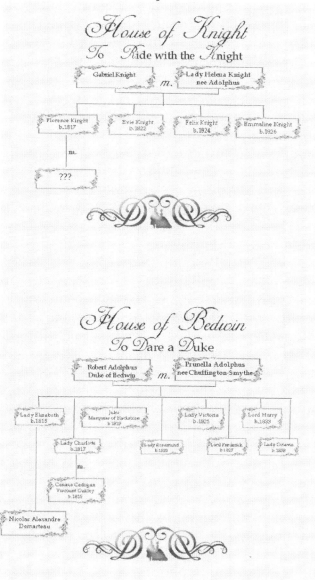

House of Knight
To Ride with the Knight

Gabriel Knight *m.* Lady Helena Knight nee Adolphus

Florence Knight b.1817 | Evie Knight b.1822 | Felix Knight b.1824 | Emmaline Knight b.1826

Florence Knight *m.* ???

House of Bedwin
To Dare a Duke

Robert Adolphus Duke of Bedwin *m.* Prunella Adolphus nee Chuffington-Smythe

Lady Elizabeth b.1815 | Jules Marquess of Blackstone b.1819 | Lady Victoria b.1825 | Lord Harry b.1833

Lady Charlotte b.1817 | Lady Rosamund b.1925 | Lord Frederick b.1827 | Lady Octavia b.1838

Lady Charlotte *m.* Cassius Cadogan Viscount Oakley b.1815

Nicolas Alexandre Demarteau

1

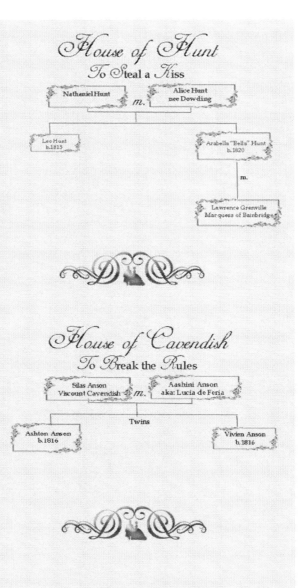

House of Hunt
To Steal a Kiss

Nathaniel Hunt — *m.* — Alice Hunt nee Dowding

Leo Hunt b.1815

Arabella "Bella" Hunt b.1820

m.

Lawrence Grenville Marquess of Bainbridge

House of Cavendish
To Break the Rules

Silas Anson Viscount Cavendish — *m.* — Aashini Anson aka: Lucia de Feria

Twins

Ashton Anson b.1816

Vivien Anson b.1816

House of Trevick
To Follow her Heart

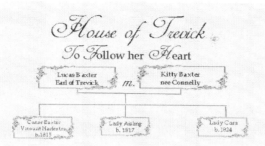

Lucas Baxter
Earl of Trevick

m.

Kitty Baxter
nee Connelly

Conor Baxter
Viscount Harleston
b.1815

Lady Aisling
b. 1817

Lady Cara
b. 1824

House of St Clair
To Wager with Love

Jasper Cadogan
Earl of St Clair

m.

Harriet Cadogan
nee Stanhope

Cassius Cadogan
Viscount Oakley
b.1815

m.

Lady Charlotte Adolphus
b.1817

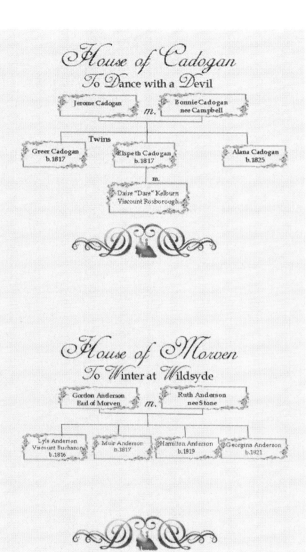

House of Cadogan
To Dance with a Devil

Jerone Cadogan *m.* Bonnie Cadogan nee Campbell

Twins

Greer Cadogan b.1817 — Elspeth Cadogan b.1817 — Alana Cadogan b.1825

m.

Daire "Dare" Kelburn Viscount Roxborough

House of Morven
To Winter at Wildsyde

Gordon Anderson Earl of Morven *m.* Ruth Anderson nee Stone

Lyle Anderson Viscount Buchanon b.1816 — Muir Anderson b.1817 — Hamilton Anderson b.1819 — Georgina Anderson b.1821

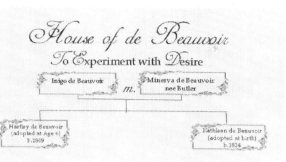

House of de Beauvoir
To Experiment with Desire

Inigo de Beauvoir   *m.*   Minerva de Beauvoir
nee Butler

Hartley de Beauvoir
(adopted at Age 6)
b.1809

Kathleen de Beauvoir
(adopted at birth)
b.1824

House of Rothborn
To Bed the Baron

Solo Weston
Baron of Rothborn   *m.*   Jemima Weston
nee Fernside

Larkin Weston
b.1816

Grace Weston
b.1821

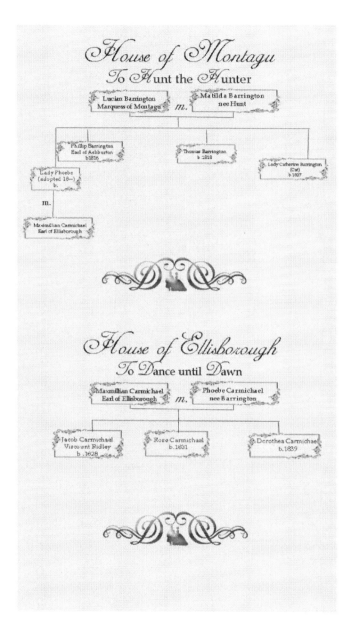

House of Montagu
To Hunt the Hunter

Lucian Barrington
Marquess of Montagu

m.

Matilda Barrington
nee Hunt

Phillip Barrington
Earl of Ashburton
b.1816

Thomas Barrington
b.1818

Lady Catherine Barrington
(Cat)
b.1827

Lady Phoebe
(adopted 18—)
b.

m.

Maximillian Carmichael
Earl of Ellisborough

House of Ellisborough
To Dance until Dawn

Maximillian Carmichael
Earl of Ellisborough

m.

Phoebe Carmichael
nee Barrington

Jacob Carmichael
Viscount Ridley
b.1828

Rose Carmichael
b.1831

Dorothea Carmichael
b.1839

Prologue

Dearest Harriet,

I am certainly up to the challenge of getting your brother married. The dear man is far too handsome and kind to spend a moment longer alone. Truly, it would be a crying shame if he does not find a wife. I agree that wretched girl did him so much damage when she jilted him. I suppose we must take what comfort there is in knowing her marriage is such a disaster. Throwing Henry over for a titled bully of a man was the most idiotic thing she could ever have done. Ambition is a strange thing that blinds some people to the reality of what their lives could be. I wonder if all her jewels and her title are a comfort to her now?

We must show Henry everything he could have, if only he gave up his bachelor's existence.

—Excerpt of a letter from Matilda Barrington, The Most Hon'ble, The Marchioness of Montagu to Harriet Cadogan, Countess St Clair.

9th August 1839, Saxenhurst Hall, Sussex.

Henry stared at the hawthorn bush and frowned. That was… odd.

"Good afternoon."

Startled out of his contemplation of the peculiar scene, Henry turned as a voice hailed him from the neighbouring field. He was on the farthest border of his estate here, a narrow strip of land that jutted out at an angle like a feather on a bonnet. It was the first time he'd walked the considerable border in a decade, not that he'd accomplished it all in one day. On two sides it was surrounded by the grand estate of Holbrook House, which belonged to his sister's husband, the Earl of St Clair. On the third, the land was owned by a gentleman farmer, whom Henry had not seen since the fellow was a boy.

"Good God. Sterling?"

A boy no longer, he gave Henry the benefit of a crooked grin and raised his hand in greeting. "Don't tell me, I've grown."

Henry laughed as the fellow climbed the stile and walked over to shake his hand. "Well, it's true! What the hell happened?"

"Ten years?" Sterling suggested wryly.

Henry looked him over, shaking his head. Sterling Oak had been a quiet, lanky boy on the cusp of adulthood the last time Henry had seen him. He had grown into the promise of the coltish figure that had been all skinny arms and legs, and now was an enormous fellow, the image of his sire.

"I was sorry to hear about your father," Henry said. Mr Oak Senior had been a good man. Taciturn and sparing with his words, but the kind to help a neighbour in need and expect nothing in return.

"Me too," Sterling said with a shrug. "Odd not having him around, telling me I'm doing it wrong."

Henry huffed out a laugh. "Oh, I know that feeling."

Except, for all his criticism, Sterling's father had been proud of his son. Henry's father had just been critical, if he'd been there at all.

"Staying?" Sterling asked.

Henry smiled, reminded of old Mr Oak, who would never use five words if one would do.

"I'm not sure," he said, staring out at the view of softly rolling hills, a patchwork of green and gold, gilded in the sunlight of the late summer's afternoon. He loved it here. It was home, and yet… "I had thought perhaps I might, but my sister has got it in her head I must marry. She's plotting and scheming with her friends. I may need to run away again simply to thwart their plans."

"Not disastrous," Sterling replied, frowning. "To marry."

"Yes, it is," Henry replied, quite certain on that point. "Some men are not cut out for it and I'm one of them. But never mind that, it's too dull to contemplate. Look at this." Henry stepped aside to gesture to the hedge and was taken aback to see the fellow shudder. Admittedly it *was* a little disturbing, but likely just some local superstition. There were seven little corn dolls suspended in the hawthorn bush, and each of them held a small section of hawthorn twig, spiked with thorns.

"Witchcraft," Sterling said, taking a step away. "Don't touch it."

Henry frowned at the fellow in consternation. "Surely you don't believe in such nonsense?"

Sterling shifted uneasily, rubbing the back of his neck. "Aye, my old gran was a cunning woman. Learnt a bit from her. Knew stuff. Someone else believes it too. Seven is a fairy number and cutting the Ogham tree like that—" He sucked air in through his teeth. "—someone is asking for help with a difficult situation. Take my advice, Mr Stanhope. Leave it be. Asking for trouble, else."

Henry looked at Sterling in exasperation but held out his hands. "Very well. I'll leave it, but it's still a lot of nonsense."

Whatever his opinion, the relief in Sterling's expression was clear. He was truly rattled.

"And what's with this Mr Stanhope business? It's always been Henry to you. Here, do you fancy a drink at The Lamb, now you're old enough?" he added with a smirk. "You can tell me everything you've been up to in my absence."

Sterling quirked an eyebrow.

"Everything?" he repeated, dry as dust.

"Well, only the interesting bits," Henry said, clapping him on the back as they walked back to the lane that led to the nearest pub.

The two men enjoyed a pint, reminiscing about years gone by, though it was Henry who did most of the talking, with Sterling adding an occasional remark or grunt of amusement. He was still a serious, introverted fellow, much like his father.

"Suppose I'd better go," Henry said, giving his empty glass a regretful glance. "Harry will have my hide if I'm late for dinner."

"Ah, eating at the big house, then, with all the man traps?" Sterling said with a devilish glint in his dark eyes.

"Thankfully, most of the women Harry was trying to pair me off with are gone now, but there's still some of her friends *and* their daughters. God help me, I think one of them has determined to set her cap at me."

Sterling smirked at Henry's morose tone. "Ah, yes. Awful testing, having a pretty young woman chasing after you."

Henry scowled at him. "She's just a silly child."

"How old?"

"Oh, I don't know," Henry shrugged. "Twenty-two, twenty-three, maybe."

Sterling's eyebrows went up. "Hardly a child. I'm only twenty-six."

"Really?" Henry frowned at the man, startled. Of course, if he'd thought about it, he'd known that. He hadn't been away that long, after all. Sterling seemed older than his years, though, but perhaps it was just his serious manner. "Well, either way, she's too young for me."

"Not by most people's reckoning. You're the biggest catch around these parts now Viscount Oakley's gone."

Henry grimaced, knowing that was likely true. "Perhaps you ought to look closer to home for a fine catch," he replied with annoyance.

"Me?" Sterling made a disparaging sound. "Not with those high-bred ladies. Too low down the pecking order to catch one of them. Don't have your pretty manners."

There was a faintly mocking tone to his words, and possibly a thread of anger which made Henry wonder. "Nonsense. You're a gentleman, educated and with a fine house, land, you're prospering nicely from what I've seen. More so than even your father managed. Perhaps you've no title, but neither have I, and you're a deal younger than me, which ought to give you an edge."

Sterling gave him a narrow-eyed look of suspicion.

"What edge? What do you mean?"

"I mean," Henry said decisively, "that you are coming to Holbrook for dinner. A handsome fellow like you is just the thing to keep the young ladies out of my hair."

"Oh, no." Sterling shook his head. "Absolutely—"

"Shan't take no for an answer," Henry replied, getting to his feet. "Harry won't mind a bit. I'll meet you at Lower Sheep House Field in an hour. Don't be late."

He flashed an outraged Sterling a quick grin and hurried away before the fellow could wriggle out of it.

Florence stared at herself in the looking glass and frowned as she submitted to her own stern, internal monologue.

You will not behave like a ninny, Florence Knight. Staring at Henry Stanhope like a besotted mooncalf and sighing will only give him a disgust of you, so this lunatic behaviour will cease and desist at once.

She sighed anyway. Well, Henry wasn't in sight, so that was surely allowed. He was just so… compelling, and handsome, and sophisticated and witty, and… wouldn't be the least bit interested in someone as young and silly as he thought she was. She wished Arabella were here. She had confided her ridiculous infatuation to her friend, who had completely understood her feelings. Arabella was happily married now, though, and had returned to Royle House to be blissful with Lord Bainbridge. Florence squashed an unwelcome and uncharacteristic surge of jealousy. Just because the fellow she had fallen ridiculously and hopelessly in love with refused to so much as look at her was no reason to be so utterly tedious as to resent everyone else's happiness. With the scolding over, she got to her feet and made her way downstairs.

Florence could not help but feel relieved when she entered the parlour. Most of the guests, including the sophisticated widows Lady St Clair had invited, had left that morning, which meant she might have half a chance of conversing with her elusive heart's desire, Mr Henry Stanhope. Assuming he ever so much as glanced in her direction. Though she had only seen him for the first time here at Holbrook just days ago, she had the strangest feeling that there was no other man who would ever capture her attention as thoroughly as he had. She did not know exactly what it was about him, only that he drew her to him whenever he was in the room, and she could concentrate on nothing else. She made her way over to Evie, who was laughing at something Louis César had said.

"Good evening, Monsieur le Comte," she said as he bowed politely. "I hope my sister isn't teasing you?"

"Yes, she is," he replied with a sad shake of his head. "She is a dreadful girl and I wish you would take her away."

Florence grinned, knowing he didn't mean it. She had been worried by the rather odd friendship between the comte and her little sister, even speaking to her mother about it. She knew Mama was keeping a close eye on them too, but now she saw what Mama had told her, that Louis César regarded Evie much as she did, as a sister. For Evie's part, she truly did not seem to see the man's stunning good looks. This bewildered Florence, who found them somewhat intimidating. She could not imagine being married to a man who was so much more beautiful than you were. It would be a constant source of stress and anxiety, as other women would always want him and try to take him from you.

"You are only sulking because I won our bet," Evie said, her plump cheeks dimpling as she gave a smug smile. "I told you Ash's waistcoat would outshine yours, and it does."

Louis César made a sound of disgust. "Being garish enough to induce a megrim does not mean it has superior attributes."

"I heard that," Ash remarked, turning around. "And of course my waistcoat is superior, it has canaries on it."

An expression of pain crossed Louis César's exquisite features as he cast Ash's waistcoat a dubious glance. "Is that what they are? I thought they were goldfish."

"With wings?" Ash retorted.

Ash's twin sister Vivien joined the conversation and squinted at the canaries. "Well, they could be fins, not wings."

"Traitor," Ash said hotly.

Vivien patted his arm. "Well, darling, really. Lime green with yellow birds is a little *de trop*, even for you."

"Philistines, every one of you," he muttered, before stalking away.

Florence chuckled, and then her breath caught as Henry Stanhope walked into the room. *Oh, good heavens.* Her heart skittered in her chest, her skin flushing hot and her stomach fluttering in the most peculiar way. She'd never reacted like this to a man before. What was it about him? He had been all she could think about from the first moment she'd seen him, grinning boyishly at his sister as Lady St Clair greeted him with happy tears and laughter after almost a decade apart. He just seemed to use up all the air in the room when he walked into it.

She tried to consider him objectively, to pinpoint what it was that attracted her so strongly. He was handsome, but not so outrageously that he made women swoon on the spot like Louis César. He was fit and strong and virile, his skin darkly tanned from his adventures abroad, and he carried an air of confidence that was deliciously appealing. But it was more than that. There was a sense of energy, of vitality, as if a flame blazed inside him that made even younger men seem somehow less in his presence. It burned from within and pulled Florence to him like he'd cast a spell over her, making her helpless to do anything but respond to him. She felt so restless she wanted to throw herself into his arms, which was dangerous and foolish, and yet she had the absolute certainty that it would be a safe place to be. If a man like Henry loved you, he would be honourable, dependable. It was also frustrating and not a little irritating when the devil refused to pay her the least bit of attention.

Henry had another fellow with him tonight, whom he'd introduced as Mr Sterling Oak, his neighbour. Florence had ridden past Thistley House Farm, which was rather grander than its name implied. It was a large half-timbered house of red brick and lime render, and very ancient. Mr Oak was a fierce-looking fellow with strong features, thick black hair, very dark eyes, and a cleft in his chin. He tugged at his cravat and gave off the impression he would rather be anywhere else than here.

"He looks rather intimidating," murmured a quiet voice in Florence's ear.

"Dreadfully fierce," Florence agreed, smiling at Grace. The girl had been so subdued and listless since she'd arrived at Holbrook, it was a relief to see her interacting at all. "Do you think he bites?"

"Only if you mention how much you love sunsets and bunny rabbits," Grace said, sliding her arm through Florence's.

Florence chuckled and sent Grace a look of amusement, but the girl was staring out of the window, a faraway look in her eyes. "Grace?"

She didn't so much as stir but tugged absently at a loose blonde curl of hair, her grey eyes the colour of an overcast summer's day.

"Grace?" Florence tried again. "Won't you tell me what's wrong?"

The girl started, looking alarmed.

"Wrong?" She laughed and shook her head. "Oh… Oh, no… n-nothing."

Florence lowered her voice and drew her into the corner of the room. "Yes, there is. You wrote and told me you'd done something stupid, and you're clearly unhappy. Won't you confide in me?"

Grace chewed at her lip, staring about the room like some wild thing caught in a snare.

"Not now," she said desperately, and tugged her arm free of Florence's hold before hurrying away from her.

Florence sighed.

The meal, as with all those served at Holbrook, was divine. Not that Florence noticed it much. The debate going on between their hostess, Lady St Clair, and her brother vastly entertained most of the guests, and Florence was no exception. Henry's opinions intrigued her. The topics were far-reaching, from Henry Fox Talbot's extraordinary exhibition of photogenic drawings at the Royal Institution—which Henry had missed but had read about with fascination—to the Chartist riot in Birmingham the previous month. Florence was beguiled by his easy manner, his breadth of knowledge, and not only pleased by his sympathy for the Chartists and what they were trying to achieve—an effort her father supported—but his agreement with his sister that women as well as men should have the vote.

"Well, as the most intelligent person I've ever met was a woman, it seems foolish to deny the possibility they might make better decisions," he observed, lifting a glass in a toast to Lady St Clair.

It seemed every time he opened his mouth, he proved himself to be the man Florence had longed to find and had begun to think as rare as a unicorn. Yet here he was, right in front of her, forthright and confident, handsome, and full of such energy and masculine vigour that he held everyone's attention.

As hard and fast as Florence was falling for him, it was astonishing how the man could be seated so close, almost opposite her, and ignore her so thoroughly. He was charming and witty with everyone else, yet barely paid her the briefest of attention. She wondered if anyone had noticed it yet, for it bordered on rudeness. Worse, the only time he'd paid her any mind was when he'd done his level best to get the taciturn Mr Oak to speak to her. The attempt had failed, as Mr Oak seemed to have little interest in speaking to anybody. It had just made her feel foolish and annoyed.

Well, if she'd had any doubts about his lack of interest in her, tonight's performance ought to have driven them from her head and made her determined to turn her attention elsewhere. It would have done if she'd had an ounce of sense. Sense seemed in short supply this evening, however, and it was all she could do not to gaze longingly at him over her bowl of syllabub. Instead, she stared at the dessert with a morose sigh and ate the whole thing without speaking a word to anyone. Oh, but it was delicious. She'd always been partial to syllabub. Sighing with pleasure, she forgot herself for a moment and licked every trace of cream from the bowl of the spoon.

Feeling eyes upon her, she looked up. Henry was staring at her, his gaze riveted on her mouth. Florence flushed. Drat the man. The one time he looked in her direction and she was behaving like a mannerless child. His jaw stiffened, and he turned resolutely away from her, plunging into conversation with the Marchioness of Montagu.

Florence felt ill, the syllabub churning unpleasantly in her stomach. She did not understand it. Everyone said how charismatic and likeable Henry was. No one had a bad word for him, and yet he seemed to despise her for no reason. It couldn't even be because she'd made a fool of herself by flirting shamelessly or setting her cap at him, for he'd not shared more than a few words with her. Miserable and confused, Florence decided she must endure the rest of the evening as best she could and go to bed. Perhaps tomorrow would be a brighter day.

Henry did his best to attend the conversation with Matilda, who was a friend of many years, but it was nigh on impossible. He was simply too distracted. Matilda kept giving him these odd, searching looks too, which was most unsettling. He tried to remember what they'd been talking about, but the sight of Miss Knight's neat pink tongue lingering over the smooth curve of her spoon was engraved upon his mind.

Stop it. Stop it. Stop it. You are not a lecherous beast. She's half your age.

17

No, she's not, a belligerent voice in his head retorted.

Too close to half for comfort.

Henry tried to understand what it was about her. Yes, she was beautiful. Her glossy black curls shone in the candlelight and, now and then, he glimpsed irritation in her green eyes that made them flash sparks like emerald fire. Oh, hell. Yes, she was lovely, and that was why he was staying far, far away from her. He'd been conscious of her from the very first moment she'd walked in the room on arriving at Holbrook. His entire being had vibrated like a tuning fork, shockingly aware of her. It was a sensation he was all too familiar with. He'd felt just same way once before, a long time ago.

He'd believed in love at first sight in those days, but he was not a green boy any longer. Women were not to be trusted with your heart and, for some people, love was an illusion that faded quickly. It wasn't that he didn't believe in it. Too many of his friends were happily married not to provide examples of the way it could be. But it was not for a man like him. As far as Henry was concerned, only lust was honest, and he was not about to turn into one of those disgusting men who chased after young women. His first love affair, his foolish, youthful folly had been forgivable, if humiliating. To fall into the same trap again at his time of life would be....

His stomach clenched, and the back of his neck felt hot and uncomfortable just considering it.

Miss Lily Johnson. No, *Lady Nettlebury* now. Christ, he'd not thought of her in years. Once, she had been the *only* thing he'd thought of. When she'd thrown him over, he'd thought he'd die of misery. He hadn't, naturally, and all too soon he'd realised his error. He'd had a lucky escape. Lily had been beautiful, blonde, and exquisite. A blue-eyed angel. It had been all on the surface, though. Beneath the lovely exterior she had been shallow, selfish, and ruthlessly ambitious. Oh, no, he was not being played for a fool again, especially by some slip of a girl. Not that Florence

Knight seemed at all the same kind of creature as Lily, despite her beauty.

It was clear she had been cosseted and indulged her whole life, but she did not appear spoiled. When she spoke, it was with intelligence and wit; hardly surprising, with Lady Helena as her mama. That was another thing… he was friends with her father. Gabriel would likely tie him to the tracks and run him down with one of his blasted trains if he had the slightest idea of Henry's attraction to his daughter. Besides, he did not wish to marry. Not ever. It wasn't for him. So that meant dallying with any respectable unwed young lady was out of the question.

There was only one thing to do, and that was to make certain he kept as much distance between him and the alluring Miss Knight as possible.

Chapter 1

Dearest Florence,

It was so lovely to see you at Holbrook and to spend time with everyone. I must confess it is good to be home, though. How strange it is that Royle House has become my home so quickly. Now that Hilda has gone to Paris and Hugo is happily married, the house is so much calmer. Of course the duke is a dreadful handful, worse than any spoilt child, but I rather adore the cantankerous old devil.

Freddie and Bertram have a new governess, who is a delightful lady, and they already adore her, though she's had a stern word with Bainbridge about the influence of that wicked parrot. I'm beginning to think he's right and the wretched bird knows exactly what to say at the precise moment to make your toes curl. I had the most mortifying encounter with the gardener last week when he brought over his prize-winning marrow to show us. Of course Bainbridge was in fits, but I did not know where to put myself.

Have you spoken to Grace yet? I have been so worried about her. Do keep me informed.

—Excerpt of a letter from Arabella Grenville, The Most Hon'ble, The Marchioness of Bainbridge (daughter of Mrs Alice and Mr Nathanial Hunt) to Miss Florence Knight (daughter of Lady Helena and Mr Gabriel Knight).

Early hours of the 8ᵗʰ of August 1839, Saxenhurst Hall, Sussex.

Henry woke with a start, his heart thudding and all the fine hairs on the back of his neck standing on end. He sat up, wondering if he'd been dreaming, and listening out for the blood-curdling sound that had invaded his sleep. It came again, rending the peace of the night and echoing through the old house. That was no dream.

Henry flung himself out of bed, snatching up a banyan and pulling it on, tying the belt as he ran from the room. He wouldn't have bothered, but he always slept naked and did not wish to traumatise the female staff any more than the scream would have done.

Naturally, the entire household was awake, the flicker of candlelight illuminating the house at intervals with small patches of golden light. Panicked whispers threaded through the strange silence that remained in the absence of that unsettling sound.

"Where did it come from, Parker?" he demanded of the butler.

"Conflicting reports, sir. Some say the north wing, but Cook says she'd swear it was the library."

"Are all the staff accounted for?"

"Yes, sir."

Henry nodded, organising the men into groups to search the property from top to bottom before running towards the library himself. Two of the footmen accompanied him but, as they burst through the door, the library was still and quite obviously empty.

"I want every inch of the house and grounds searched," he said, but had hardly finished the sentence when a crash sounded upstairs.

Henry and the men flew from the room, taking the stairs three at a time. On the landing that led to the nursery and schoolroom was a smashed vase.

The search went on for several hours until Henry was satisfied that no corner of either the house or the garden had been missed. They found nothing. The staff went back to bed to snatch what little sleep they could before morning, muttering about ghosts and ill omens. Henry did not believe in ghosts or ill omens any more than he believed in witchcraft, but he did believe people could do ridiculous things for a myriad of reasons. Someone was playing silly buggers, and he intended to find out who.

Despite telling herself she was an idiot for getting her hopes up, Florence was looking forward to today. Lady St Clair had gained an invitation from her brother for their guests to picnic at Saxenhurst Hall. Whilst the Hall was nothing like as grand as Holbrook House, it was a very fine building. A moated manor house on the very edge of the border between Sussex and Kent, it dated back in parts to the thirteenth century. Florence wondered if it was haunted, and if Henry would allow them a tour. For the moment they were picnicking on a high spot, where views reached far across Kent: miles and miles of fields and woodland as far as the eye could see. It was a glorious day, with tiny wisps of cobwebby clouds touching the cobalt sky.

Florence was relieved to discover it was a proper picnic, too. She had been to some grand affairs where the entire dining room was simply transported out of doors, which was a poor sort of picnic in her view. Henry had done it properly, with blankets spread on the ground and enormous wicker baskets stuffed full of delicious food that were at once indulgent and easy to eat with your fingers. It was one of the things she liked about him, that he was down to earth, with easy manners. Henry was a gentleman of means and used to moving in the highest circles of society. He had wit and charm and exuded confidence, but he had also gone out of his way to put Mr Oak at ease today. Mr Oak was a gentleman, if a little rough about the edges, but he did not seem at home among Henry's guests and was clearly cursing Henry for having persuaded him to attend. Despite this the friendship between them was obvious and Henry did his best to draw the taciturn fellow into the conversation. Florence could not help but believe that the broad-shouldered Mr Oak would far rather be about his farm doing something physical. The thought made her smile.

Henry caught her eye at that very moment and followed her gaze to Mr Oak. Florence blushed and looked away, embarrassed. Dash it all. The fellow had the worst timing. Now he would think she was interested in Mr Oak. She groaned inwardly.

"What is it, darling?"

Florence turned at her mother's enquiry; her unease must have been visible. Mama was somehow managing to look supremely elegant whilst eating a chicken leg. It was a gift Florence had yet to master. She set her own down and wiped her greasy fingers on a napkin.

"I was thinking about you and Papa, actually," she said, as it had been on her mind of late. "About how you met and married."

Her mama laughed. "Goodness, what a long time ago that was, and yet it seems like yesterday."

"Papa didn't like you at first, did he?" Florence asked, comforted by the knowledge.

"Oh, I love this story," Grace said with a wistful sigh. "Do tell us, Lady Helena."

Mama gave them an indulgent smile.

"No, your Papa did not like me one little bit, darling. He thought me spoiled and shallow, a pampered heiress who was only interested in him because he would not give me the time of day. He was right, of course," she added, laughing merrily.

"But you didn't let that put you off, did you, Mama? Because you knew he was the one," Florence pressed, needing to hear that she wasn't being a complete fool for believing in something, or someone, when there was no reason to do so other than some sixth sense that nagged at her heart and whispered in her ear.

"No. I was rather shameless, I'm afraid. Something I do not encourage you to emulate," Mama added, her expression growing stern. "Things are far stricter for you girls than in my day. Even so, I was lucky that Gabriel was an honourable man, with strong principles, and that he truly cared for me. Not all men are the same. If I had not chosen so well, I might have ended in a great deal of trouble."

Florence considered her mama, who stared thoughtfully out at the view before them.

Grace frowned down at her plate, tracing a pattern in the crumbs. She seemed to have the weight of the world on her shoulders. Florence looked between them. Had Grace taken a chance on someone?

"But if you'd not taken a chance, if you'd not dared him to race you to Brighton, you'd never have won him, would you," she urged, wanting to hear her mother agree to give her reassurance.

Her mother shrugged, her green eyes taking on a faraway look, her beautiful mouth curving with a soft smile. "Oh, I don't know about that. I think I would have found another way. It might have taken me longer, but... I'm nothing if not persistent."

"It is a family trait," Louis César murmured, gaining himself an elbow in the ribs from Evie, who had also been listening.

"Someone has to stop you from misbehaving. I think of myself as the voice of your conscience," Evie said airily. "Without me you'd go to the devil in no time."

Louis César snorted at that and cut a neat slice of apple, handing it to Evie before cutting another for himself. "Between you and Agatha, I shall be willing to enrol myself in the nearest monastery before the year is out, just to get a little peace."

"Piffle. You enjoy the attention. Oooh, look, macarons! My favourite."

"At least you are easily distracted," Louis César observed, reaching for the plate and setting it in front of her. "Do not eat all the pink ones."

"Why not?"

"I like them best," he replied with a wink. He turned to where the children were playing some game of their own devising across the field and called out. "Aggie, *viens ici, mon enfant.*"

"You're teaching her French?" Evie asked. "You're supposed to be helping me, you might remember."

Louis shrugged. "Yes, but your accent is shocking. It gives me a headache."

"You're a very rude man," she said, laughing. "But I shall forgive you because it's true. No doubt I try your patience horribly."

"Beyond enduring," Louis agreed amicably, waving at Aggie to come and join them.

Florence sighed, her gaze inevitably moving across the assembled company towards Henry. He was sitting as far from her as it was possible to get, laughing with Ash and Lord St Clair. Even Mr Oak looked more at ease now, which was surprising, as the austerely handsome Marquess of Montagu was also among their group. He was usually enough to make any man feel self-conscious. She turned her attention to their conversation. It sounded as though Henry had been telling them of his time in India.

"I swear, a ruby almost the size of a hen's egg. I'd seen nothing like it in my life before, but the prince was so vastly wealthy it was a mere trifle. His palace was extraordinary, incredibly beautiful. Indeed it was a magical place, like a fairytale, though I admit the heat was hard to tolerate."

"Was he dreadfully handsome?" Lady Montagu asked, voicing the question all the women were thinking and causing her husband to arch one perfect blond eyebrow at her. "What, darling? I'm interested. I want to know more about him. Was he an interesting man? I'm sure he must have been quite splendid."

Montagu sighed and shook his head. "I knew the day would come. A marquess is a poor substitute for a prince."

Lady Montagu laughed, her eyes glittering with adoration. "Foolish man."

"Not in the least foolish, as you were born to be a princess," he said with the utmost gravity, taking her hand and raising her fingers to his lips.

Lady Montagu blushed at the devilish look glinting in her husband's eyes and Florence sighed, wondering if she would ever have that. The kind of connection she saw between Lord and Lady Montagu was the same she saw between her own parents, yet none of them had gained their heart's desire without a fight... Lady Montagu especially. Well, then, she must not give up too easily. She did not know for certain that Henry didn't like her. Perhaps he was shy, or perhaps he thought he was too old. He was a friend of Papa's, after all, though younger than him. Indeed, now she thought about it, her father might not like the match. Florence chewed at her lip pensively as she considered this. The idea had merit, for she knew Henry was an honourable man. She stilled, suddenly aware of eyes upon her. Florence looked up, finding Henry watching her with an intense expression. He looked away at once, busying himself with opening another bottle of wine. But Florence had seen. Her heart beat hard, hope flickering to life in her chest.

Oh, no, she wasn't giving up yet. She'd only just begun.

Fool, Henry cursed himself, tugging the cork free with more force than was required. He might make himself sit as far from her as he could get but keeping his eyes from her was another matter. It was as if she radiated some magnetic force, and he was helpless to resist turning towards her, like a sunflower raising its face to follow the light. The moment he let his guard down, he found himself looking for her, listening for the sound of her voice. It was intolerable. Memories of the days after Lily had jilted him filled his mind, and he embraced the memory of hurt and humiliation to remind himself of the danger. He remembered too well, remembered the pain, as if his heart had been torn from his chest, remembered the mortification that burned so badly he'd hidden himself away at Saxenhurst and refused to see anyone for months. Irritated, he flung open the lid of the basket beside him, looking for the glasses, and stilled as he saw what lay within.

"Don't touch it!" Sterling snapped, seeing what Henry had seen.

"Whatever is it?" Ash asked, peering to look at the basket.

Though his back was to her, Henry was aware of Florence getting to her feet, too curious not to investigate. She looked over his shoulder, and he was ridiculously aware of her closeness, certain he could feel the warmth of her body through his coat, which was absurd.

"Why, it's just a little corn doll," she said in surprise, clearly wondering what they were both looking so shocked about. "A pretty one, too, though Lammas Day was almost two weeks ago."

It was beautifully crafted, no bigger than his hand, the corn stalks woven together with the frilly ends where the grain bloomed making the doll's skirts.

Florence reached to pick it up.

"No!" Mr Oak said sharply, but it was Henry who reached out, grasping her wrist before she could touch it.

Her gaze snapped to his as something that felt like electricity crackled between them. The shock of recognition lanced straight to Henry's core, and he sucked in a swift breath, dropping her hand as if the contact had burned him.

"What the devil is going on?" Montagu asked, staring at the corn doll with suspicion. "That's the kind of thing Pippin makes—our old cook, that is—but I've seen no one look so anxious about it before."

"Witchcraft," Mr Oak said succinctly. "You'd best tell them, Henry."

Henry shook his head, irritated. "No, it's a load of nonsense."

"Someone breaking into your house and causing havoc is not nonsense."

Mr Oak's words had everyone's attention, including Harriet's.

"What's this, Henry?" she demanded.

Cursing Sterling, and with a sigh of resignation, Henry told them about the dolls in the hedge and about the events of last night.

"Someone wants to hurt you."

Henry's heart gave a little skip in his chest at Florence's words, at the worry in her eyes. He waved her concern away.

"With a corn doll?" he retorted, a mocking tone to the words.

She put her chin up, holding his gaze. "It wasn't just a doll, though, was it? A woman screamed in the night, a valuable vase was broken. Someone is trying to scare you, at the very least, and who is to say this isn't just the beginning? Perhaps they will get bolder."

"Well, I'm not easily scared, Miss Knight, certainly not by handicrafts and amateur theatrics." Henry plucked the doll from the basket and tossed it into the grass. "Who wants wine?" he asked, reaching for the glasses he'd wanted.

Florence hesitated, her hands twisted in her skirts. He could sense her agitation, her concern for him, and it warmed him as if he'd stepped in front of a fire after a long day out in the cold. It was seductive, that heat. A chill ran down his spine as he recognised the danger to his heart. *No.* No, he would not tread this same path again and make a damned fool of himself. Florence, though, was not done.

"Mr Stanhope, I think you ought to speak to your staff at once. Surely they ought to know how it got in the basket. What if someone in your household holds a grudge? You might be in danger and—"

"Miss Knight, much as I appreciate your concern, I fear you've read one too many Gothic novels. You're becoming hysterical."

Henry hated himself the moment the words left his mouth, his tone hard and derisive. His self-loathing burned harder still when Florence blushed, swallowing hard as everyone stilled in shock.

"Forgive me," she mumbled. "I… I am sorry my concern is such a trouble to you."

With great dignity, she turned and walked away, sitting down with her back to him on the far side of the guests.

There was an uncomfortable silence and Henry was too aware of the weight of disapproval directed towards him. God, what an arse. More so because now he owed the wretched girl an apology.

Somehow the silence was broken, and conversation began once more, but the convivial atmosphere had been tarnished and the picnic broke up not long after. Henry was unsurprised when his sister accosted him on the walk back to the house.

"What the devil is wrong with you, Henry?" she demanded, her eyes sparkling with anger behind her spectacles. "I've never seen you act so badly. Poor Florence was mortified. How dare you speak to her so, and in front of everyone? Surely you know how fragile a young woman's self-esteem is, and for you to belittle her in front of her friends and family...."

"I know, I know," Henry gritted out. "I'll apologise."

"I should think so," Harriet snapped, scrutinising him with the delicacy of a rapier. "But what I don't understand is why. You've never been rude to anyone in your life, certainly not a young woman."

Henry groaned, wishing his sister were a little less perceptive.

"I suppose these blasted dolls have rattled me more than I wish to admit," he lied, grasping at straws quite literally. "And I didn't get a lot of sleep last night for obvious reasons. I... I'm tired and bad-tempered. Forgive me, Harry. I'll make it up to her, I swear."

Harry snorted. "Indeed you will. You're only lucky I'm here speaking to you and not Helena. She's furious, I might add."

"Oh, Lord."

Well played, you stupid bastard. Now, not only must he give a heartfelt apology to the woman he'd been doing his utmost to avoid, but he'd offended her mother, who would no doubt tell her husband about it too. So, his friend, Gabriel, would also be angry with him. No, strike that. The way Gabriel protected his daughters, he'd be lucky not to have his tongue ripped out for speaking so to Florence.

"I'll speak to her at once," he promised, only to have Harriet shake her head.

"No, you won't. Helena is taking her straight home for she has a headache, and no wonder. You may come tomorrow morning, by which time I hope you will have come up with a better excuse than the one you offered me."

With that, his sister stalked off, clearly in high dudgeon.

Henry turned as a friendly hand slapped him on the shoulder. Harriet's husband, Jasper Cadogan, the Earl of St Clair, grinned at him.

"Buck up, old man. The fair sex ever did turn a man's brain to treacle."

Henry frowned at him, not understanding.

"I was awful to poor Harry for years," Jasper whispered, before winking at him and striding off after his wife.

Hell and damnation!

Chapter 2

Dearest Arabella,

I am so glad you are happy at Royle House, not least because you may have another house guest soon.

Oh, Bella, I'm so mortified. Henry gave me such a set down yesterday at the picnic, and in front of everybody, too. It was all I could do not to cry or throw something at him. There was a large apple pie which would have made an excellent weapon, but then I reminded myself that I have manners, even if he doesn't, the brute. Except he does, with everyone else.

Why does he hate me so? I don't understand it, and now I must endure an apology from him, which will be simply excruciating. I know he's only doing it because everyone is cross with him, not because he means it, and that just makes it worse. If things don't get any better, I shall come and stay with you and learn every one of your parrot's dreadful words. Perhaps he can teach me something to insult Henry badly enough that he won't forget it, or me.

—*Excerpt of a letter from Miss Florence Knight (daughter of Lady Helena and Mr Gabriel Knight) to Arabella Grenville, The Most Hon'ble, The Marchioness of Bainbridge (daughter of Mrs Alice and Mr Nathanial Hunt).*

10ᵗʰ August 1839, Holbrook House, Sussex.

Florence spent a great deal of time getting ready the next morning, but she was determined to look her best. Damn Henry Stanhope for making her feel too much. She was angry and out of sorts, restless and frustrated, and it was all his fault. Why had she become infatuated with a man who couldn't stand the sight of her? It was thoroughly absurd and so annoying to feel this way. Why couldn't she make it stop? She was an intelligent woman and perfectly capable of rational thought. Yet she could not stop her heart from wanting a man who clearly held her in contempt. She was besotted, there was no escaping it, and there seemed to be nothing she could do about it, either. Perhaps it was a family trait, to be drawn to people who did not want or like you. Perhaps Mama had just been supremely lucky with Papa, and this strange fascination she had for Henry was nothing but a malfunction in her brain. She sighed as her maid put the finishing touches to her hair.

"Thank you, Maisie. It looks lovely."

"You're welcome, miss. You look good enough to eat, if you don't mind me saying so."

Florence smiled gratefully at Maisie and took one last look at herself in the mirror. Her gown was a soft lilac and went well with her green eyes, somehow making the colour brighter by contrast. Not that it mattered, Henry was not coming to see her because he wished to, but to execute an unpleasant but necessary task. Like getting a tooth pulled, she thought with a grimace. Ah, well. Best get it over with.

She made her way down to the library to find her mama waiting for her.

"Oh, darling. Oh, you do look lovely," Mama said, giving her a warm smile.

Florence blushed a little, wishing she'd not gone to so much trouble.

"I wondered if you would like me to stay with you?"

"Oh, no," Florence said at once. She didn't doubt Henry was dreading this as much as she was. Having to apologise in front of both her and her mother would be too embarrassing for words, and he'd hate her even more. "No, I'll be fine. Really."

Mama nodded, frowning a little. "It's the strangest thing, though. I've never known Henry to be rude to anyone before in my life. I—"

"Oh, well, you know how it is. Some people just rub you up the wrong way for no reason," Florence said, wanting the conversation over as quickly as possible. "He probably thinks me an empty-headed ninny who was interfering in men's business."

Her mother bristled at once and Florence sighed, realising she'd said precisely the wrong thing.

"If he does—"

"Oh, Mama, ignore me. I'm just nervous. You cannot get angry at the man when we have no idea what motivated him, especially as he is coming to apologise. Perhaps he has things on his mind that we know nothing about, and he did not mean to lash out at me at all. Everyone says how out of character it was for him to do so, therefore there must be an explanation."

Shame burned in Henry's chest as he stood in the open door of the library and heard Florence defend him for no good reason he could think of. He cleared his throat, and she whirled around. Oh, God help him. His breath caught, a dart of longing stabbing at his chest. Her eyes were thickly lashed, and they widened at the sight of him. Henry stared into them, discovering they were the most astonishing shade of green and ever so slightly tilted, giving her a somewhat feline appearance.

"Miss Knight, Lady Helena," he said, bowing.

Lady Helena gave him a cool, considering look that lingered for a second longer than was comfortable. She patted her daughter's arm.

"I'm going to take a walk down to the lake with Harriet if you want me, darling. *Henry*," she added as she walked past him, a warning note in the sound of his name he did not miss.

Helena left the door ajar, but they were alone now, and Henry had never been more aware of the fact in his life. His senses seemed heightened somehow by her proximity, every part of him orientated towards her. *Concentrate, you blithering idiot.*

He cleared his throat again, feeling like a snotty schoolboy and not a man who had seen more of the world than most.

"Miss Knight, I…." he began, forcing himself to remember the words he'd rehearsed on the ride over here. "I must begin by—"

"Why don't you like me?"

Henry stopped, staring at her in alarm. No, no. This was all wrong. She wasn't supposed to ask questions, she was supposed to listen to his apology, make him feel wretched a bit longer, and then accept it so they could both go about their business.

"Er…." Oh, very eloquent, and he was supposed to be the sophisticated man about town.

She sighed and gave him an impatient glance before walking to the window and staring out.

"You don't like me," she repeated, except it wasn't a question this time. "You avoid me, never speak to me, even when I'm right in front of you. Have I done something, offended you somehow…?"

"*No!*" he said at once, appalled it had been so damned obvious. What a blasted imbecile he was. "No, of course not."

She glanced back at him, such hurt in her eyes that he felt that awful stabbing sensation in his chest again. God damn it.

"Miss Knight, it isn't… I don't…." Henry muttered an oath and ran a hand through his hair.

Every instinct was yelling at him to go to her, to tell her…tell her what? That he wanted to kiss her from her perfect little nose to her innocent toes, and every splendid inch of skin in between, that he wanted to feel her body against his and make her cry out his name. Oh, yes, her parents would love an apology of that nature. Christ. This was bad.

"It's all right, Mr Stanhope," she said, with something that looked horribly like sympathy in her eyes. "I suppose it simply isn't possible to like everyone. Perhaps I remind you of someone else who was unkind to you in the past. Either way, it is of little consequence. I know you are sorry, so there is no need to prolong the agony. Good day to you."

"No. Wait," he said the words escaping him before he could consider the consequences. "*Please.*"

She paused, watching him warily. Damn, but she was perceptive, this young woman, for how else could she know how she stirred the memories of his past? Not that she reminded him of Lily's golden, blue-eyed beauty. In looks they were like night and day, except Florence Knight was far lovelier, for she had a good heart, a heart he had wounded. She did remind him of his past, though, of the fact that he could be hurt, hurt very deeply, and that made him angry. He did not want to remember a time when he'd been vulnerable. He never wanted to be vulnerable ever again. Yet he owed her something.

Nausea churned in his guts, but he forced the words out.

"You do remind me of someone," he said, not entirely truthfully, but it was as close as he could get, as much as he dared give her. "And I wish to offer my sincere apologies for... for punishing you for another's sin. It was unforgivable, and I regret it, Miss Knight. I swear that I do."

Her expression softened and he saw compassion in her eyes, which only ignited a spark of defensive pride in him. Damn it, he didn't want her pity. Yet he promised himself he would hold his temper in check, no matter what, she deserved that much. Strangely she seemed to sense the change in his mood and her expression became bland, her voice soft but not too kind, avoiding the sort of well-meaning sympathy he could not tolerate.

"I understand, and I thank you for your apology, Mr Stanhope. I only hope you can forgive me for reminding you of something painful. Sadly, I do not know how to make amends for that, but I shall try. Good day to you."

She left the room and Henry stood rooted to the spot, wishing he'd had the courage to tell her the truth, and then cursing himself for having no more sense than he'd had all those years ago. Florence Knight was a danger to him, whether or not she meant to be, and that was all there was to it.

Henry rode home, feeling strangely frustrated and annoyed with himself, and with Florence. It was irrational to be angry with her. He knew that. The girl did not know what she did to him and so could hardly be held accountable. Only it was so damned inconvenient. Why couldn't he have felt a surge of lust for one of the lovely women Harriet had selected for him? At least with a widowed lady of his own age, he might have enjoyed a brief affair with no consequences and got the whole thing out of his system.

That was hardly an option with Florence. If he so much as kissed her, they'd have to marry, and that would be him nicely trussed up for the rest of his days. He refused to allow himself to consider the idea, reminding himself that marriage was the very last thing he wanted. What in God's name did he want with a wife and an end to his freedom? And then there would be children, interfering with his well-ordered life and squalling at all hours of the night and day. No, thank you very much.

He was so sunk in despondency and irritation that it took a moment before he noticed the rider approaching. Henry reined his horse in, waiting as he saw Sterling cantering towards him.

"You'd best come," the fellow said, his expression grim.

Henry muttered a curse and followed him.

They rode to Tun Slip, a five-acre field that bordered Sterling's farm.

"I came up to check the fences," Sterling said, gesturing to the dead sheep.

He stared at the dead animal, wondering why Sterling was so unsettled. Sheep were notoriously stupid creatures that got themselves killed for no good reason and were prone to a myriad of diseases and troubles that seemed to manifest on a regular cycle. The occasional dead ewe was hardly cause for the concern in his friend's eyes. Henry dismounted for a better look.

"Poisoned," Sterling added, before Henry had the chance to see for himself.

Frowning, Henry crouched down to inspect the sheep, noticing the glossy green leaves on the grass beside it. He picked one up. "Rhododendron."

Sterling voice was grave. "I've ridden around, there's none anywhere close to this field."

That meant someone had brought those leaves here and fed the animal on purpose.

"Is this the only one?" Henry asked, scanning the field to where the rest of the flock was grazing, untroubled by their dead companion.

Sterling nodded. "For now."

Henry frowned down at the sheep. "God damn it."

"Reckon Miss Knight had a point."

He looked up sharply. "What do you mean?"

"Someone's out to scare you."

Henry huffed out a breath, shaking his head. "But it makes no sense!"

Sterling shrugged. "Any enemies? Someone who bears you a grudge?"

"No!" Henry stood, raking a hand through his hair. "Damn it, Sterling, I've not even been in the country for the best part of a decade."

The man stood and stared at him, his expression unreadable.

"You really think this is personal? That someone is targeting me for a reason?"

Sterling let out a slow breath, staring at the sheep before looking back at Henry. "Reckon so."

By the time Henry had spoken to the shepherd, ensured the rest of the field was clear of poisonous leaves, and returned to the Hall, he was not in the best of humour.

It was a state not helped as he walked through the gates and saw a corn doll dangling from the wrought-iron railings, swaying gently in the warm breeze.

A hangman's noose was drawn tight about its neck.

Chapter 3

Dearest Flo,

You poor lamb. I am dreadfully sorry the wretched man embarrassed you so. Bainbridge asked me to tell you he is at your disposal should you wish him to break anyone's head for you.

Of course, I should be delighted to have you stay, whenever and for however long you wish. Oh, we shall have a marvellous time if you come. I have so much to show you. Only, I think I ought to point out, darling, that men never truly grow up. So you ought perhaps remember that the boys who like you the most are usually the ones who pull your hair, drop worms in your lap, and throw mice under your petticoats.

—Excerpt of a letter from Arabella Grenville, The Most Hon'ble, The Marchioness of Bainbridge (daughter of Mrs Alice and Mr Nathanial Hunt) to Miss Florence Knight (daughter of Lady Helena and Mr Gabriel Knight).

11th August 1839, Holbrook House, Sussex.

Florence smothered a yawn as the vicar addressed the congregation, not that he was a boring fellow. Indeed, as vicars went, Reverend Martin was rather entertaining. He was also young and handsome, as had escaped not one of the women in the audience. There was a deal of whispering and giggling among the younger females as he spoke, causing the older generation to mutter and scold at intervals. Florence was tired, though, and no matter how entertaining the vicar, she only wanted to go home for a nap. Last night she'd slept ill, her mind filled with worry. She was certain Henry was not taking the events he'd described as seriously as he ought. Someone was making a point and, if Henry did not get to the bottom of it quickly, who knew what the person responsible might do. If they kept getting away with their pranks with no consequences, surely they would only grow bolder.

Then there was Grace.

Though her own troubles had filled her mind of late, she had not forgotten her friend. Yet Grace refused to confide in her, at least for the moment. Goodness, but when had life become so complicated? Florence stared at the back of Henry's neck. He sat with his sister and her husband in the family pew at the front of the church, close enough to touch. Florence's fingers itched with the desire to reach out and stroke his hair where it curled over his collar. It was thick and glinted in differing shades of gold. His sister's hair was a light brown, as was Henry's, but so much time in the sun had bleached it, turning some locks a bright blond, others a soft amber, and still others all shades in between. She sighed.

Vivien, who was sitting beside on her right, leaned closer.

"I'm tempted to do something wicked, just so he'll come and save me," she whispered.

Florence followed her gaze to Reverend Martin and giggled, only to be severely hushed by an old woman in the pew behind them. Naturally, this only made Vivien snort with amusement, which in turn made Florence want to laugh harder. She bit her lip to hold it in.

Henry turned, his hazel eyes meeting hers just as Vivien added, "You've got to admit, Florence, for a man of God, he's quite edible."

Florence ignored Henry and looked at the vicar.

"Yes," she said, her words very deliberate. "Yes, he certainly is."

Henry glowered at the pulpit. The smug young pup. He didn't doubt the man knew full well that all the young women in the church were fluttering their eyelashes in his direction. Not that Henry cared. It was of no consequence to him who Florence Knight found handsome. Not in the least. He'd not give it another thought. Indeed, Reverend Martin was exactly the kind of man Florence ought to be interested in, though she could look far higher than a mere country vicar. Her mother was the Duke of Bedwin's sister, and her father one of the richest men in the country. With her beauty, connections, and vast dowry, she could snag a titled fellow with ease. She could certainly do far better than a vicar, or him for that matter. Henry battered down an unwelcome surge of resentment and reminded himself he was being ridiculous. She was in her twenties, and he'd just passed forty. Whilst that was hardly an unusual age gap, it was... he just... well, it....

Her father would kill him.

Finally grasping at a reason which was solid and undeniable, he relaxed. Besides, he did not wish to marry, and any entanglement with Florence Knight would end with a swift trip to the altar, the one destination in the world to which he had no desire to travel.

The interminable service over at last, they filed out of the church. Henry stood with his sister and her husband, Jasper, as people milled about chatting and came to speak to them. They were popular among the local people, he realised, noting how many of the congregation wanted to speak with the earl and his lady. Two young women came arm-in-arm, one—an attractive blonde—clutching a posy of flowers.

"Good morning, Lord St Clair," they chorused, blushing rosily at the handsome earl.

Jasper smiled at them. "Susan, Nancy. Good day to you both."

"I wanted to thank you, my lord, for letting me have the day off tomorrow to visit my sister. It's very kind of you," said Susan, the blonde girl with the posy of wildflowers.

"Think nothing of it. Please send your sister our regards and tell her we miss her at Holbrook."

"If you would like to go the kitchen this evening, I've had Cook make up a basket for you to take to her," Harriet added, smiling kindly at them. "New mothers need their strength building up."

"Oh, my lady," Susan said, her eyes sparkling. "That's so very kind of you."

"A pleasure, Susan. Please tell your sister we miss her at the house, but hope she is very happy in her new life. Her husband is treating her well, I trust?"

"Oh, yes, Lady St Clair. Rachel married a fine fellow. If only we'd all be so lucky," she added with a sigh and a wistful glance at the earl.

"Those are pretty flowers," Henry observed, some sixth sense telling him Florence was watching the exchange. "From a sweetheart?"

The girl blushed and lowered her gaze, avoiding his eye.

"Oh, no, sir," she said, staring at her toes. "They're for my gran."

"Come on, Susan," her friend urged, tugging at her arm. "We'll be late back if we're not careful."

The girls dipped curtseys and walked away, only pausing to lay the flowers on a gravestone before they hurried off. As they went, Henry noticed a dark figure, standing beneath the shade of an ancient yew tree, leaning on a spade. The man called a greeting to the girls, winking at them. They both put their noses in the air and ignored his remark. The fellow laughed, his gaze drifting next to Florence, who was standing apart from the others, some distance away. She was talking intently with another young lady. There was something about both girl's posture that made him frown. They seemed upset.

Henry glanced back to the man, who must have been the gravedigger for the church, and did not like the lascivious look in the fellow's eyes as he admired Florence and her friend. A prickling sensation rolled down Henry's back. Following his instincts, he extricated himself from Jasper's company as the fellow had got himself deep into a conversation with the blasted vicar. By the time he turned back, however, the girls were nowhere in sight.

"Oh, darling. Please won't you tell me what's wrong?" Florence begged Grace. The poor girl was pale and miserable, on the verge of tears. She took her arm, dragging Grace farther away from the others around the corner of the church where they could not be seen. "Is it... is it a man?"

Grace burst into tears and Florence gathered her into her arms.

"Oh, love."

"I've been such a fool," she sobbed into Florence's shoulder. "Such a stupid, stupid fool. I've r-ruined everything. I've ruined myself."

Florence's heart sank as she heard the words, her worst fears realised. "Then...?"

Grace looked up, her grey eyes filled with tears. She nodded. "I'm with child."

Florence held her breath, struggling to find the words. Even though she'd been prepared for it, it was still a shock. Grace was so young, only seventeen. What kind of man could have taken advantage of her so badly?

"The father?" she asked, hoping against hope, but Grace only shook her head.

"He wants nothing to do with me. He says he never loved me, that I threw myself at him and he only did it because he felt s-sorry for me."

"The brute!" she exclaimed, outraged that a man could be so cruel.

"I th-thought he loved me, Florence. He told me he did, and I believed him, but it was all a l-lie."

"Oh, Gracie. Oh, my dear. I'm so dreadfully sorry, but you're not alone. You have friends and we will all stand by you. I promise we—"

"No."

Florence stepped back, holding Grace by the shoulders as she stared at her, puzzled. "What do you mean, no?"

Grace drew in a deep breath and gathered herself. She wiped her eyes and blew her nose, then tucked the handkerchief back up the sleeve of her gown. Suddenly she looked older, the weight of pain and experience colouring her stormy sky eyes. "You cannot see me once this becomes public, Florence. None of you can. If you do, you will be tainted by association. You know this as well as I do. I must take responsibility for my actions, and I won't have any of you damaged by my shame."

"But…." Florence began, only to be silenced as Grace pressed a trembling finger to her mouth.

"You've no idea how much it means to me, that you would support me in this, but you cannot. We both know you cannot, Florence. Please don't be naïve and give me promises you simply cannot, *must* not keep. You cannot help me now. No one can."

Florence swallowed hard, wanting to deny it, wanting to shout and rage that it wasn't fair, but the truth of the words hung between them, taunting them with their cruelty. Any chance Florence had for making a good match would be badly damaged if she were seen with Grace.

"What will you do?" Florence asked, her throat growing thick as she tried not to cry.

Grace returned a sad smile. "I shall enjoy the last weeks of summer. I shall dance and have fun and do all the things that young women are supposed to do, and then… and then I shall confess all to my parents. It will break their hearts. Especially…." Her voice trembled, and she took a moment to swallow and steady herself. "Especially darling Papa. He'll be so upset, but I shall go away. Perhaps to Scotland. I've always wanted to see Scotland. Such a romantic place. I'll have my baby and… live quietly. Perhaps in a year or two, you'll be able to come and visit me."

"Oh, Grace," Florence said, shaking her head as she struggled to keep her composure. The thought of Grace all alone with a baby was too much to bear.

"I'm stronger than I look, Flo," Grace assured her, and Florence saw the steel in her grey eyes, the strength that belied her slender figure and fine features. "I'll be fine, so please don't worry about me. I don't want to spoil your summer any more than I do my own. Forgive me, but… but I'd like to be alone for a bit. If you don't mind, I'd prefer to walk back by myself."

She gave Florence a swift hug, kissed her cheek, and hurried away, just as Henry Stanhope came around the corner.

Henry paused as he saw the girls embrace, saw Miss Weston hurry away, and Florence wipe the tears from her cheeks. She was crying. Why the devil was she crying?

"Miss Knight?" he said.

She muttered something under her breath, which he thought might be a curse, as she turned away from him.

"Miss Knight," he said again, walking to her. "Is something wrong? Has someone upset you?"

If anyone had hurt her, he'd bloody crucify them.

She shook her head, refusing to look at him. Henry put his hands gently on her shoulders and turned her towards him. Miss Knight looked up at him, her green eyes swimming with unshed tears. The desire to take her in his arms and hold her to him, to protect her from the world, from whatever had put that look in her eyes, was like nothing he'd ever known before. It stole his breath, made his chest hurt and his skin ache with longing.

"Why are you crying?" he asked, keeping his voice gentle, his hands lightly holding her shoulders.

She returned a tremulous smile. "It's nothing, truly. I'm fine, though I thank you for your concern. You're very kind."

He snorted at that. "No, I'm not," he said, terse with regret. "I've treated you very ill."

Henry stilled as a thought struck him, making him feel sick to his stomach.

"Hell, it's... it's not because of me? Because if it is...."

She laughed a little and reached out, touching a tentative hand to his chest for a moment. She snatched it back, blushing a little.

"I'm not crying over you, Mr Stanhope." Another look slid into her eyes, something warm and gently teasing, full of promise. "Perhaps you would prefer it if I were?"

Henry dropped his hands from her shoulders before he was tempted to pull her closer.

"Miss Knight," he began, a warning note to his voice that was entirely for his own benefit.

Use your head, Henry, you fool! What the devil are you playing at?

"Mr Stanhope," she repeated, mocking him, a breathless note to his name that made his heart skip.

"I see you have recovered," he said, striving to make his voice cold and indifferent, which was damned hard when he wanted to kiss the smirk from her lips. Damn the chit. If he did as she clearly wanted him to, she'd have a bloody shock, for he wasn't some fumbling boy who didn't know what he was about. "I shall escort you back to your friends. You ought not be alone out here."

She stared at him and, for a terrifying moment, Henry got lost in her green eyes. So very green. The churchyard was surrounded by trees, from the dark, forbidding yews to ancient oaks and elegant beech trees. The sun filtered through their branches, turning their leaves to emerald, yet her eyes were the most lush shade of all… and the only thing he could see.

"I'm not alone. I'm with you," she whispered, as if that were the only place in the world she wanted to be.

Henry swallowed. "You ought not be."

She stared at him for a long moment. "Is that what you really think?"

Henry knew this was the moment that he ought to say, *yes, yes, that is what I really think*, but the words would not come. He heard himself saying the words in his mind, but he could not force them to his lips. He could only stare at her with his heart thundering. He felt like a boy again in the presence of his first love, a sensation so horrifying it was all he could do not to turn and run like a frightened child.

Miss Knight smiled, a knowing smile that sent a thrill of sensation prickling down his spine, and then she turned and left him standing by himself in the churchyard. Henry watched her go, frowning. He wasn't the only one. The gravedigger watched her go too, then stared at Henry for a long moment before tugging at his cap and carried on digging the grave.

Chapter 4

Brother,

I hope you are well and enjoying your time at Holbrook. I was sorry that I missed seeing you once again before you left. Do give my regards to Miss Smith and all our friends. Eliza sends her fond regards as well. We hope you will come and visit us very soon.

I have not had the opportunity to speak to you privately since we returned. The school has kept us very busy, alongside a dozen and one other projects Eliza is determined must run alongside it. I swear I have never met a more exhausting woman in my life. As a private conversation with you at present is not possible, I felt it best to write and let you know I saw Wolf when I was in France. He is well, and the same as ever, though I have the unsettling suspicion that he is growing bored. Though I pressed him, he will not allow me to repay my debt to him in another manner, as I had hoped. At some point he determines to return to England, and he will be a guest in my home. I cannot begin to imagine the trouble this will cause, but I pray, brother, that you will stand by me (I do not ask that you do so publicly but in spirit at least) when the time comes. I shall need all the friends I can get.

—Excerpt of a letter from Mr Nicolas Alexandre Demarteau to his brother, Louis César de Montluc, Comte de Villen – translated from French.

15th August 1839, Holbrook House, Sussex.

Florence checked her appearance in the mirror before hurrying to find Evie. Happily, her sister was already at breakfast, looking pretty and as fresh as a spring morning in a pale green riding habit.

"Hurry up, Flo," Evie chided her. "We're supposed to be leaving in ten minutes."

"I'm here!" Florence exclaimed, accepting a cup of tea. She reached for a warm bread roll and tore it in two, buttering it too thickly in her haste. Not that she cared. "Is everyone else down already?"

"Everyone except Louis, of course," Evie said, rolling her eyes. "Actually, I'm wondering if I should send someone to knock for him. He hates getting up early, you know."

"That's because it is a dreadful habit and bad for a delicate constitution," the man himself said, looking as immaculate as ever in his riding attire, even as he smothered a yawn. He sat down and declined breakfast with a grimace, but accepted a cup of coffee.

"You're not delicate, only idle," Evie remarked.

"Evie!" Florence exclaimed, a little shocked at her speaking so rudely to him.

She knew that Evie and the comte were friends, but her sister's manner towards the man seemed far too easy. The teasing way they spoke to each other revealed a close relationship, more like with a brother than a friend, but if others who did not know them heard, they would assume a different story.

Evie blushed and looked to the comte, who regarded her over the rim of his coffee cup and shrugged.

"Well, you're not wrong," he said, grinning at the relief in her eyes. "But your sister is right too. You must watch that dreadful tongue of yours, child, or people will talk."

He drank his coffee, watching Evie, who sighed heavily.

"I suppose," she said reluctantly.

They ate in silence for a while as the comte finished his coffee and got to his feet. He laughed again at the look of consternation on Evie's face and reached out to tweak her nose.

"Brat," he remarked, before leaving them to finish their breakfast.

Evie met Florence's considering gaze, a surprisingly defiant glint in her own. "We're friends, Flo. He's all alone now his brother is married and busy with his own life. Louis doesn't make friends easily, but… we get along. He can be himself with me because he knows I'm not interested in him like that. It's… comfortable, that's all."

Florence nodded, hearing the truth in her sister's words. "I know, love. I just don't want to see you get hurt, and you know people will think the worst if they see the ease of manner between you. My word, just hearing you address him as Louis would be enough to ruin you. You must remember to be more formal in company. Promise me you'll be careful?"

"I promise," Evie muttered, looking very much as if she wanted to roll her eyes.

They finished their breakfast and hurried out to the stables, where everyone else was already assembled. They were riding out to Hever Castle today, a trip Florence had been looking forward to. She'd not seen Henry since Sunday at church, but he was supposed to be accompanying their party today. Most of the men hereabouts had been out with their guns, since the twelfth of August had marked the beginning of the shooting season. Shots had been resounding constantly across the countryside and Florence had sent up a prayer to the poor birds, hoping more of them were surviving than it sounded like.

There was quite a party for their trip and the weather promised to be perfect, for it was warm and bright, but with a playful breeze that rustled the treetops and kept the heat from being oppressive. Florence had also worn a green riding habit, but hers was a slightly brighter shade than her sister's. She had a matching hat, which she wore at a jaunty angle with a plume of yellow feathers. Mama had said she looked very dashing.

The stables were all a-bustle as everyone waited whilst the grooms dashed back and forth, ensuring all the guests were mounted correctly for the day. Florence hurried over to Grace as soon as she saw her.

"Are you well?" she asked in an undertone, noting she was not in her riding habit.

Grace smiled and nodded. "I shall travel in the coach with Lady Montagu and the children," she said, reaching out and taking Florence's hand. "Don't worry so. Let us enjoy a lovely day. *Please*."

Florence stared at Grace in wonder. The girl was facing an unimaginable future, yet she stood with dignity, determined to enjoy her last weeks of freedom.

"Very well," Florence said, squeezing her fingers.

She turned to see Mr Oak watching them, a look in his eyes she could not decipher. Henry arrived then, moving to greet Mr Oak, who nodded at him.

"A fine day for it." Henry gestured to the clear blue sky above them.

Mr Oak gave the sky a frowning glance.

"For now," he said ominously.

Henry laughed, looking perplexed. "Sterling, there's not a cloud to be seen."

"There will be a storm before evening."

"You can't possibly know that," Henry replied, his scepticism obvious.

Mr Oak just shrugged, his gaze drifting to Grace once more. Florence frowned, moving away from him, unsettled and uncertain as to whether she liked the fellow or not. He was always so aloof. Hearing her name called, she hurried over as her horse was led out for her.

Florence was delighted when she saw the beautiful palomino mare with a golden coat and white-blonde mane. The horse was lively, dancing a little in her eagerness to be off as the stable boy brought her out.

"Can you handle her?"

Florence turned to see Henry regarding the mare with a slight frown. For a moment she bristled with irritation that he believed her incapable, but then she realised he was concerned for her safety. The thought warmed her, and her annoyance dissipated.

"Yes. I'm a proficient rider, I assure you."

Henry nodded and went to turn away.

"Won't you help me up, please?" she said quickly, not about to let the opportunity slide.

He stopped and Florence stared back at him, challenge in her eyes. Something stirred in those hazel depths, and she felt her pulse quicken as a smile played at the corners of his mouth. There was something predatory in that not–quite-smile and Florence swallowed, a little less sanguine now. She stood, waiting for him, assuming he would make a step of his hands to help her up, as was usual. He did not. Instead, he strode towards her, grasped her by the waist, and tossed her into the saddle.

Florence squealed and grasped the horse's mane to steady herself. Not that she was in danger of falling as his large hands still gripped her waist.

"I'm so sorry, did I startle you?" he asked, all innocence, the rat.

Doing her best to catch her breath, Florence made a performance of checking her hat was in place and gathered up the reins.

"Not at all. Thank you, Mr Stanhope," she said, irritated to discover she was breathless.

"You're welcome, Miss Knight," he said, smirking a little.

Florence relaxed. At least now he would walk away and see to his own mount. She hooked her leg over the fixed head of the side saddle but instead of walking off, Henry hiked up her skirts to reveal her ankles and made it his business to place her supporting foot in the stirrup.

"Mr Stanhope!" she hissed in outrage. "I am perfectly capable of arranging…"

He looked up at her and the words died in her throat. His hand rested on her ankle still, the warmth of it burning her even through the soft leather of her ankle boot. There was a look in his eyes that made her want to leap down from the horse again and press her mouth to his. Her stomach got that peculiar fluttery sensation that always began when he was near, and she prayed no one was looking, for she was certainly blushing. At last he dragged his gaze from hers and was suddenly all business, tugging her skirts into place to cover her ankles.

"Enjoy the ride, Miss Knight," he said curtly, and walked away.

Good heavens.

By the time they set out, Florence had composed herself once more, though she could not keep her eyes from Henry, who seemed to be making a project of staying as far from her as possible once again. This time, however, the thought made her smile. He was not indifferent to her. The look in his eyes earlier had shown her that, which meant he was avoiding her for an entirely different reason.

Except... he'd said he'd been unkind to her because she reminded him of someone else, someone who must have hurt him very badly. Had that been the reason he'd left England all those years ago? Had a broken heart driven him away? If that were the case, then had that look been for the woman he'd loved before, perhaps loved still? Or had it been for her?

"You look very serious."

Florence looked up to see Vivien's twin brother, Ash, regarding her with interest. She smiled at him warmly. Ash was a good friend and she liked him very much. She trusted him too, so....

"Ash, do you know anything about Mr Stanhope?"

Ash shrugged, giving her a quizzical glance. "Not really. I mean, I saw him now and then before he left the country, but I was only a boy then."

Florence nodded. "But have you heard anything, about why he left, I mean? Was... Was there a broken love affair?"

Ash frowned, considering this. "Yes, now you mention it. Wasn't he jilted by his fiancée? Yes, that's it. She eloped with some titled fellow instead, just days before they were due to wed."

"Oh," Florence said, her heart aching. If that were true, Henry would not only have been heartbroken, but he'd also have been mortified. It was the kind of blow a young man's pride would struggle to recover from. "Do you know who the lady was?"

Ash shook his head. "You be better off asking your mother. She'd know."

Florence nodded, having no intention of asking Mama. She was far too perceptive, and Florence did not want her putting a spoke in her wheel if she did not approve the match. Far better it were a foregone conclusion. Florence turned back to Ash, discomforted to discover he was watching her with interest.

"Something to tell me, Flo?" he asked, lifting one dark eyebrow. His golden skin glowed in the sunlight, his thick black hair tousled and gleaming blue like a crow's wing.

"Whatever do you mean?" she asked, striving for nonchalance.

"Oooh, I see it," he said, giving a low chuckle. "You've a *tendre* for him."

"No, I…." Florence began, and then gave up with a huff. "Well, perhaps I do."

Ash grinned at her. "I knew it."

He turned to regard Henry, who was riding a little ahead of them to their right.

"Don't look," Florence said urgently, which had no effect whatsoever on Ash, naturally.

"I suppose I can see the appeal," Ash said, considering. "A handsome fellow, sophisticated and urbane. All that self-assurance and experience must be a lure. Hmm, I wonder if *I* ought to try to look older."

Florence snorted. "From what I hear, you do not need the help."

Ash turned back to her with a wide-eyed look of naivete that was patently false.

"*Moi*?" He placed a theatrical hand to his chest, which was currently encased in a garish purple waistcoat with red silk spots on it.

"Yes, you. So stop smirking at me. Oh, promise you won't tell anyone, Ash, please?"

He shrugged. "Viv will know. I can never keep secrets from her."

"Oh, Ash, please! Try, will you?"

"What's it worth?" he asked, waggling his eyebrows at her.

"Ash!" she said in alarm, but the devil only laughed at her.

"Oh, stop fretting. I shan't say a word. Your secret is safe with me."

Florence let out a slow breath and smiled at him. "Thank you, Ash. You're a good friend."

"I know," he said with a sigh, before winking at her and riding ahead to join the men.

It was a lovely ride to Hever, and there was plenty of time to explore and see the castle before lunch. Florence wandered from room to room, enjoying the history of the place that had been Anne Boleyn's home, but the castle was not so quiet and romantic as she remembered from a previous visit as a child. The north-east corner of the castle had collapsed under the weight of a large fifteenth century chimney which had been built on top of the kitchen flue. Now builders worked to move the kitchen into the Great Hall, as the tower was showing signs of cracking. Just another phase in the life of this historic building that had stood for centuries. How strange to think it would still be standing, proud and immutable, generations after all those here today had turned to dust. It made one think about time, about what one wanted from life, and about taking chances.

Lost in her own thoughts, Florence found she was wandering by herself, having been abandoned by Ash and Vivien for dallying too long as she stared out the window at the view over the moat and the landscape beyond. She was in the west wing now and remembered this was where Anne Boleyn's private parlour had been. As she got to the doorway, she stopped with a little gasp, struck by the scene before her.

Montagu was here with his wife, the two of them in a fervent embrace. Florence stared in shock, taken aback by the obvious passion between them. Goodness, they had three children, two of them full grown, and yet the love and desire between them seemed undiminished.

"Shhh," murmured a voice in her ear.

Florence's heart jolted as a flutter of warm breath moved over her cheek. She turned to see Henry watching her with amusement. He pressed a finger to his lips and took her hand, curving his fingers around hers. With a tug, he pulled her away, not speaking until they were out of earshot. He guided her to the morning room: a cosy, dark, and intimate room with ornate panelling.

"Do you know their story?" he asked, still holding her hand. "The Montagus, I mean."

Florence was riveted by his touch. He wore no gloves, and she could feel how warm he was. She wanted to remove her own gloves so badly she hardly understood the question he asked, but forced herself to concentrate.

"Of course. The Duchess of Bedwin wrote about it in *The Eagle and the Lamb*. Everyone knows their story."

He nodded, smiling. "Then you must know this was one of the places they met, before they married."

"Ah," she said, letting out a breath, understanding now. "I had forgotten. How romantic."

He gave a short laugh and let go of her hand.

"You don't think so?" she asked him.

"Of course, it's romantic now they are happily married. At the time I doubt it felt romantic at all—rather desperate, I should think—but I had forgotten how important a great romance is to girls."

"To girls?" she repeated, quirking an eyebrow at him. "I hardly think it is only important to girls, and, besides which, I am *not* a little girl, Mr Stanhope."

He snorted at that and moved to the window, staring out. "Is that so? No doubt you think you're all grown up, but you're not."

Florence regarded him curiously, noting the tense set of his shoulders. He had brought her here instead of taking her to be with the rest of their party. She could see most of the others were outside now, enjoying the sunshine. How strange men were. It was clear he wanted to be alone with her, but it made him uneasy, so he tried to keep her at a distance whilst bringing her nearer. Foolish man. She smiled and he turned, noticing her expression.

"What?" he demanded.

Florence shook her head, not about to share her observations. He glowered at her. The urge to laugh was tempting but she fought it, moving to the fireplace. She took off her gloves and touched the initials carved into the stone. H.W. for Henry Waldegrave, whose family had owned Hever Castle from the fifteenth century until the early seventeen hundreds. She traced the H with a fingertip, up and down, caressing the cool stone. He watched her, his gaze following the path of her finger.

"Have there been any more strange goings on?" Florence asked, needing to break the peculiar atmosphere. It was becoming hard to breathe. "Things that go bump in the night?"

Henry hesitated and she felt her heart skip as she realised there had been. He frowned, saying nothing, which seemed answer enough. She hurried towards him.

"What?" she demanded. "What now?"

He gave her an impatient glance and shook his head. "I shan't tell you, for you'll turn it into some Gothic horror."

"Mr Stanhope, you are the most pig-headed man. Can you not see? I don't need to turn it into a Gothic horror, it's already begun. What has happened?"

She stared into his hazel eyes, noticing this close that they were a complex shade of gold and bronze and amber. His skin was darkly tanned, and she could not help but wonder if he was that colour all over. After a long moment, he let out a breath.

"Someone poisoned one of my sheep with rhododendron leaves, and there have been more corn dolls. One was hanged by the neck on my front gates and I...."

He hesitated, clearly not wishing to tell her.

"What?" she asked, almost breathless.

He sighed and ran a hand through his hair, tumbling the thick locks into disorder. "I found one on my pillow when I woke up this morning."

"Oh, Henry!" Florence rushed forward, too shocked and afraid to think of what she was saying or doing as she moved closer to him, grabbing the lapels of his coat. "You're in danger. Can't you see that? Someone was in your bedroom whilst you slept. They killed your sheep already. The hanged corn doll was a warning, a threat.... Oh, please, you must take care."

"It was only a sheep," he said in consternation, making light of it, the wretched man.

"For now!" she exclaimed, horrified that someone might really mean him harm.

"Do you worry for me, Miss Knight?" he asked, his voice soft, such warmth in his eyes as he reached out to touch her cheek.

Florence closed her eyes, shivering under his fingertips. It was barely a touch, feather-light, and yet she felt it to her toes, and felt an answering spark of flame ignite at the question his touch posed... the one he would never speak aloud.

"Of course I worry about you. Someone means you harm."

He dropped his hand but did not step back. Standing close enough to kiss her, he did not move but just stared down at her. Florence was too aware of the rise and fall of his chest, the sound of his harsh breath suddenly the only thing she could hear above the thudding of her heart in her ears. The scent of him enveloped her, fresh linen and horses, leather, and the subtle musk of his body, drawing her in, muddling her senses. She wanted to touch him, to have him touch her, so badly it was a pain beneath her skin, a longing so profound it hurt to be this close without physical contact.

"Henry," she said, too aware that there was pleading in the sound of his name on her lips, that her voice begged *kiss me, please kiss me,* without her ever uttering the words.

Something flickered in his eyes, there and gone before she could read it. He took a step back, any emotion wiped from his face.

"You ought not be alone with me, Miss Knight. Come, I shall return you to the others."

She stared at him in shock, at the indifference in the tone of his voice, the nonchalant way he dismissed her.

"I don't want to return to the others," she said, aggrieved that he could ignore the force of whatever it was between them, as if it were nothing. "And I'm only alone with you because it's what you wanted. You brought me here."

"A mistake," he said crisply. "One that won't happen again. Come along."

Florence glowered at him. "I'm not a child," she snapped. "I can find my own way outside and, unlike some, I am not a coward."

With that parting shot, she turned and stalked away.

As exit lines went, she was rather pleased with herself, though less so when she discovered she'd gone the wrong way and had to retrace her steps. Muttering crossly about the male of species, she was in a fine temper by the time she made it outside, to find everyone was waiting for her. Her spirits were further lit by the look of amusement in Henry's eyes as he turned away from her.

Oh, the fiend. He would pay for that look, and the fact he made her act like a complete lunatic.

The party made their way the short distance to the pub on the corner, the Henry VIII. It was a handsome property. In traditional Kentish style, the bottom half of the building was made of warm red brick, the upper half tile hung, and the middle punctuated by a half-timbered gable. Impressive chimneys soared into the sky and the leaded light windows shone brightly, promising a clean and well-run establishment.

The proprietor was a Mr Moon, who was clearly delighted to have such exalted company as the Marquess and Marchioness of Montagu, the Earl and Countess St Clair, Lady Helena Knight, and even a glamorous French comte in his pub. Mr Moon greeted them eagerly and showed them to a large, private parlour where they were waited on promptly and their orders taken.

"Whatever is the matter?" Vivien asked once everyone was settled. "You look positively murderous."

Florence tried to rearrange her face, but her mouth felt too stiff to smile, so she doubted it had done much good. She glanced at Ash, who just shrugged.

Vivien looked between them, her dark eyebrows drawing together. She gave her twin a hard stare. "What do you know that I don't?"

"N-Nothing," Ash stammered, doing his best to appear innocent and looking as guilty as hell.

Florence sighed.

"Oh, you may as well tell her, Ash," she said, resting her head on her hand and glowering at the far side of the room.

Henry was laughing with the earl, the two men chuckling over something amusing. Probably her idiocy, she thought gloomily. Was he telling the earl all about the silly chit who was in love with him?

Vivien followed her gaze and let out a squeak of triumph. "You are in love with Mr Stanhope."

"Good Lord," Ash exclaimed. "How do you do that?"

"Do what?" Vivien asked, swivelling back to look at Ash.

He had folded his arms, his expression fierce. "I never even got the chance to tell you!"

Vivien shrugged. "There's hardly any need when she's gazing at the man like a lovesick puppy."

"I do not look like a lovesick puppy," Florence objected, sitting up straight again.

"You do a bit," Ash murmured, a touch apologetically.

"I do not!"

"Well, a kitten, then," Vivien allowed, patting her hand. "It's rather nauseating, whichever you choose, love."

"Oh!" Florence wailed and put her head in her hands. "I don't know what to do."

Vivien considered her with interest. "What do you *want* to do?"

Florence snorted, muttering under her breath. "I don't want to do anything. I want Henry Stanhope to admit he's madly in love with me and carry me off into the sunset, but he's far too maddening to do anything of the sort. I think he thinks he's too old for me."

"Well, he is a friend of your father's, Flo, and your papa is known for being, er... somewhat protective of his girls," Ash observed, tracing the scarred top of the well-polished table with a finger.

Florence glowered at him. "Not helping."

Vivien considered her with a frown of concentration, which was a little unnerving as she was always so intense. Being the centre of her attention was a bit like standing in the heart of a storm, just waiting for the chaos to begin around you.

"What was your dare?" she asked, her tone thoughtful.

Florence regarded Viv warily, her senses prickling. "Tell a lie for love."

Vivien grinned.

"Oh, God," muttered Ash.

"I don't like it," Florence admitted. "The idea of telling a lie to someone I care for is... it's just not right."

Ash nodded sympathetically. "It does sound rather unpleasant."

Vivien gave an impatient tsk and shook her head. "You're both missing the point. You must remember the spirit of the dares, what our mothers did it for. They were written in the spirit of hope and expectation. It's not that you must tell a lie to cause hurt or to cover a secret. It's more a lie that you know will be found out, a little deception to get what you want."

"Like what?" Florence asked, not quite understanding.

Vivien pursed her lips and studied her nails with an expression that was far too innocent to sit easily on her stunning features. "Oh, like... making out your horse has bolted, or... falling off and pretending you've sprained your ankle and can't ride, so you can be alone with a certain fellow who's been playing hard to get."

Ash groaned and put his head in his hands. "Viv!"

"What?" she demanded, wide-eyed. "It's quite brilliant if you ask me, but I suppose it's up to you, Flo. What do you think?"

Florence grinned at her.

Chapter 5

Dear diary,

It is always such fun to be at Holbrook House, especially this summer, for Aggie is here too. She really is the dearest creature and my very best friend. I feel sad that she lives in an orphanage, not that she seems to mind, for she says it is a palace compared to her life before. She says the teachers are all lovely and kind and she likes being with all the other girls. Of course she also has the Comte de Villen as her guardian, who is very glamorous and spoils her a good deal.

I asked Papa if I might give her one of my new gowns, as I know she won't have anything so fine, and I have lots to choose from. He kissed me and said I was just like Mama, which I think means I may do as I please, for he loves Mama above all things.

Lord Fred bought Aggie more books too, so I think she is having a splendid time.

I saw Grace Weston crying this morning. She was all by herself in the orchard and looked so desperately unhappy I did not like to intrude. I wonder if I ought to tell someone. I don't want to be a tattletale.

—Excerpt of an entry to the diary of Lady Catherine 'Cat' Barrington, (youngest daughter of the Marquess and Marchioness of Montagu).

Still the 15th of August 1839, en route from Hever Castle to Holbrook House, Sussex.

"Are you going to tell me about her, then?"

Henry slowed his horse as Jasper Cadogan, the Earl of St Clair, rode up beside him.

"About whom?" he asked, narrowing his eyes. He had the uncomfortable suspicion he would not enjoy this conversation.

"Don't be thick, Henry. I've known you since you were in short trousers."

Henry returned a quelling expression, which only made Jasper snort.

"Miss Knight, you dolt, and stop pretending ignorance."

Henry glanced about them to see if they could be overheard.

"There's nothing to tell," he replied, aware he sounded terse. "The silly chit has a *tendre* for me, that's all."

"Really?" Jasper replied, raising his eyebrows. "I always found Miss Knight to be a well-educated, sensible young woman, not the least bit silly. Not surprising, really, with Lady Helena for a mother. She's very keen on the education of women. A fan of Mary Wollstonecraft, I believe. Don't get her started on *A Vindication of the Rights of Woman*, for you'll be in for a long evening. Not that I disagree, naturally."

"Naturally," Henry replied dryly.

Jasper laughed. "Well, really, Henry! I am married to your sister, and we'd both need to be exceptionally witless not to realise she's got more brains than the two of us put together."

Henry muttered an oath of exasperation and raised his eyes skyward. "Is there a point to this conversation?"

"Naturally there's a point."

"Well, do you think we might get to it via a more direct route?"

"You know, I have noticed that men who deny they are in love when all evidence is to the contrary are remarkably bad-tempered."

Henry glowered at the man who had been his best friend since boyhood. "That would be a no, then."

Jasper grinned at him, quite unrepentant.

"I am not in love with her."

"Well, you're something," Jasper observed with a smirk.

Henry felt his temper flare.

"Very well," he said, his voice harsh. "She's beautiful, and I want her. Every time I see her, I want to drag her into a quiet corner and...."

He broke off, disgusted with himself. "I'm sure Gabe wouldn't mind," he added viciously, in case Jasper was in any doubt of his predicament.

"If all you wanted was to indulge your lust, I don't doubt he'd hunt you down like a dog," Jasper remarked, studying Henry with interest. "But that's not all you want, and that's why you're in such a lather. Admit it, man, you're running scared."

"Oh, I'll admit I'm running scared. I'm terrified I'll give into temptation, which is all too possible when the girl so obviously wants me to kiss her. What scares me the most is that the moment my lips touch hers I may as well post the blasted banns and have done with it."

Jasper gave a little huff of laughter and returned a look which was one part sympathy, two parts pity. "Henry, you're a jolly good fellow and a great friend, despite abandoning us all for a decade, but you're also being deliberately obtuse."

"Am I, indeed?" Henry replied through gritted teeth. "And what is it I'm being so dull-witted about, pray tell?"

Jasper shook his head, looking like he too was holding onto his patience now. "Very well, and I say this as your oldest friend, and someone who wants to see you happy. The fact is, you *want* to get caught, to have the decision taken away from you so you need not admit it's really what you want and need above all things. For God's sake, man, just court the girl, will you? Gabriel won't kill you if your intentions are honourable. Knowing the trouble she's just endured with her last suitor, he might even be pleased."

"What suitor? What trouble?" Henry demanded at once.

Jasper only laughed at him, his amusement too obvious.

"Why don't you ask her?" he said, still laughing under his breath as he rode away.

Henry scowled at his friend's back.

"Idiot," he muttered. It was fine for Jasper, he'd been in love with Harriet since he was a boy. He'd always known his lot in life would be to settle down and take on the earldom with a suitable wife. Whilst Harriet had not given him an easy time of it—to say the least—Jasper had known what he wanted, and what was expected of him, from the start.

Henry had thought he'd known once, too. His father had been a brilliant academic who travelled the world, studying ancient civilisations. As a boy he'd assumed he'd follow suit. His father had certainly wanted that. Except it had soon become clear that Henry was not suited to academia. Sitting still, writing lengthy essays had driven him to distraction when he wanted to be out of doors, exploring and discovering the world. Whilst his love of travelling was certainly a trait required for such a future, learning history in the depth required was simply beyond him. His father had made no secret of the fact Henry's less than pristine school record caused him great disappointment. Not that he took any pride in Harriet either, who was far cleverer than he'd ever been… simply because she was a girl. Indeed, the late Mr Stanhope had been forthcoming about the fact his children were useless and hopeless until the day Harriet had married Jasper, the Earl of St Clair. He'd looked on her with pride for that, much to Harry's contempt. Henry did not think she'd ever forgiven her father, and he did not blame her in the least.

Henry had thought that he might have done the right thing when he'd begun courting Miss Lily Johnson, the daughter of a viscount. His father had been thrilled by the connection with another powerful family and had, for once, looked upon Henry with something approaching pride. Then his father had died, and they'd had to delay the wedding whilst Henry was in mourning. Henry had wanted the wedding to go ahead, but Lily said she did not want a dull, gloomy affair and had insisted they delay. At least his father had never seen what had happened next, when Lily had jilted him, and not gently either. Henry had often wondered what would have happened if his father had lived and he'd married Lily. He suspected it would have been the greatest mistake of his life, but perhaps that was because he'd become old and cynical in the years that had followed.

When she'd eloped with the Earl of Nettlebury, just days before their wedding, the scandal had been far greater than Henry could have imagined. He'd been humiliated and he wasn't certain his pride had ever recovered. It was why he'd stayed away for so long. Longer than he'd wanted to, if he were honest, for he'd been homesick. Coming back to face everyone again had been hard. But here he was, hardly back in the country for a couple of weeks and he had some young woman making doe eyes at him and the man he'd always considered his best friend encouraging him to court her.

Well, there was no way on God's green earth he was walking down that same path once more. He'd die a lonely old man before he let himself get hurt like that again. He'd guard his heart this time, so there was no way some wretched woman could pluck it from his chest and throw it down in the dirt before grinding it beneath her heel. Never again. No matter how temptation beckoned, or how lovely the woman was. This time, he'd listen to his head, not that idiotically flawed and tattered organ that passed as his heart.

"Are you quite sure about this?" Ash asked Florence quietly. "We can stop it if you're not."

They had already dropped far behind the others, dawdling and pretending to chatter and admire the scenery. The rest of their party had now moved out of sight, having passed a thick copse of trees.

"I think so," Florence said, when in fact she wasn't the least bit sure. Her dare needed completing, though, and this was the only idea that might give her a chance to be alone with Henry. She was certain he was attracted to her now, after that scene in the castle, not to mention this morning. If only she could induce him to kiss her, she felt certain things would go her way. This was her best chance to make that happen.

"Right then, this looks perfect. Florence, you'd best dismount and arrange yourself as though you've taken a tumble," Vivien said, gesturing imperiously for her to get on with it.

"Do you need help?" Ash asked.

"No, I can do it." Florence kicked her stirrup free and slithered to the ground, not altogether elegantly.

"Right, well, lay down over there, like you've fallen from your horse."

Florence looked at the patch of grass Vivien indicated and did her best to organise her skirts and limbs in an appropriate pose. "Like this?"

"Hmmm, I think you should put your hand up behind you—yes, like that—and the other over your heart... oh, jolly good. Now close your eyes. Yes! That's perfect. You look lovely, like a tragic heroine. Ophelia, perhaps."

"Didn't she drown?" Ash asked sceptically.

"Don't split hairs," Viv retorted, waving this away. "Ophelia, once she'd been hauled out of the river and dried off, if you insist."

Ash sighed.

"Right, well, we shall ride off and take our time catching up with the others. We don't want him to find you too quickly. You need to be a way behind us, so you get some time alone with him. Just don't waste it. We'll bring your horse with us and make up a story that sounds plausible."

"And why haven't we returned to search for our friend?" Ash asked with the quirk of a dark eyebrow. "A fine fellow he'll think me."

"Oh, not for long. Flo will tell him the truth before they get back, won't you, Flo?"

Florence blanched a little at the idea of admitting what she'd done to Henry, whom she doubted would see the funny side of it, but she nodded gamely. "Of course."

"Very well, then," Ash said, with the fatalistic air of one who was in the grip of one of Vivien's *ideas* and knew he'd be mown down if he tried to stop her. "If we must, let's get it over with."

Vivien gave a little squeal of excitement. "Yes! Let the drama begin. Don't forget to play your part, Flo. If he doesn't kiss you before you get back, I'll be most disappointed in you."

Florence sighed from her position in the grass and waved them off, wondering just how long she would have to wait for Henry to find her.

"Mr Stanhope!"

Henry turned at the sound of his name. Miss Anson was hailing him from some way back, her brother riding up behind her. How the devil had they got so far behind? He turned his mount, trotting back to them.

"Oh, Mr Stanhope. I just must speak to you about those corn dolls. You know, our grandmother might have something to say about them. You see—"

"Viv! Viv, where's Florence?" called her brother as he drew up alongside them.

Miss Anson frowned at him. "Flo? Why, she was with you."

"Well, she's clearly not with me, Viv. What the devil have you done with her?"

"I've not done anything!" Miss Anson replied hotly, glaring at her brother.

"Wait!" Henry interrupted, a sick feeling stirring in his guts. "Do you mean to say Florence has disappeared?"

"Well... I... I suppose so," Miss Anson said, her expression growing anxious. "Oh, Ash, you don't think... could she have had a fall?"

At this moment the pretty palomino mare Florence had been riding trotted around the corner without her rider.

"Hell!" Henry said, urging his horse forward. "You, retrieve the horse. *You*, tell the others," he instructed each twin in turn, before riding off.

He would not sit about listening to those two twits trying to figure out what to do next. If Florence had fallen she might be hurt or in pain. She would certainly be frightened if no one returned to help her. He glanced up to where thick, smothering clouds were rolling in at an alarming rate, turning the sky a sickly greyish yellow. The glorious day was turning into a very sombre afternoon, and Henry cursed himself for not having taken Sterling's words more seriously. They would have a storm very soon, judging by the way the wind had picked up, and they would need to get to cover fast.

It took him the next fraught quarter of an hour to find her, the entire time spent with his heart in his throat, terrified he would find her crumpled and bleeding. Visions of her lying broken and bloody filled his suddenly overactive imagination as he rode flat out, searching the ground for any evidence of a fall. When he finally found her, he could have wept with relief, a sensation swiftly overtaken by the urge to wring her blasted neck.

"What have you been playing at, you little nitwit?" he demanded, seeing her walking through the meadow with a disconsolate air and no little difficulty, hindered by her heavy skirts. "I told you that horse was too much for you."

A look of deep irritation crossed her lovely face, and her green eyes flashed sparks at him that could have ignited the dry grass about her. "No, you did not. You asked *if* she was too much for me. I said she was not. I was correct, by the way."

"Then why did you fall off?" he demanded.

"I didn't," she admitted, a sudden flush of colour pinking her cheeks in a way that was quite delicious.

Stop noticing her, he warned himself crossly.

"Oh really?" he asked, not bothering to hide his contempt at her lie. "Then why are you on foot?"

"For you, you idiot man!" she exclaimed, the temper erupting in time with an ominous rumble of thunder.

"What on earth...?"

"Oh, it doesn't matter," she said with a dismissive sweep of her hand. "Just go away. You clearly can't wait to be rid of me."

"I'm not leaving you here alone," he retorted.

She sent him a volcanic glare.

"Then send Ash and Viv back with my horse," she said through her teeth.

"No. Not until I understand what you mean that you did it for me."

She rolled her eyes as though she were all out of patience with him which, given the circumstances, was rather rich. "Oh, to get you alone, of course. How dim-witted are you? It was a dare."

Henry blinked at her, thoroughly lost, though the mention of a dare stirred an uneasy memory. "A dare?"

Florence nodded. "Like our mothers did. We've been taking turns to draw a dare from the hat."

"*The* hat?" he asked in astonishment. "The actual hat? You mean that still exists?"

"Yes," she said with a sigh. "And all the original dares. Our parents all met and married happily because of those dares, and it worked for Eliza and Elspeth, and Arabella. I thought it might work for me too but... but then I realised it was a rotten trick to play on you, especially as you don't even want to like me, or anyone come to that. You're too angry with the world, or at least with the female portion of it, to fall in love. And I knew you'd just be cross, so... it seemed best to tell you the truth at once. I'm sorry if I worried you," she added, though with an unmistakeable note of defiance as her chin went up.

Henry did not know whether to laugh or put her over his knee, too stunned by her precise summation of his state of mind to think clearly. In lieu of a response, he asked, "What was it?"

"What was what?" she asked, her voice dull.

"Your dare."

"Oh," she sighed, staring out over the acres of meadowland around them. "To tell a lie to someone I loved. I suppose I failed the dare too," she added with a huff of unhappy laughter.

Henry felt his heart squeezed in his chest. The foolish child believed she was in love with him, and, God help him, she looked so forlorn. "Well, you can't stay out here by yourself, and that storm will be upon us at any moment."

He dismounted and walked his horse over to her. She gave him a frowning glance, which for some reason made Henry desperate to kiss her, to chase away the woebegone expression that dulled the brightness of her eyes.

"Come on, up you get."

"But you've not got a side-saddle," she objected.

"No, so you'll have to make do."

Before she could object, he picked her up, throwing her up onto the saddle as he'd done this morning.

"Oh!" she said, scrambling into place before she slipped off and glowering down at him. "I do wish you would stop manhandling me."

"But I thought that was what you wanted," he returned before he could think better of it.

She blushed again, brighter this time, and he found he could not regret his words. The pink of her cheeks was perfectly charming. He climbed back into the saddle, and she gasped as he tucked her in front of him. Though Henry suspected it was not terribly comfortable, she did not complain, though he regretted the position at once, for he was obliged to put his arm around her to hold her steady, pulling her against his chest. She was too close. Her softness pressed against him, the scent of her teasing his nostrils. He was uncertain whether she wore perfume or if it was simply the soap she used, but the faint scent of roses enveloped him. It beckoned him, tempting him to press his nose to her hair, the tender skin behind her ear, or the curve of her neck and inhale, to see if he could find the source of the delicious aroma. He wanted to search everywhere until he was certain. Instead, he reminded himself severely of what he wanted from his future, and tried to get a grip on his sanity before it unravelled.

"You don't love me."

She turned her head, the ridiculous feather on her hat tickling his chin as she did so. "How can you be so sure?"

He shrugged. "I've been home more days than weeks; we've had a handful of conversations. You don't know me."

"Perhaps not," she admitted, and he could feel the weight of her green gaze upon his face, avoided it for fear of what he might see there. "But I know you are kind and loyal and I admire your opinions, and I know how you make me feel."

He frowned at that, his eyes finding hers despite his reluctance.

"How?" he asked, even knowing he ought not, that he did not want to know the answer.

You damned liar, Henry.

"Safe," she said softly. "You make me feel safe."

Henry looked away, trying to scoff at her answer and finding himself unable to do so. The word seemed to creep beneath his skin, to invade his blood, to settle in his heart.

"Why?" His voice was too rough, but something primal and possessive was thrashing about inside him and he couldn't stop it. She was looking for a man who made her feel safe, but why? Who had made her feel less than safe? If someone had hurt her, he'd....

"Because the future scares me."

He could not help but meet her eyes again, even though he knew it was dangerous. He saw the truth shining there, the fear.

"Why would you fear the future? You're young and beautiful, you've a vast dowry. Surely you could have anyone you wanted?"

She snorted at that, a flicker of scorn showing in her lovely features. "Oh, yes, because an heiress will always attract the best men."

Henry felt his brows draw together. "Well, yes. Obviously, there will be fortune hunters, but there are decent men too, aren't there?"

He felt rather than saw her shrug. "Decent men who will control me, own me, take my money and dictate who I see and when, what I may wear, what I may speak of... Oh, yes, there's plenty of those."

The despair in her words was unmistakable.

"You're young yet, Miss Knight, give it time...."

Her laugh was bitter, and he wanted never to hear such a sound from her again, this vivacious young woman who ought always to be full of joy.

"Perhaps another three years, and then I'll be considered an old maid. You know it's true as well as I do. I just—" Whatever she'd been going to say, she bit off the words and shook her head. "Never mind."

"Tell me," he said, when he ought to have kept his mouth shut. He did not want to know about her troubles, her fears for the future, for there was not a damned thing he could do to help her. It seemed he could no longer control his wretched tongue, though, nor his desire to discover more.

She took a breath. "You're always so proud of Harriet and never in awe of her cleverness. So many men dislike women who like to think for themselves, but from what I have seen you enjoy a spirited discussion, a woman who challenges you instead of agreeing with your every word. I feel you are the sort of man who would not crush the woman he married but… but be a friend to her as well as a lover. A man who would encourage her freedom but always remain a… a shelter from the storm."

Henry cursed the sensation that lanced through him at her words: the unacceptable but undeniable desire to be everything she wanted, to be *her* shelter. Jasper was right, she was no child, but a woman with a mind of her own, one that would test him, that would never allow him to be complacent, one who would remind him what it was to live, to love….

No.

No.

That way led to misery and despair, for she would soon realise her mistake, realise she wanted a younger man, one her own age, not a fellow nigh on two decades her senior. He tried for an amused tone in reply.

"Well, I think a more tangible shelter from the storm is required, Miss Knight, and sooner rather than later."

As they'd been talking, the sky had turned the colour of pewter and the temperature plummeted. The first fat drops of rain fell heavily, hitting the dry ground with distinctive thuds that came faster and faster. Henry muttered a curse under his breath, knowing they would need to shelter from the storm. Now he was in for it.

Chapter 6

Dear diary,

I am in despair. I am wearing a jovial mask, trying to be brave, to pretend all is well and my life does not hang in tatters. I am so frightened when I consider my future, of living in obscurity to hide my shame. I do not know how long I can keep up this façade, but I am afraid to face those I love most with the truth. Not because they will be angry, or condemn me, but because they will be heartbroken on my account, and I cannot bear to hurt them so.

—Excerpt of an entry to the diary of Miss Grace Weston (daughter of Jemima and Solo Weston, Lady and Baron Rothborn).

Still the 15ᵗʰ of August 1839, en route from Hever Castle to Holbrook House, Sussex.

"Hell!" Henry muttered, as thunder rumbled overhead. They could not shelter beneath a tree in a storm, but they were miles from any village yet. "I think I saw a shepherd's hut not far from here. We'd best take cover until this passes. Hold on."

Cursing the fates and the far too tempting young woman in his lap, he urged the horse into a canter as the rain fell with ever increasing vigour. In a matter of minutes they were soaked to the bone and the daylight subsumed in an unhealthy dirty grey glow as the sky glittered and cracked overhead. Henry urged his horse on, grateful that the lightening lit the way for long enough to show the low shape of a rustic wheeled hut up ahead through the torrent of the rain.

"Get inside," he yelled over the din to Miss Knight as he towed the unhappy horse around to a rickety shelter. It was not in the best of upkeep, but it afforded the poor creature some respite from the wind and rain.

Henry relieved the beast of its saddle and settled it as best he could before hurrying back to the hut. He paused inside the door, a little surprised to discover Miss Knight had set about lighting the fire and got a creditable blaze going.

"What?" she asked, a defensive angle to her chin as she glared at him. "I know fashionable women are supposed to be defenceless and swoon at every opportunity but I'm simply not the helpless kind."

"So I see," he said dryly. "That must be why you're making such heavy weather of finding a husband."

She covered her heart with her hand and gasped, a theatrical gesture that did not lack for sarcasm. "My word, Mr Stanhope, do you really think that could be it? Why I would *never* have guessed."

"Or that sharp tongue of yours puts them off," he added wickedly, earning himself another glare.

He smothered a grin, unable to deny the delight he took in provoking her. She was too delicious when she was cross with him.

"You are a very rude man," she observed.

Henry nodded gravely. "I am, which begs the question of why you like me so much?"

Idiot!

Henry wanted to bite his tongue out. For the love of God, they were alone, unchaperoned in a damned shepherd's hut with a storm raging overhead. It was the basis of a dozen or more overblown romantic Gothic novels and would end with him caught in the parson's mousetrap if he weren't very careful. He must pray the storm would blow itself out quickly and they could catch up with the rest of their party. The last thing he needed was to go encouraging the growing intimacy between them, but it was too late. He'd asked, and he could not deny that he wanted to know the answer.

She placed another piece of wood on the fire and then stood, dusting off her hands. She was wet through, her riding habit moulding itself to her lush form. He tried not to notice the hard peaks of her nipples beneath the sodden fabric and failed, too aware of her proximity, and of the fact they were all alone. He swallowed, reminding himself that this was everything he did not want, and so closing the gap between them would be utter madness.

It didn't matter. She came to him before he even had the chance to give in to idiocy, and Henry found he could not move away. No matter how the panicked voice in his head screamed the risks at him, reminded him of weddings and tenants for life and squalling babes and an end to freedom, his feet remained planted to the floor. Before he could come to his senses, her hands smoothed over his chest. Desire speared to his loins like an arrow thwacking a bullseye. Dead centre.

"I don't know," she whispered, answering a question he could no longer remember while need uncoiled low in his belly, his blood heating and surging in his veins. "I only know I have wanted you to kiss me from the first moment I saw you, but as you won't oblige…."

83

She grasped his lapels and tugged and, fool that he was, he bent his head, too weak to resist the lure of her sweet mouth, too lost in wanting her to remind himself he did not want her at all.

He knew the depth of his mistake the moment his lips touched hers. It was like being struck by lightning, but with way more force than the storm raging outside could possibly muster. It stole his breath, set his blood on fire, and had his cock standing to attention and demanding he take action.

Now, damn it.

It was such a brief touch, barely a kiss at all, yet it shook him to his bones, rattled his composure, and reminded him with a cacophony of alarm bells just why she was so bloody dangerous.

She'll make you act the fool for her, Henry.

For a moment, fear overrode passion and Henry wrenched free, putting distance between them. He stared at her in bewildered shock, as though she were some foreign species of creature that he'd not known existed before.

No. No, no, no. Not happening. Bad, bad idea.

"Henry," she said, and the sound of his name on her lips, the intimacy of it....

"No."

He was too aware of the ragged quality of his voice, too aware of the fragile veneer, thin as tissue paper, that stood between acting like a gentleman and taking advantage of this young woman and what was on offer. Oh, God. He wanted her, so badly that he felt giddy with it. He wanted to show her what it was she was so intent on getting from him and....

Breathe, Henry, Breathe.

"Why not? You want to kiss me."

He gave an outraged bark of laughter. "You little fool. I want a deal more than to kiss you. You're just too damned naïve to be afraid."

The wretched creature just shook her head. "I promise you I am in no way naïve. Inexperienced, perhaps, but not ignorant, nor as foolish as you might suppose, and I'm not afraid of you. I could never be afraid of you."

"Then you're an idiot."

"Sticks and stones, Mr Stanhope," she retorted, her amusement obvious.

She looked so damned smug, a knowing glint in her eyes that told him she knew he was all talk, that he was too honourable to do anything to frighten her. Irritation burned. He wanted to shake her composure until it was as wrecked as his own.

It wasn't as if he decided to do it, but before his brain had time to catch up, he'd grabbed hold of her, pressing her against the cold wall of the building with his body, holding her by her wrists, pinning her in place.

Mistake. Mistake. Mistake!

He shook with the force of the struggle going on inside him, the battle between what we wanted and good sense. Bar the tremble in his limbs he kept utterly still and breathed in that maddening rose scent, fighting a silent war against desire, fighting to remain calm, to behave as he ought. His longing to shock her fought his need to behave like a gentleman as his composure fractured by degrees. His lips touched the smooth skin of her brow, his breath moving over her as he fought to control his need, to bring himself back to his senses. She shivered against him but made no protest, her chest rising and falling rapidly, her softness pillowed against his harder frame.

Stop this. Stop this. You are behaving like a madman. You'll frighten the poor girl.

Henry drew in a shaky breath and pulled back, trying to find words to make an apology. Another mistake. A mistake to look into her eyes, expecting to see fury, but finding the emerald green dark with wanting.

"Please," she whispered.

Henry closed his eyes, praying for patience, for sanity, for the strength to ignore the pounding of his heart, the way his blood was rushing through his veins, and the desperate throb of his aching cock. He wanted... so many things, with a longing too profound to comprehend.

"Henry. *Please...*"

He groaned, knowing he was in deep trouble, unable to resist that wicked *please* that would lead him to ruin. For that was the crux of the matter, it was not her in danger of ruination, it was him.

His hands moved up from her wrists, their fingers interlacing as he lowered his head and took her mouth. She opened for him at once, letting him in with no resistance and whatever sanity remained in his thick head shrivelled and died. He took and took, and she met him at every turn, giving everything he demanded with enthusiasm. Not her first kiss, he thought dimly, and though he'd wager she'd little experience, she learned quickly. Her lithe body pressed against his in invitation, her hands sinking into his hair.

Henry drew back, and she made a whimpering sound of protest.

"Hush," he murmured, stripping off his sodden coat and waistcoat.

They were soaked through, and she did not need to be made any colder. Henry returned to her and took her in his arms once more, stealing another kiss, devouring her like a starving man offered the sweetest of treats. He became aware of the damp material of her gown through his thin shirt. Surely, she'd catch a chill if she didn't take it off? She should take it all off. He could keep her warm. The idea had merit, melding too well with his every desperate desire. He wanted to take her here on the floor of this damned hut, to make her his, to keep her with him....

Wait, what?

He dragged his mouth free of hers, but she'd tugged his shirt from his trousers and her soft, cold hands slid over his skin. Henry gasped at the shock of it, and not just the temperature of her fingers. He felt branded, his flesh burning for her, wanting, *needing* to feel her body against his. Christ, he'd not felt this out of control since he was a lad. What the devil was wrong with him? If he didn't get a grip, he was going to have her and then he'd be honour-bound to marry her. No. *No.*

Henry stared down at her, struggling to find words to stop this.

"Florence...." he began, his voice ragged. "Florence, we can't. I must not...."

She looked up at him, her cheeks and throat flushed, her lips red and swollen from his kisses.

"Henry," she said, a helpless plea. She trembled in his arms, her hands moving over him restlessly as she pressed against him, seeking, wanting. "Please... I'll run mad...."

Henry heard the desperation in her voice and understood all too well what she was feeling. Though he'd made himself forget, it was too easy to unearth the memories, those days he'd fancied himself in love with Lily, the certainty that he'd lose his mind if he could not be with her, touch her... *Christ.*

He could not hurt Florence like Lily had hurt him. He needed to put a stop to this. Now.

"Easy, love," he murmured, pressing her head against his shoulder, and pulling her to him. "This is a mistake."

He forced the words out, reminding himself that she was not only an innocent, a lady, but his friend's daughter, for the love of

God. He would not be this man, the kind who would take advantage of a young woman's misguided passion.

"It's not a mistake," she said, anger in her voice, though it was muffled against his chest. She looked up and his breath caught at the fierce burn in her green eyes. "*I* am not a mistake!"

Henry swallowed, reaching out to smooth a damp coil of dark hair from her forehead.

"No," he said gently. "But I am."

"No!" she insisted, the stubborn creature.

Henry took hold of her shoulders and gave her a gentle shake. "Listen to me. There's some handsome young fellow out there waiting for you, someone as full of enthusiasm and joy as you are, someone who wants a life with you, children, and a home and all the things you deserve, but it's not me. I don't want those things. I don't want a wife."

She pushed at his chest and Henry released her, taken aback by the anger in her eyes.

"Liar!" she exclaimed, facing him head on. No tears, no tantrums… just a cool fury that refused his placations. "You're a liar, Henry Stanhope! And, worse than that, you're a coward."

Henry jolted as though she'd slapped him. "Now, wait just a moment—"

"I won't wait, and I won't listen either. If you didn't want me, it would be different, but you obviously do. I know you were hurt before and I understand why you're afraid, but you can't spend your whole life running away. You came back, Henry. You came back for a reason, so don't take to your heels just because claiming everything you thought lost means you must take a chance."

"I came back to see my sister, to check on my property," he retorted, though the words rang as hollow as his chest had felt of late. He'd come back because he was homesick, lonely, because….

Florence gave him a look of such pitying disgust that his temper flared.

"If I had come back to marry, I'd hardly be looking at one of my friend's daughters to fill the position! What the devil do I want with some silly child barely out of the schoolroom?"

He saw the hurt flare in her eyes at his words and waited for the tears, for her angry words. Perhaps she'd throw something at him. God knew he deserved it. Instead she just let out a breath of laughter, though not the happy kind. She turned away from him and went and sat by the fire.

"You know as well as I do, I am no child. Many of my friends married four or five years ago, some have children already. It's just an excuse you are using to keep me at a distance. One day you'll look back upon your life and remember this day. One day, when you're alone and it is too late to change the mistakes you've made. If you won't be honest with me, you should at least be honest with yourself."

"What on earth makes you think you know my mind better than I do? You barely know me."

"Am I wrong?"

She stared at him, challenging him, daring him to look her in the eyes and deny all the things he had once wanted and hoped for, to deny that he wanted them still, despite everything. Something hurt and angry boiled inside him. He wanted to lash out at her for making him face it again when he'd thought such feelings long since buried.

He'd resigned himself to a bachelor life. It was a good life, one he'd enjoyed, one he did not want to give up now, not even for her. He heard the lie and knew he could not say those words aloud and not have her hear it too. Panic uncoiled in his guts, cold and uncomfortable, making him reckless.

"And what if I do as you think I ought? What if I marry you and in twenty years, ten even, you realise you made a mistake in marrying a man so much your senior?" he demanded, shocking himself with the anger in his voice, with the realisation that he feared this above all things… that he might let himself care for her, love her, only to have her regret her decision and despise him for it.

He would not put himself in such a position again. Never again would he be made to feel a fool for loving a woman who didn't want him.

Her expression softened, her eyes growing bright.

"Oh, Henry…." she began, but he could not stand it.

He did not want her care, certainly not her pity. He wanted no part in this… this ridiculous notion that they could possibly have a future together.

"Don't," he snapped, snatching up his coat and waistcoat and tugging them on, which was difficult when the material was so damp. He fought his way into them with sharp, angry movements. "I'm going to check on the horse," he muttered, and hurried out of the blasted hut before things could get any worse.

Thank God the worst of the weather seemed to have cleared, for now at least. The rain had slowed to a thin drizzle and the thunder was only a distant grumble, barely audible. Henry hurried around to his horse, who seemed undisturbed by his less than salubrious accommodation and was snoozing peacefully. He leaned against the beast and let out a slow breath, trying to release the tension singing through his bones. His shoulders were stiff and taut, but the pain did not end there. Though he wanted to deny it, his heart felt bruised, too exposed, and that was before he considered the thrum of unfulfilled lust that still burned in his blood.

"Hell and damnation, Henry," he muttered. The horse turned its head to regard him with mild curiosity. He shrugged at the beast. "I'm an idiot."

The horse grunted and Henry groaned. This was bad. Very, very bad.

"Henry!"

Henry turned as a familiar voice hailed him and saw Sterling riding towards him with Florence's mount in tow. Thank God.

"Is she well?" he asked as he came level with the shack.

"Yes, fine. Just took a little tumble," Henry lied, not about to say anything about Florence's absurd scheme to get him alone. "Thanks for bringing the horse."

Sterling shrugged.

"We got caught in the storm," Henry added unnecessarily.

"Reckoned," Sterling replied, giving him a considering look. "We made it to the inn on Saint's Hill. Don't think the storm's done yet. Best make haste."

Henry nodded and set about readying his horse.

Chapter 7

Dear Viv and Ash,

I hope you are both well. I am so sorry that I didn't get to see more of you this summer, but Papa had so much to do at Trevick that we had to return. I am so looking forward to next season when we can all be together again. I had a letter from Arabella telling me all about her life at Royle House. It sounds terribly romantic—well, apart from the parrot— and I am horribly envious. A little bird told me a story about a hat and a dare, Viv. You'd best write and tell me everything at once. I cannot believe you have not already done so. Some friend you are, keeping me in the dark. You'd best wait until we are together before you attempt it, or I shall be very cross.

Ash, I do hope you like the enclosed waistcoat, I thought the embroidery rather fine if I say so myself. The embroidered stockings are for Viv, of course. I hope you like them. I had a dreadful time not bleeding on the white silk as the roses were so fiddly. Trevick is a romantic place but deadly dull at times, so these have kept me occupied. I am making something as a belated wedding gift for Arabella now. By the way, do you think Bainbridge would wear a waistcoat with parrots on it?

—Excerpt of a letter from Lady Aisling Baxter (daughter of Luke and Kitty Baxter, The Earl and Countess of Trevick) to Mr Ashton Anson and Miss Vivien Anson (son and daughter of Aashini and Silas Anson, Viscountess and Viscount Cavendish)

Still the 15th of August 1839, Holbrook House, Sussex.

Florence sank into the hot bath with a sigh of relief. She'd never been so cold in her life. After a stop at the inn on Saint's Hill whilst the storm rumbled about menacingly for another hour, they returned to Holbrook without further incident. She knew Henry's sister had persuaded him to stay the night instead of riding the extra distance home though she was surprised he'd agreed to it. No doubt he wanted to run away from her. After what had happened, Florence didn't doubt Henry would go back to ignoring her and staying as far from her as possible. How depressing. She did not know what to do about him.

On the one hand, if he did not want her, she ought to respect his wishes and keep away. On the other, the foolish man clearly *did* want her, he was just held in check by the events of his past, events that would keep him chained to a lonely future if she didn't set him free. Surely, she ought to help him past that, even—and this thought made her swallow hard—even if it only freed him to find someone else. Not that she was going to hand him over without a fight.

Florence closed her eyes and sighed as she remembered the muddle of sensations being in his arms had provoked. Good heavens, but the man could kiss. It had not been her first kiss. When Mr Yates had been courting her, she had allowed him to kiss her. It seemed foolish not to kiss a man one was contemplating marrying. It had been one of the many things that had disappointed her about him. At first, she had believed he was as inexperienced as she and thought perhaps they just needed practise. It quickly became apparent he cared little for her pleasure, though, too intent on taking what he wanted and groping what parts of her he might in the brief moments she had endured it. His kiss had been wet and hard and unsettling, and not in a good way. Kissing Henry had been nothing like that. Though he had taken control, demanded more and more, it had never felt as if he was overpowering her, only asking her to meet him, to follow where he led. His kiss had been challenging, yes, but it had also been tender, his hands had been careful, holding her as if she meant something, like she was precious.

Florence sighed, aware of a restless simmer beneath her skin, of the need to be with him, to feel the weight of his body upon hers. He was so big and capable and… she groaned and rested her head on her knees. *Henry Stanhope, I will make you pay for this insanity, for kissing me and giving me a taste of what we could have and making me want to act like a lunatic.*

That first taste of him had been intoxicating, and it would never be enough.

"Something must be done about Henry," Harriet said, her brow crinkled endearingly as she pushed her spectacles up her nose. "I fear he is determined to live the rest of his days a bachelor. I shall have to think who else we can invite who would make him a good wife, though he didn't take the slightest notice of the eligible women I invited for him."

Jasper, Earl of St Clair, regarded his wife with amusement, only a little surprised that the disturbingly prescient woman had not noticed the obvious.

"Didn't he, dear?" Matilda said with an enquiring lift of one eyebrow that was far too nonchalant.

Ah, someone had noticed, and he could hardly be surprised if it was the Marchioness of Montagu. Matilda had been the mother hen of their group of Peculiar Ladies, and the one responsible for many of the matchmaking schemes that had found the close-knit group of friends happily married. Harriet, never usually slow on the uptake, frowned at her friend.

"Who?" she demanded.

Matilda pursed her lips.

"Well," she began cautiously. "It wasn't someone you invited *for him*, but... but I felt perhaps there was someone who captured his attention."

Jasper grinned as Matilda glanced up at him.

"You've noticed it too," Harriet accused him. "Oh, Jasper, you never said!"

"Didn't feel I could, Harry, my love. The poor devil is fighting it tooth and nail and... well, to be honest, I wasn't certain how you'd feel about it."

"Why are you both talking in riddles?" Harriet exclaimed, she let out a breath, staring from one to the other of them as though she could see into their brains if she looked hard enough. "Why would I not be pleased if someone here has captured his attention? But, wait... Matilda, you said I didn't invite the woman for *him*, so...?"

Jasper poured himself a drink and sat down, amused as he watched his wife's astonishing brain at work. The trouble was, as clever as she was, affairs of the heart were really not her forte.

"Well?" he pressed, seeing Matilda fighting not to laugh at Harriet's frustration.

"I don't know!" Harry exclaimed irritably. It was an answer that never failed to make her wild with frustration.

"Put her out of her misery, for heaven's sake," Jasper advised Matilda.

"Well, my dear. I cannot help but think he has feelings for Florence Knight."

Harriet stared at them both and then gave an exasperated huff of irritation. "Don't tease. Though I cannot fathom why, he doesn't even seem to like poor Florence much. For heaven's sake, he had to apologise for being so rude to her the other day. That hardly seems like…." She broke off as Jasper exchanged a glance with Matilda. "What?"

"He's annoyed with her because she provokes him," Matilda said, keeping her voice gentle. "She's made no secret of her interest in him. Indeed, Florence is a single-minded young woman, and she has set her sights on your brother. She's beautiful and eligible and very clever, and poor Henry knows he's in trouble. He feels trapped and so he's come out fighting."

Harriet gaped, before turning back to Jasper for confirmation who nodded.

"He's afraid he's too old for her, but I think he's also terrified of getting hurt again."

"Florence," Harriet said in wonder, shaking her head. "I never would have guessed."

Jasper made a sound of affectionate amusement. "My darling, I was hopelessly in love with you for years and you never suspected a thing. You must admit it's not your strong suit."

The look Harriet gave him was filled with such aching regret that he wished he'd not said it.

"Oh, Jasper," she said, hurrying to sit beside him and take his hand.

"There, there, love. All's well that ends well. The point is, Florence is falling for Henry hard if I'm any judge, and I think Henry is in more than a little danger himself, no matter his protestations."

"Henry and Florence," Harriet said, as if trying the names together and seeing if they fit. "She is much younger than him, it's true, but she's no child. I have always found Florence to be forthright and strong. Indeed, she's a courageous young woman, intelligent too. She'd never bore him with tedious conversation, she'd be an endless challenge. With Gabriel as their father, those girls have suffered their fair share of slights by the *ton* and yet Florence has never shied away, never backed down. She's a force to be reckoned with, and...."

Jasper waited whilst Harriet worked it through. She looked up at him and then at Matilda.

"You really think Florence has feelings for him?"

Matilda gave a little laugh. "Darling, she can hardly keep her eyes from him. I admit I am slightly disappointed, as I was looking forward to matchmaking, but there's nothing to be done except to wait for things to play out. Just you watch when they are next in the same room."

Harriet nodded, clearly taking Matilda's observations as beyond doubt. "We need to speak with Helena, but assuming she does not disapprove the match.... Yes. I think that this will do very well indeed."

Though he'd been wet and cold and weary, Henry was regretting his decision not to carry on back to the Hall. Though Holbrook felt homey in a way his house did not, and the meal before him was excellent, he did not feel at ease. He had the distinct feeling he was being watched, and it was an uncomfortable sensation. He could not figure out who was watching him, either. Florence appeared to be ignoring him, which he thoroughly deserved but did not like a bit, and no one else seemed to want to meet his eye, which was odd.

Perhaps he ought to have made himself go home, though he really hadn't wanted to. If he were honest, waking up to find a corn doll on the pillow beside his head had been extremely unsettling and Saxenhurst Hall was not the most welcoming of homes at the best of times.

His fault, of course; he'd left it empty all this time and he'd never been happy there, even as a boy. Harriet felt the same, he knew. Holbrook House had been home, Jasper's mother the epitome of everything a parent ought to be. He'd been more upset than he'd expected when she'd passed away.

Their mother had never had the knack of making a house a home, and Father always seemed to prefer to live in a museum, so that was how the house had felt growing up. Once he'd inherited, Henry had tried to change it, donating many of the collections his father had amassed to various museums and doing his best to make the place somewhere that his wife would wish to live in.

Of course, back then he'd assumed he would marry Lily, that the house would ring to the sound of children's voices. She'd had great plans for the property, he knew, though looking back he realised she'd wished to make it bigger and far grander than it was. Her ambitions were greater than he'd ever realised, more fool him.

When that dream went to hell, he'd stalked the empty house, not caring what the hell it looked like or if it fell down around him. All that had mattered was licking his wounds in private. Once that had become intolerable, he'd left, turning his back on it all for the best part of a decade. One could hardly wonder at it if the place was less than welcoming, and that was before one counted screams in the night and some mad fool dabbling in witchcraft or whatever mischief it was they were set upon. Henry sighed, picking halfheartedly at a delicious steak and kidney pie that he ought to be devouring, and only belatedly noticing he was being addressed.

"I beg your pardon, Helena," he said, forcing his attention back to the present. "I was wool gathering."

"So you were," Helena said, smiling at him, a considering glint in her eyes that made him want to check his hair and cravat and tug at his waistcoat. It seemed... measuring somehow, as if she were estimating his worth. "I was just curious what you thought about Caroline Norton?"

Henry searched his tired brain for the name which seemed vaguely familiar, though not as an acquaintance. "The Custody of Infants Act?" he wagered.

Helena gave him an odd smile, a bit like a parent who'd assumed their child too dim to get the answer correct and was pleasantly surprised. "The very same."

"Erm...." he began, a little hesitant. "I think she was stuck in an unhappy marriage with a man who tried to control her, and then tried to ruin her when he discovered she was too strong for him. She fought back and gained some measure of control over the right to her own children, which her idiot husband had no right to keep from her. Her fight has changed the law for many women in similar straits, and I believe she ought to be commended."

There was a profound silence around the table which Henry could not read. He cleared his throat, feeling rather uncomfortable.

"Of course, I don't know the ins and outs of it in detail. Only what I've read and heard via friends."

Helena nodded, which seemed to be a gesture of approval, so he relaxed a little. He had the distinct impression he'd just passed a test but, for the life of him, he didn't know what it was.

"Do you remember, Harry, the days when we said Henry couldn't chaperone a sponge cake?" Helena asked.

His sister, who had just taken a sip of wine, choked. Jasper sprang to his feet and went to pat his wife on the back.

"There, there, Harry. Here, have a sip of water."

Harriet took the glass from her husband with a grateful smile, casting Helena an accusatory glance.

"Very amusing, I'm sure," Henry muttered, looking suspiciously around the assembled company.

Only Florence met his gaze, a challenging look in her eyes that made something hot and impatient stir in his guts. *Christ*. He ought to have gone home, corn dolls be damned. Between someone playing silly devils, screaming in the night and murdering sheep, and being anywhere near Florence Knight, he knew damned well which was the most dangerous.

Finally, dinner was at an end and Henry thought perhaps he could escape to the safety of his own room. Jasper had other plans for him.

"Fancy a drink, old man? I need a nightcap. Yes, yes, you can keep me company for a few minutes, can't you?"

Henry sighed. Jasper clearly had something on his mind. He may as well get it over with.

Chapter 8

Dear Aisling,

Ash adores the waistcoat, naturally. Where in heaven's name did you find that gruesome shade of orange? I swear you two have the most lamentable taste. The sunflowers were extraordinarily well embroidered, though, I must admit. You have a spectacular talent. I only wish you wouldn't display it quite so vividly upon Ash's person. He really does not need the encouragement and I believe my eyes are suffering under the glare. If I am forced to wear spectacles, I shall hold you entirely responsible.

I have no information pertaining to Bainbridge and waistcoats with parrots, further than hearing from Arabella that he prefers parrots stuffed and mounted as a rule.

We long to see you too, darling, and I swear I will wait for you to commit my dare. I may need a partner in crime.

—Excerpt of a letter from Miss Vivien Anson (daughter of Aashini and Silas

*Anson, Viscountess and Viscount
Cavendish) to Lady Aisling Baxter
(daughter of Luke and Kitty Baxter,
The Earl and Countess of Trevick).*

**Early hours of the 16th of August 1839, Holbrook House,
Sussex.**

Florence closed the door behind her as quietly as she could
manage. Grace was sleeping at last. She'd known her friend had
been unhappy by the way she had laughed and chattered so
determinedly. Though she was no wallflower, Grace was inclined
to be reserved, which always made her sharp sense of humour even
more amusing, as it took one by surprise. Not that she was shy, but
Grace preferred to observe people and enjoyed listening to others
talk. If she joined in a conversation, her input was always
unexpected and intelligent. Grace had a way of seeing the world
differently from other people, certainly from Florence, who would
admit to sometimes seeing things as rather black or white rather
than shades of grey.

Now, though, Grace was deeply unhappy and afraid, not that
she would say as much. She was too determined to be brave, to
shoulder the burden of her secret alone. It broke Florence's heart to
see it, and she wished she could do something, anything to help
her, but she simply did not know how. She had promised to stand
beside Grace when the time came and she told her parents, though
Grace had stoically shaken her head and kissed Florence's cheek in
thanks for the offer. So Florence had done what she could and
stayed with her, talking and keeping her company until she had
finally fallen asleep.

Florence smothered a yawn. It must be after midnight for she
had heard the chimes what seemed like ages ago. As if on cue, a
clock somewhere struck one o'clock. Wearily, Florence turned to
walk back to her room, which was two doors down, and found
herself staring up at Henry.

She gave a little squeak of alarm and clutched at her heart. "Lud, but you gave me a start! You ought not sneak up on a person in the dark."

"I didn't sneak," he said, an indignant tone to his voice, which sounded different than usual. "And what the devil are you doing wandering about in the dark, in your nightgown? Whose room is that?" Florence narrowed her eyes at him. She could smell brandy on his breath and realised he was foxed. It might be best if he did not know she'd been with Grace, for he'd want next to know why and she did not want him watching Grace with curiosity.

"None of your business who or why," she said crisply, stalking past him.

It was really too awful of him to ignore her all blasted night and then interrogate her, the wretched man.

His hand grasped her wrist before she got two paces and she stilled, turning to face him. The feel of his warm hand upon her skin was electrifying. All she could think about was how it had felt to put her hands on him earlier. How on earth she'd had the nerve to slide her hands beneath his shirt she would never know, but she wouldn't ever regret it. Lord, but it had felt marvellous. His skin had been so hot, and surprisingly silky, the play of hard muscle beneath her hands so invigorating she'd wanted to tear his shirt from his body, and would have done if he'd not gone all honourable on her and told her she was making a mistake, the insufferable lummox.

"Whose room is that?" he asked again, an intense expression in his hazel eyes which seemed far darker in the dim light of the hallway.

"What does it matter to you?" Florence demanded. "It's not as if you want me, is it?"

He made a harsh sound that sent little prickling sensations shivering down her spine.

"Not want you?" he repeated, a dangerous note to the words that had all her instincts standing to attention.

"No," she said, when a more sensible young woman might have just admitted she'd been chatting with Grace, and they'd lost track of time. "I'm a mistake, remember?"

A sensible young woman would have paid attention to that dangerous note and the matching gleam in his eye and decided a quick apology and faster retreat was in her best interests. Sadly, any sense Florence had been born with seemed to melt into a puddle of warm treacle, alongside anything resembling a brain whenever this irritating, intoxicating man got within twenty paces of her. In those circumstances, provoking him seemed a simply marvellous idea.

"I never said—"

"Yes, you did. A mistake. I remember it quite clearly. So, I may saunter about the house in my nightgown, and visit the devil himself if I so choose, and you may not say a word about it, for it is none of your affair. If I wanted to, I might go outside and dance naked in the fountain, and you could not stop me."

"Could I not?"

She wondered how his voice had become that low growl. In fact, at this precise moment, he put her strongly in mind of the full-size grizzly bear in the earl's study. Of course, that one was stuffed whereas Henry was very much alive, but still....

"Do you know why it is a very bad idea to roam about the halls of a house like this in your nightgown, Miss Knight?"

"Hmmm, let me think," Florence said, making her eyes wide and round and pressing a finger to her mouth in a parody of strong concentration. "Could it be because I might run into some wicked man, who's had too much to drink and harbours nefarious intentions about what he wishes to do with me?"

She blinked up at him, which admittedly might have been the straw that broke him. It had certainly been calculated to do so. Even so, she was a little startled when he picked her up and flung her over his shoulder.

"Henry!" she said, as loudly and as urgently as she dared. "Henry, put me down this instant!"

"Or what?"

"Or… I'll scream, and then everyone will see, and you'll be forced to marry me. Now there's a fate worse than death," she added, with extra sarcasm just to be certain his brandy-soaked brain understood she was mocking him.

"Needs avoiding at all costs," he agreed, sounding quite amicable now as he strode downstairs.

Wait. Downstairs?

"Where are you taking me, you great oaf? I know men regress when they've been drinking, but there's no need to return to your caveman origins. I value my hair and do not wish to be pulled about by it."

His shoulder shook beneath her belly, and it took her a moment to realise he was laughing.

"*Oh!* I hate you. I don't know what I ever saw in you. I plead temporary insanity, for I must have been out of my idiotic mind. No woman in their right mind would see you as husband material. You're a pig-headed, irritating, stubborn, insufferable cretin and I wish I'd never met you!"

"Sticks and stones, Miss Knight," he returned, sounding far too pleased with himself.

With some anxiety, Florence realised they had reached the entrance hall and Henry was making for the front door. She tugged at his coat, which was awkward to do while upside down.

Cool air drifted about her bare ankles, and she became rivetingly aware of the fact she was naked beneath her nightgown and Henry's hand was resting on her calf to keep her steady as he strode... towards the lake.

"Henry, drat you. You've made your point. Put me down, will you?" she pleaded.

"What point is that?"

Florence frowned. She'd hoped if she seemed to agree with him, whatever bee he'd got into his bonnet would buzz off. Apparently not, for she had not the slightest idea what he was doing. She sighed, bouncing as he walked. Really, it was a most undignified mode of transportation and not to be recommended.

"Oh, I don't know!" she wailed. "That you want me. That you *don't* want me. That you want me to want you, but not want me in return. That you want me but don't want to, or don't want to marry me, at least. Who knows? I don't know. Does anybody know? I wish they'd tell me. I wish *you'd* tell me. I fervently, truly wish I *did* know but I don't, so why don't you tell me?"

"Very well," he said, and she heard the brandy in his voice, the unmistakable thread of excitement and amusement fired by alcohol. She wondered which of them would regret this most in the morning. "I'll tell you. You provoke me, Miss Knight. You are the most provoking female it has ever been my misfortune to come across. If it isn't bad enough tripping over you whenever I turn my blasted head, you're laying traps for me, lying in wait for me, provoking me on purpose."

Well, she supposed she could hardly deny it. "And what do you hope to achieve by... by whatever this is?"

"To make myself feel better," he said, before he dumped her unceremoniously in the lake.

To be fair, it was only a few feet deep, but the shock of the cold water, and that he'd done it at all, made Florence reel backwards in shock. Henry grabbed for her but too late and she fell backwards, submerged beneath the icy lake for a moment before strong hands grasped hold of her and hauled her out again. She came up, spluttering and gasping.

Henry's expression was a combination of regret and a man trying very hard not to laugh. She gave him a hard shove, and he stumbled back a pace.

Florence pushed her dripping hair from her face and glared at him.

"F-Feel better now?" she demanded, teeth chattering.

But his expression had changed dramatically, all the laughter gone from his eyes. He was very still, except for the way his chest rose and fell, somewhat quicker than before. Florence frowned, not understanding for a moment why he was staring at her so intently. Heat surged through her like a tide, welcome after her dip in the frigid lake, and the inevitable result of realising Henry was staring at her as if he wanted to eat her in one bite. Her nightgown, a dreadfully expensive and fine cotton, was clinging to her body. Florence glanced down and realised it was transparent.

A proper young lady would probably have fainted, or at the very least tried to cover herself up. Mind you, a gentleman might have offered her his coat. Neither of them seemed to be making much effort at proper behaviour of late.

Henry swallowed. She saw the way his Adam's apple bobbed, saw the way his fists clenched and knew he was fighting the same battle he'd waged in the shepherd's hut. He'd wanted her badly then. He wanted her badly now. That time he'd won.

She took a step towards him slowly, as if she were approaching a wild animal, though she was uncertain if he meant to bolt or pounce on her. From the savage look in his eyes it could go either way.

"Don't," he warned her, giving the slightest shake of his head. "I've been drinking, Florence. I.... Don't."

"Why not?" she demanded, realising the question was full of pleading. She was breathing hard and desire was thrumming beneath her skin, chasing away the chill of the lake.

"Not like this," he managed, the words seeming to cause him pain. "Christ, Florence, go. *Please*."

"Why should I? Why should I run away? I don't want to. I want this. I want you."

There, she'd said it as explicitly as she could. Not that he could have been in any doubt.

Henry closed his eyes and let out a low moan. "God, you're determined to send me to the devil."

"I am not," Florence said, hotly, indignant that he should still equate her with sins and mistakes. "I just want—"

"I know what you want, but this isn't it," he said, and there was anger in his voice. "And this is not the way to get it. Don't you see? If there's to be anything between us then... then it has to be...."

Florence stilled utterly. *If there's to be anything between us.* Had he...? Yes, he had said that. He'd allowed the possibility. She held her breath, waiting for him to go on with such impatience the urge to fidget was hard to deny.

"Not like this," he said at length. He opened his eyes, gazing at her, but not allowing his attention to stray from her face. "Florence. I'm sorry. Go back to bed. Please, love."

Florence's breath caught at the endearment. "Yes, Henry."

He stripped off his coat and handed it to her. "Quickly, before anyone sees."

Florence nodded, taking the coat and shrugging it on. She stared at him for just a moment, trying to read his expression but it was too guarded. Nonetheless, he'd said *if,* he'd called her *love*.

She smiled, swift and tentative, and then hurried past him, hope fluttering in her chest as she ran back to the house.

Chapter 9

Dear Nic,

Thank you for the warning regarding Wulfric. The world is never quite safe when that man grows bored. Though what the devil you mean by asking me if I'll stand by you, I cannot fathom. And what do you mean by "not publicly"? I ought to call you out for such an insult, you damned fool. You seriously believe I would disown you in a scandal? I hope you have warned Eliza and her father, however. I am of the strong opinion the duke does not like surprises. Besides which, as he has supported us in the past, perhaps he would be an ally if we spoke to him? I do not understand what Wolf hopes to gain by coming here but then the past catches us all up eventually, I fear. Something that nags at us to lay old ghosts. I'm afraid I understand the impulse too well.

—Excerpt of a letter from Louis César de Montluc, Comte de Villen to his brother, Mr Nicolas Alexandre Demarteau.

16th August 1839, Holbrook House, Sussex.

The next morning Florence's maid came to tell her they had all been invited to visit the Hall. According to Maisie, the other ladies had decided that they would go by carriage as it was promising to be a scorching day and none of them were keen to be trussed up in riding habits. Florence chose a pale lilac muslin with a belted waist and full bell skirt. The off-the-shoulder neckline had a wide lace collar which she fastened with a gold-and-amethyst brooch her father had given her.

"Such a picture you make, you do me proud. You'll have all the gentlemen sighing over you, as usual," Maisie said as she handed Florence her bonnet. It had an upturned brim, trimmed with sprays of purple flowers. Florence tied the bow and then waited patiently as Maisie adjusted it to her satisfaction. "Oh, and don't forget your parasol. It's going to be so dreadfully hot, I fancy you'll need it."

"Thank you, Maisie," Florence said, giving her maid a grateful smile as she took the lacy lilac parasol that matched her gown.

Of course there was only one gentleman whom she wanted to sigh over her, and she could not wait to see him again.

When she went down to breakfast, she was disappointed to discover Henry had already gone home to prepare for his guests. Lord St Clair told them about the building as they breakfasted.

"Saxenhurst is a fascinating place. There used to be a small castle on the spot in the thirteenth century, then Henry III granted a charter to build a Chantry. The castle fell into disrepair and the manor built in its place in the next century. It's been rebuilt and added to many times over the years. My wife's family bought it towards the end of the fifteenth century and have been there ever since. It's a handsome building, though, rather a gloomy old place," the earl had added. "It has never really felt like a home. Harriet and Henry's parents were barely there, always off on their travels, and they weren't exactly the warmest and most welcoming of people when they were. Henry is in desperate need of some advice on how to make it a home to my mind. It needs a woman's touch, don't you agree, darling?"

Lady St Clair had choked on her tea at that, causing Lord St Clair to spring to his feet and run to pat her on the back.

"Drat you, Jasper," she muttered, glaring at him though it appeared she was trying not to laugh.

All very peculiar.

Still, Florence could not deny the little bubble of happiness floating about inside her. Henry had invited them all, yes. Not just her, but he had invited them knowing she would come, and after his words last night.... Had he changed his mind? Though she had always considered herself too sensible to lose her head over a man, she could not deny the giddy excitement surging through her. Not least because she would finally get to see the Hall which she had longed to do. For surely the place where he had grown up and spent most of his life would give her some insight into the man himself?

"Is he going to ask you to marry him?"

Florence jolted out of her reverie at her sister's question. She looked wildly around, only to discover the breakfast room empty.

"They left a few minutes ago, not that you noticed," Evie remarked, picking up her teacup and taking a sip. "You wouldn't notice if an elephant lumbered through the room. Well, unless Henry Stanhope was riding it."

"Evie!" Florence exclaimed, and then let out a sigh. She ought to have realised she could not keep such a secret from her sister. "I don't know, Evie. I don't think he knows what he wants either. Half the time he seems cross with me because he doesn't want to like me, so I'd be surprised. Mr Stanhope says he's too old for me. He also says that he doesn't want to marry at all, but I think he's lying to himself. I think he is afraid to try because he was jilted so publicly before. Whether he wants *me,* though…I don't honestly know."

"Don't you?" Evie said dryly. "I think he wants you very much, and I doubt I'm the only one who's noticed."

Florence flushed, remembering the look in his eyes last night. Oh, he wanted to bed her all right, but marriage…. Then she realised what her sister had intimated. "Oh, Evie, you don't think Mama…?"

"Of course I think Mama. Honestly, Flo. If you would only stop gazing at the man like a lovesick puppy—"

"Have you been speaking to Ash and Viv?" Florence demanded, folding her arms.

"No." Evie sent her a puzzled look. "Why would I, before I'd spoken to you? But, really, you are a dolt. Why on earth do you think Mama was quizzing him last night about Caroline Norton?"

Florence shrugged. "Mama always quizzes men about things like that. She likes to ruffle their feathers, to make them cross and to force them to think about injustice."

"Or perhaps she was testing a potential suitor to see if he measured up?"

Florence gave her an odd look. "Mama has been friends with Henry for years."

Evie shrugged. "Not close friends, and he's been gone a long time. I think she was testing the water before you plunge in headfirst. Unless… oh, Flo, you've not done anything rash, have you?"

"No!" Florence exclaimed, irritated, although it was a fair question after her behaviour last night, though Evie did not know about that, thank heavens. "No, I haven't."

Unless kissing him whilst trapped in a shepherd's hut in a storm could be considered rash, which it obviously could… but she did not see why she must admit that to her little sister.

"Hmmm."

Evie gave her a look which suggested she was unconvinced, but did not press her further, for which Florence was grateful.

One of the earl's neighbours, a Miss Dudley, was to be joining them for the visit, along with her friend, Miss Hatchet. They were both spinsters of middling years, though could not be more different in character. For the life of her, Florence had never understood why they were friends.

Miss Dudley was a sweet, kind lady, who drove everyone mad by crying at the drop of a hat, for she found everything desperately romantic, sad, or tragic. She swooned at the least provocation, but had such a generous heart everyone forgave her for her eccentricities, trying as they sometimes were. Everyone was fond of her, despite her fussy ways, and she was often a guest at Holbrook.

Miss Hatchet was a tattlemonger. There was no other way of saying it. Whether she set out to cause harm by her words or not was moot, as that was the inevitable result. She could not bear to leave a juicy morsel of gossip unsaid, no matter how much better for everyone it would be if she held her tongue. Most people who knew her held her in contempt, and only bore with her for Miss Dudley's sake. Her presence was an unwelcome blight on the outing, but one there was no polite way of avoiding.

It was a pleasant ride to the Hall, and they arrived precisely at the appointed hour, to find no sign of Henry.

"That's odd," Jasper said. "He was very clear about when we should be here. I know he was a little foxed last night, but I find it hard to believe he has forgotten."

Or changed his mind. Florence felt a flicker of doubt as she wondered if he'd decided it was all a mistake after all. He *had* been foxed, as Jasper pointed out. Perhaps… No. She would not put words in his mouth or let him get away with changing his mind again. She would speak to him first, which meant she must find him.

Jasper hurried inside the house to speak to the staff, none of which seemed aware of their arrival.

"Perhaps he's at the stables?" she suggested. "I'll go and look."

Florence turned and walked away before anyone could stop her, though she heard her mama call after her and knew she was being followed. She hurried around the back of the house as fast as she could but, before she even reached the stables, she saw a dark shape upon the ground in the shadow of a barn. For a moment she hesitated, uncertain what she was seeing, and then the figure groaned, a hand going to its head.

"Henry!" she exclaimed, running to him and kneeling by his side, unheeding of her skirts on the dusty ground. "Henry, darling, are you hurt? Speak to me."

"Florence?" he muttered, blinking up at her dazedly. "Christ, my head. That bloody ladder. Must have knocked myself out cold when the rungs broke."

"Oh, Henry, you're bleeding!" Florence cast about her skirts, searching for her pocket and the clean handkerchief there. "Here, let me…."

Henry gave a hiss of pain as she gently pressed the handkerchief to the back of his head where his dark gold hair was sticky with blood.

"Oh, darling, I'm so sorry."

"Florence, get up," hissed a voice in her ear as her mother grasped her arm and hauled her to her feet.

"But Mama!" Florence protested. "Hen—"

She snapped her mouth shut as she saw they were not alone. Lady St Clair, Evie, and Grace, and many of the others had followed them, including Miss Dudley. Next to her, Miss Hatchet was watching the proceedings with obvious delight.

"Mr Stanhope is hurt," Florence said, trying to calm her thundering heart.

Henry *was* hurt, but as he was clearly in no danger she forced herself to step back and watched the comte help him to his feet.

"What on earth happened?" Louis César demanded.

"The ladder broke," Henry muttered, touching tentative fingers to his head and wincing. "The rungs must be rotten."

Florence fought the desire to tend to him, to hug him and then scold him soundly for giving her such a fright. Afraid she might give herself away in front of Miss Hatchet, as if she'd not already done so, she turned to look at the ladder and frowned. There were two broken rungs near the top.

"Why were you climbing the ladder, Mr Stanhope?" she asked, for surely he'd known they were arriving at any moment.

"I...." He stared up at the large opening on the upper floor of the barn, used to stow hay for storage, his expression quizzical. "Oh, Lord! I heard someone call for help. A woman."

Florence experienced a chill that began at the nape of her neck and ran down her spine like a trickle of iced water. "Don't look so appalled, I very much doubt she's there now. The rungs aren't rotten, they've been cut. Someone lured you up there on purpose."

There was a faint moan and a rustle of skirts and Louis César moved so fast Florence was quite astonished. He caught Miss Dudley before she too cracked her head on the cobbles.

"Oh, well done!" Evie said to him, gaining herself a quick smile from the comte.

Florence swung back to Henry, caring too little for Miss Dudley and her vapours when he was in danger, her fear for him making her forget to guard her tongue.

"I *told* you! I told you, you were in danger you stubborn man! Now will you listen to me and act before someone kills you? Please, I... I couldn't bear it if—"

Mama gave her a swift pinch. Florence gasped, but swallowed the words she'd been about to say. Not that it mattered, there had been too much emotion in her outburst, and Miss Hatchet had no doubt seen her kneeling in the dirt beside Henry too. Even if she hadn't seen, Florence's dusty skirts would be enough to tell the tale.

"Indeed, Mr Stanhope, none of us could bear it if you were badly injured," her mother said smoothly. "You have been a friend to our family for so many years. I believe my daughter is right to be concerned for your safety. Someone clearly means you harm."

"Oh, Henry, who could it be? I don't believe anyone holds you any ill will," his sister exclaimed.

Henry sighed and stared up at the ladder for a long moment, then he turned back to Florence. "I feel I owe you another apology, Miss Knight. Though I have already apologised for my rudeness, idiot that I am, I confess I still did not believe your concerns had any validity. It seems I was foolish to not to listen to you, and to dismiss your opinions, and you, out of hand. I shan't do so again, I assure you. Can you forgive me?"

Florence could not stop the hopeless smile that curved her lips, nor no doubt the lovesick puppy expression her friends accused her of wearing. But, really, it was impossible. He'd apologised before everyone for not listening to her, and with such sincerity, *and* he'd promised to never dismiss her opinions, or her, again. How could she not fall hopelessly in love with him?

"Thank you, Mr Stanhope. That was very prettily said, and I do indeed forgive you."

"That's all well and good and I'm pleased you are taking this seriously now," Lady St Clair said, her expression pinched with worry. "But someone tried to kill you, Henry."

Henry waved this away. "Calm down, Harry. It's not that bad. If they'd wanted me dead, that was a feeble way of doing it. It wasn't much of a fall, really, just unlucky for me that I cracked my skull. Though I agree they meant me harm, I think the objective was to scare me rather than put an end to me."

"Well, for my part I can say it's working," his sister said, snatching her spectacles off her nose and wiping them vigorously on the silk shawl draped over her shoulders. "Oh, where is Jasper?"

"Here, love," the earl said, hurrying up behind his wife. "What's amiss?"

In concise, clear words, Harriet told her husband what had occurred, and his expression grew serious as he heard.

"Well, I'm afraid you will not like this much either," he said, reaching for his wife's hand. "Henry, you'd best follow me."

Thoroughly spooked, the party followed Jasper to the front of the house and inside. It became apparent why no staff had come out to greet them as they all stood around muttering unhappily, staring at a strange object in the centre of the dining table.

"I came in to lay the table for your guests, Mr Stanhope, and there it was," said a young footman. The poor fellow looked thoroughly rattled, as well he might. "Not only that but half the silverware has disappeared. We've been finding it all over the house, behind curtains, in vases, and all the wine glasses were in your bed."

"All the spoons were in the linen closet," one of the maids piped up, wringing her hands. "And the napkins were in the potting shed."

"It's witchcraft, evil doings," someone muttered at the back of the room.

Henry glowered and walked to the table.

The corn doll was much larger this time. It stood about two feet high and was intricately woven. It was dressed in a simple white gown. Its head and hands protruded from the gown and were made of the whiskery ends where the grain grew, giving the doll an unsettling, nightmarish appearance that made Florence not want to touch it. Still, she moved closer, noticing a pattern beneath the doll.

"What's that, underneath her? Someone has scratched a design in the tabletop."

"Damnation, that table is ancient," Henry cursed, leaning forward to move the doll aside.

Florence almost exclaimed, to tell him not to touch the horrid thing, but reminded herself sternly that she did not believe in such supernatural nonsense. That idea was tested somewhat as she saw the design beneath the doll. Three circles had been drawn one inside the other and, in the smallest, a simple daisy-like pattern filled the space.

Florence jumped as slim fingers curved around hers and turned to find Grace at her side.

"I don't know what it means, but that is surely witchcraft," the young woman said under her breath.

Before Florence could respond a gruff voice sounded from the open doorway.

"What's all this?"

"Sterling! Thank God. Look at this." Henry gestured for the man to come in.

Sterling Oak stared about the assembled company for a moment, appearing reluctant to enter. At Henry's insistence he moved forward, and his eyes widened at the sight of the corn doll.

"What do you make of this?" Henry asked, gesturing to the carving on the tabletop.

Sterling stared at it. He seemed uneasy. "A hexafoil."

Henry's eyebrows went up. He waited but Sterling said nothing further, so he gave an exasperated huff.

"Which is?" Henry demanded.

Mr Oak shrugged. "To trap evil spirits."

Henry made a sound of irritation and rubbed a hand over his face. "So I'm dealing with a blasted lunatic."

Mr Oak sucked air in through his teeth, plainly disliking Henry's observation. "Wouldn't say that."

"Well, what would you say?" Henry asked, losing his patience.

Mr Oak glanced around the assembled company and frowned, shaking his head. Clearly, he did not wish to speak in front of everyone.

"For heaven's sake, Sterling," Henry said. "If you know something—"

"I never said that!" he retorted.

"I think perhaps Mr Oak would rather speak to you in private, Mr Stanhope," Grace put in, before the two men could lose their tempers. "Perhaps he does not think the conversation fitting for female ears," she added, though there was a hint of mockery in her eyes.

Mr Oak's attention was suddenly riveted on Grace, and with such intensity Florence felt he no longer saw anyone else. It was as if they'd all disappeared.

"That's not it," he said, his deep voice rumbling through the room.

"What, then?" Grace asked.

He studied her, really studied her, as if he could weigh the elements of her soul if he stared long and hard enough. Grace returned his gaze with a quiet calm, apparently unruffled.

"That there corn doll represents the Maiden. The cunning folk know things we don't, Miss Weston. My Gran did. There's stuff out there older than us, things we don't understand."

"You surely don't believe in witchcraft?" Henry said, clearly aghast at the idea.

Sterling met his gaze steadily. "I don't say as I do, but I don't say as I don't either. There are more things in heaven and earth."

Grace seemed interested in this, her head tilting to one side to study Mr Oak. "You've read Hamlet, Mr Oak?

"Aye, why not?"

"I meant no offense. Only that I supposed farmers have little time for such things."

"The winter months are long and dark, miss."

There was something in the way he said it that made Florence's skin prickle. She cleared her throat, eager to dispel the strange atmosphere in the room.

"Whether or not any of us believe it, why would someone put a corn doll in this room, with that symbol beneath it? What are they trying to say, Mr Oak?" she asked.

Mr Oak's attention slid unwillingly from Grace to Florence. "I couldn't say, Miss Knight. Generally, corn dolls are positive symbols. You must know that much."

"Of course. The last sheaf is said to hold the spirit of the corn. It's plaited into a corn doll to give the spirit a place to live until the next harvest, then it's ploughed back into the soil. They are supposed to bring good luck, I think?"

"That's right."

"So why does it feel like a threat?"

Mr Oak shrugged. "Perhaps it's the spirit of the corn that's in danger."

Henry made a pained sound, so Florence glared at him. He rolled his eyes to the ceiling but held his tongue.

"Or perhaps the Maiden represents someone, a woman in danger," Grace offered.

Mr Oak looked back at her. His eyes were a very dark brown and he regarded Grace with a speculative but approving expression. "Could be," he agreed, not taking his eyes from her.

Grace flushed and took a step back, so she was slightly behind Florence.

"Look," Henry said, and Florence felt he was counting to ten. "I know there are some riveting and bizarre customs among the locals. Indeed, on my travels I have discovered there are stories like this all over the world. Every culture has its witches and superstitions, some more outlandish than others. No doubt there is a kernel of truth to be found here or there," he allowed.

Mr Oak snorted and folded his arms.

"But honestly, Sterling. Whatever the origins of this... this *Maiden*, her use has clearly been appropriated to put the wind up me."

No answer from Mr Oak was forthcoming past a noncommittal shrug.

"So I need to find out who and why. Yes? Do you have any ideas?"

Mr Oak considered this for a lengthy moment. "No."

Emma V Leech

Henry threw up his hands. "Well, as fascinating as this all is, what the devil am I supposed to do with that thing? Burn it?"

"No!" Mr Oak said, with such vehemence Grace flinched. He cleared his throat and spoke again, looking somewhat apologetic. "No. Don't do that. Keep her safe. If she represents a real person, it's best you keep her with care, just in case."

"Do I invite her to dinner? Make up a bed for her?" Henry asked, apparently at the limit of what he could take.

"Don't burn her," Mr Oak advised, his voice holding a clear warning.

With that, he turned and strode out of the room.

Chapter 10

Dear Pippin,

I hope you and that wicked husband of yours are keeping well and enjoying the peace our absence must surely afford you. If by some strange quirk of character, you miss our unruly presence in your life, I wondered if you might like to take a few days holiday here at Holbrook House? Cat will be beside herself with joy, especially if you bring that old rogue with you. She believes her skill at cards is waning in his absence.

The earl assures me you would be most welcome and made very comfortable. I believe we urgently need your rather specialist skills to solve a mystery that is becoming a matter of some concern. Tell me, what do you know of corn dolls and their use in witchcraft?

—Excerpt of a letter from Lucian Barrington, The Most Hon'ble, The Marquess of Montagu to his old cook "Pippin", Mrs Bertha Appleton.

16th August 1839, Holbrook House, Sussex.

Florence took Grace for a walk about the gardens whilst the staff set about restoring the dining room to order for their meal. She wondered where Henry would put the Maiden for safe keeping, and then about Mr Oak and the things he'd said. He was a very forbidding looking man, so stern and not a little intimidating. She did not much like him and was uncertain he was trustworthy.

"What do you think of Mr Oak?" she asked Grace.

Grace looked up. She had been staring down at an ornamental fishpond at the centre of the formal gardens they were strolling around, stooping to trail her fingers in the cool water. Her skin was flushed, and she pressed her damp fingers to her throat with a sigh. The heat of the day was becoming quite unbearable.

"I'm not sure. He's rather taciturn, but I wonder if that's just his manner. Some men simply do not feel at ease in company."

Florence pondered this. "He makes me nervous."

Grace let out a huff of laughter. "Yes, I know what you mean. He does always look like he's about to bite your head off. Though...."

"Though?" Florence pressed, curious.

"Oh, I don't know. Only that he reminds me of Papa."

"Not really?" Florence exclaimed, appalled. "Your father is an absolute sweetheart."

Grace smiled, a wistful expression crossing her face. "He is, isn't he? But that's because you know him well, Flo. He's dreadfully fierce with strangers. Mama is always telling him off for it."

"I've never noticed that," Florence replied.

"Well, he doesn't really socialise outside of the village, and all the same people your family are friends with, so you wouldn't."

"Don't tell me you think Mr Oak is all soft and melty beneath that gruff exterior?"

Grace sent her an appalled glance. "Good Lord, no. What an idea. Only that perhaps he does not realise how intimidating he is, and that he needs someone to show him life need not be quite such a serious ordeal."

"Ah, Grace," Florence said, giving her friend a swift hug. "How good you are."

Grace made a rather bitter sound which was so out of character Florence's heart ached.

"Not so good as all that," she said with a twisted smile, and walked on.

Florence followed behind and they carried on along the path. A trickle of perspiration slid down Florence's back and she took her fan from her pocket, trying to stir the heavy air to a breeze. They were in full sun here and it was becoming intolerable. How she longed to cast off her corset and stockings. Ahead of her, Grace raised a hand to her head and swayed.

"Grace!" Florence exclaimed, hurrying to catch her up and slide an arm about her waist.

"I'm well. Don't fret so," Grace said, her expression pinched. "I'm just hungry, that's all."

"Did you not eat any breakfast again?"

Grace shook her head. "I can't eat first thing. It just makes me sick."

"Well, let's get you inside, into the cool. It's far too hot out here. It's making me feel cross, and that's a dangerous thing, as you know."

Grace laughed obligingly and Florence guided her into the shade. Feeling eyes upon her she turned to see Mr Oak watching them. A prickle of alarm ran over her, and she turned her back on him with something like defiance, returning Grace to the house as fast as was possible.

Henry did his best to be an entertaining host, but the afternoon seemed interminable. He'd woken with a hangover, and cracking his skull on the cobbles had hardly helped. His head throbbed like the very devil and, as fond as he was of most of his guests, he could wish them elsewhere.

Except for Florence, drat her.

What was he to do about Florence Knight? He could no longer pretend there was nothing between them. Hell, he didn't want to pretend. Though he still felt certain he was a poor choice for her, she wanted him. Heaven knew why, for there were surely far younger and more eligible men than he who must be falling over themselves for her attention. He'd not even been kind or nice to her, yet she persisted in seeing beyond his idiotic behaviour. He could not fathom why, but she saw him, understood him, with no need for Henry to explain himself.

It was strange, wonderful, and terrifying. Yet he could not make himself stay away from her. He wanted her and, if she persisted in seeking him out, eventually he would be forced to offer for her to atone for some reprehensible behaviour on his part. Then, of course, Gabriel would tear him limb from limb. So, perhaps he ought to just give into the inevitable and marry her.

Marrying her would not be so bad. It would satisfy Harriet, for one, and stop this ridiculous matchmaking. Then Florence could live here, at the Hall. She would give him children and create a home for them. The idea filled him with equal parts warmth and panic. Well, he need not be here all the time. Once she was settled, he could go travelling again. Jasper would keep an eye on her and any children, and they'd be well provided for, and... and that way he could keep some distance between them. Not just geographically, but with this feeling she evoked inside him, the strange, aching need to be with her all the time, every second. If he spent some of his time away, that peculiar urgency to be in her company would dissipate, and things need not become too....

"... around the house?"

He blinked, aware that he'd not been attending the conversation at all.

"Your guests would like the tour of the house you promised them, Henry," his sister repeated with a touch of impatience. She'd clearly been speaking to herself for some time.

"Oh, of course. My pleasure," he said, getting to his feet.

"Oh, no. I think I shall retire to the parlour, if you don't mind me being a bother, Mr Stanhope. That nasty doll and all the goings on.... Oh, I shall never sleep again, I'm sure." Miss Dudley fanned herself vigorously, shaking her head with distress.

"Fear not, Miss Dudley, I shall accompany you home in my carriage if you would prefer," Jasper said, which was almost enough to make Miss Dudley swoon again. "Though, of course, Miss Hatchet must accompany us for propriety's sake," the man added with a twinkle in his eyes.

Realising that he was being saved from an interminable afternoon, Henry sent his oldest friend a look of deep gratitude. Miss Hatchet, who was likely afraid she'd miss out on some delicious bit of gossip, looked less than pleased but could do nothing but accept such a gracious offer. No doubt she'd enjoy telling anyone that would listen all about the earl's splendid carriage, which would be some consolation.

In the end there was only a small party who gathered for the tour: the Comte de Villen, Evie Knight, Florence, Grace Weston, and rather to Henry's surprise, Sterling Oak.

They began in the library, which had always been Henry's favourite room in the house. It was the one place that got anywhere close to feeling homey, at least when the fire was lit. The furniture was ridiculously old and rather shabby, but it had a lived-in, familiar feel, which was welcome when the rest of the house was so bare and cold.

He could not help but watch Florence as he guided them around, explaining the history of the place. She seemed delighted by the library, exclaiming about the lovely view from the window and the handsome oak panelling lining the only bit of wall not smothered in books.

"Is it true one of your ancestors was involved in smuggling?" Miss Evie asked as they made their way up the grand staircase to the next floor.

Henry bit back a smile at the look of delighted interest that flashed across Florence's face at this information.

"Not really?" she demanded eagerly.

"Yes, that's true," Henry admitted. "The family finances were in dire straits and one of my paternal grandfathers decided something must be done."

"And is it true there is a secret tunnel leading from the house to a pub in the village?" Miss Evie persisted.

"No." Henry shook his head, rather sorry to disappoint Florence, who was looking enraptured by the story. "No, there are a few hidden doors and hidey holes, as with most ancient houses, but there's no tunnel. Believe me, as a boy I searched high and low for it too, but no one has ever found evidence to suggest it's true. I think it's just that it was an open secret—about the smuggling, I mean—but no one ever found any evidence to convict the old devil. It was assumed there must be a tunnel for him to get away with it so effectively and for so long, but perhaps he was just very well organised."

"What a pity," Evie said with a sigh. "Just imagine finding a hidden tunnel to explore."

Henry turned back to Florence, who was frowning, her previous enjoyment no longer visible.

"Miss Knight?"

"What if you're wrong?" she asked, staring at him with such concern Henry wanted to reach out a hand and draw her close to him.

He held onto the banister to stop himself from doing so. "Wrong?"

"About the tunnel. Think about it, Henry, about screams in the night and corn dolls on your pillow."

"On your pillow?" Sterling repeated, staring at Henry. "You never said they'd been in your room."

Henry shrugged. "It was just a doll, and I cannot believe there is a tunnel when so many people have searched for so long."

Sterling stared at him, shaking his head. "It wasn't just a doll. It was a warning. We need to find out what this is about before whoever is doing this goes too far."

"I agree." Florence was staring at Sterling with interest. "What do you propose to do about it, Mr Oak?"

Henry heard the challenging note in her voice and wondered at it. He realised now that it was not unusual for people, especially women, to take a dislike to Sterling. The man did not have an easy manner, or anything resembling charm, and seemed to rub people up the wrong way. It was clear Florence did not like him.

"I'll ask about," he said, holding Florence's gaze. "See if I can dig up any old stories, resentments against the family."

"Good," Florence said with a tight smile. "I know all of Mr Stanhope's friends will rally around to keep him safe. Whoever is doing this will not get away with it."

"Mr Oak, would you mind giving me your arm? I think I've had too much sun."

Miss Weston's intervention was purposeful and timely, breaking the brittle atmosphere.

"Aye, you're red as a beet," Sterling said with his usual lack of tact. "I suppose you've not drunk more than a thimbleful of water? Come along. I'll take you back downstairs and get you a drink."

"How gallant you are, sir," Miss Weston said, though her dry tone was lost on Sterling who offered her his arm without a word.

Henry watched him escort the young woman down the stairs.

"Miss Evie, come and see."

Henry turned to see the comte had discovered the large stained-glass window on the south side of the building. Evie made an exclamation of delight and hurried after him, leaving Henry alone with Florence.

"I don't like him," Florence muttered.

"The comte?"

She tsked and gave him an impatient glower that made him want to smile. "Mr Oak!"

"Sterling's a good fellow. He's just a bit brusque, that's all. He's not used to the company of ladies. Spends most of his time with cattle or crops."

"Hmph."

"You look very beautiful, Florence."

Her cross expression melted at his words and a tinge of colour touched her cheeks.

"I'm surprised you noticed," she said, diffident now.

He made an incredulous sound, wondering how she could be so foolish. "You must be fishing for compliments, Miss Knight, for I do not believe you are unaware of the effect you have on me."

A smile tugged at her mouth, but she struggled to meet his eyes.

"The feeling is mutual," she said quietly, glancing up at him.

Henry's mouth was suddenly dry, the desire to kiss her so strong that he ached with the need to reach for her. The way she was staring up at him now was a clear invitation to do so. Henry glanced across the galleried landing to the comte and Evie and muttered a curse. Oh, to the devil with it. He grabbed Florence's hand and dragged her with him, around the corner and along a corridor, snatching at the first door he came to and flinging it open. Henry pulled her inside and closed the door.

She stood staring at him, breathing as though she'd run for a mile.

"Well," she said, impatience ringing out in her words. "Are you going to kiss me or not?"

Henry gave a huff of laughter. "God, you're bossy."

Florence nodded. "I have opinions, too. Lots of them."

She held his gaze, defiance burning in the green of her eyes.

"I'm glad to hear it," he said, excitement thrumming beneath his skin. "What is your opinion about the fate of young women who enter bedrooms with unmarried men?"

She looked around, her eyes widening as she noticed the large four poster bed.

"I did not realise it was a bedroom," she retorted.

"Would it have made a difference?"

There was a brief pause.

"No," she said, and reached up, sliding her arms about his neck and pressing closer.

"Are you certain this is what you want?" Henry asked, wishing that hadn't sounded so damned hopeful.

There was something hurt and vulnerable twitching anxiously inside his heart that wanted him to turn away from this, from her, before she had the chance to answer, to damage him all over again.

"Henry," she whispered, a thread of helpless laughter in her voice.

He lowered his mouth, so close their breath mingled. "Are you certain?"

"Yes," she murmured, brushing her mouth against his, unaware of how that brief touch made need and desire hit him with such force he almost staggered under the impact. "Yes, Henry. Yes, please. I'm very certain this is what I want."

Thank Christ for that.

He kissed her, trying his utmost to keep things under control. Just a kiss, he promised himself. He wasn't at the mercy of his passions, no longer a green boy. He could keep himself in check. God, but it was difficult. She was so sweet, so eager, holding nothing back, giving him everything, giving him ideas. He pulled back, hauling in a breath.

"Stop," he said, though he had to be firmer when she lifted her mouth to his once more. "No."

"Henry," she pleaded, tugging at his neck.

It would have been so easy to give in, too easy. She was worth more than that. He pulled her close, stroking her hair. "I must speak to your father and ask for permission to court you."

Her eyes widened in surprise.

Henry grunted, shaking his head. "You thought we'd continue to sneak about, stealing kisses? I'm not some spotty youth, Florence. The sooner you rid yourself of those kinds of ideas, the better."

She looked indignant, as well she might, and he cursed himself for sounding such a stuffy old prig. He was the one who'd dragged her into the bedroom, after all.

"I'm only surprised that you're admitting you wish to court me," she said, temper flashing in her eyes.

He reached out, the urge to touch her irresistible. His fingers caressed the elegant line of her jaw, her throat, her skin like silk beneath his touch. He longed to lean down and kiss his way along the path his fingers had taken, but he did not dare. The temptation to go too far would be unbearable. Hell, it already was.

"I can hardly deny it, but I won't rush things. Your father will likely tell me to go to the devil as it is, but assuming I can bring him around I don't doubt it will be a condition. He'll think you've just formed a *tendre* for me that will wane in time."

"That's what you think too, isn't it?" she said.

Henry shrugged, unwilling to say it aloud, as if acknowledging his fears would bring them to life.

"It isn't true."

There was such certainty in her eyes he wanted to believe her with no reservations, but he was not a fool, and he would not hand his heart to another young woman, only to see it trampled into the dirt once again.

"Someone once told me I was her great love and that there would never be another, that she would love me until the day she died. I believed her."

Disgust flashed in her eyes, such anger on his behalf that he was rather stunned by it.

"She was the biggest fool that ever lived for jilting you, and I'd put money on her having regretted it ever since."

Henry snorted, toying idly with a thick lock of her black hair. It was so soft. He raised it to his mouth, enjoying the feel against his lips. "Riches and a title were what the lady wanted, and what she got. I imagine she's well pleased by the bargain."

"I don't. I imagine she's discovered jewels and a title are cold and unloving when she looks at her life and considers everything she might have had."

"Are you certain of that? Your father is one of the richest men in the country, Florence. I am not. Oh, I'm hardly a pauper. The estate is productive, and I invested in several schemes during my time abroad, which will provide a steady income for years to come. You'll lack for nothing and always be able to hold your head up in society, but I cannot compete with the likes of Gabriel Knight, and I have no intention of trying to. I cannot provide you with a private railway carriage, or a grand house in every county."

"And you think those things are important to me?" One imperious black eyebrow rose, her expression one of disdain.

Henry smiled, though he could not pretend it was not something that weighed on his mind. "I think you've been indulged by a doting father, who would give you the moon if you asked for it."

She pushed away from him, which was a relief, even though he missed the feel of her body against his and longed for her to return to him. "You think me spoiled and foolish."

"I do not think you foolish," he said, amused by the furious glare she shot him. He walked away from her, leaning against the wall, folding his arms as she stalked to the window and looked out. "What was your last birthday present?"

Her shoulders stiffened. "I shan't tell you," she retorted.

"That's what I thought."

She stared out at the landscape, at the sun gilding the surrounding countryside, burnishing it to a crisp, brittle gold as the usually green and pleasant land shimmered in the extraordinary heat.

"Do you know what I want, Henry?"

She turned then, meeting his eyes, and Henry's breath caught at the sight. The light hit her profile just so, her beauty so exquisite in that moment it was like an arrow shaft straight to the heart. How would he bear it if he allowed himself to love her, and could not hold her?

"What do you want?"

His voice was rough, a little angry as he berated himself for always wanting more than he could have. He'd known Lily could do better than him, she'd been the season's diamond, and no one had been more surprised than he when she'd accepted him. Except she'd come to her senses and taken a far better offer in the end. He was doing it again, wanting something that ought not be his. Florence's father might be a self-made man, but he was too wealthy to be ignored, and her mother was sister to a duke. Florence was also a beauty, intelligent and kind, and so much more. A woman like her could have any man she wished with a snap of her fingers. So what was it she wanted from him?

"I want what I see when my parents look at each other. I want a man who will stand by me, no matter what, who will never let me down. A man who keeps his promises and honours his wife and family, a man who is proud of me for having opinions, even if he doesn't always agree with them and never tries to silence me. I want a man who will discuss instead of arguing, who will seek my counsel before deciding on things that affect our family, who will allow me to make decisions for myself instead of telling me what I must do. Someone who will love me for who I am, the good and the bad, not just the pretty face I must present to society and the fat purse marrying me will give him. That is what I want."

Florence faced him with defiance and Henry let out a breath. Well, then.

"I can do that."

He held out his arms to her and she ran into them, clutching him about his waist and holding on tight.

"I know," she said, her voice muffled as she buried her face against his chest. "And that is why I want you."

Chapter 11

Dear Miss Smith,

Are you having an enjoyable stay at Holbrook House? I wish we had been able to visit too, but Father has responsibilities which take us away for August and he does not like to be absent from Mama. Mama won't be parted from the rest of us for long, so we've all been hauled off to the estate in Hampshire. Not that I'm complaining, it is a marvellous place, the fishing is excellent and there's lots to do. Only I do miss everyone. I hope you will come and visit us here one day, I'm sure you'd like it, and Cat too, of course.

—*Excerpt of a letter from Lord Frederick Adolphus (younger son of Robert and Prunella Adolphus, their Graces, The Duke and Duchess of Bedwin) to Miss Agatha Smith.*

16th August 1839, Holbrook House, Sussex.

Grace accepted the glass of water from Mr Oak with a polite nod. Though she was glad she'd diffused the awkward atmosphere, she rather wished she'd not been such a martyr. For now she was alone with Mr Oak, and she had not the faintest idea what to say to him. Why Florence had been so antagonistic to him she did not know, but she well understood he was not an easy man to be around. Partly it was the way he looked at one. The way he was looking at her now, as if… as if he *knew*….

"How far gone are you?"

Grace choked, her shock so profound she almost dropped the glass. Mr Oak lunged for it, taking it from her slack grasp before it hit the floor. He knelt beside her and gave her a couple of firm pats on the back.

"Breathe," he said. If Grace had been able to, she'd have demanded what on earth he thought she was trying to do, but she could do nothing but gasp. "Try to relax. No, don't fight it. In… and out. That's it. Steady, now."

His large hand rubbed slow circles on her back and the warmth of his palm burned through her gown, somehow even through her corset, yet it was a reassuring touch, if outrageously inappropriate.

She met his eyes, determined to deny everything and rail at him for voicing such a dreadful, ruinous, damaging accusation to an innocent young lady. But she looked into his eyes and got lost somehow, the angry words snagging in her throat. His eyes were so dark, a deep rich brown, thickly lashed and watchful. They watched her now, without condemnation or sympathy. Perhaps that was why she burst into tears.

Mr Oak got to his feet, and for a moment Grace believed he meant to walk off in disgust and was gripped by such overwhelming panic her chest grew tight. Then she saw he had only gone to close the door that he'd left open for propriety's sake. Well, that horse had bolted right enough.

He returned to her and handed her a clean handkerchief. She took it and wiped her eyes, blew her nose, and tried to get herself back under control.

"What must you think of me?" she wondered aloud, not expecting an answer, which was just as well, for she did not get one.

"How many monthlies have you missed?"

Grace felt a blush scald her cheeks and glared up at him, scandalised. "You cannot ask me such... personal.... Really, it's too—"

"How many?" he demanded.

"Two."

What was the point? Now he knew he'd probably tell everyone. Why in the name of everything holy had she answered him? Why had she tried to stop the argument between him and Florence? Why had she been such a stupid, reckless ninny and given herself to a man who didn't give a snap of his fingers for her?

"Reckoned as much," he said, shoving his hands in his pockets, his gaze unwavering.

"Who told you?" she asked, angry now.

Only Florence and Arabella knew, and she knew they would never have told. She'd thought perhaps her maid suspected. Had she tattled to someone? Surely not.

"No one told me," he said, his voice sure and calm. "I know what a breeding female looks like."

"I'm not a cow!" she objected, hot with indignation.

His lips, always set in a rather grim line, twitched slightly.

"No," he agreed.

Grace put up her chin. She may as well know the worst of it. If he thought to blackmail her, he was to be disappointed. She did not wish to tell her parents yet, but she would if she must.

"What are you going to do?"

"I rather think that's the question I need to pose, Miss Weston. Who is the father?"

"None of your business!"

"Will he marry you?"

Grace clenched her teeth together, willing herself not to cry. She would not cry. This was her doing. Her mistake. She had no one else to blame. It appeared her silence was all the answer he required.

"Damned bastard."

There had been ire enough in the words to make her look up, let alone the fact no man had ever deliberately sworn in her presence before. It was rather shocking. Mr Oak was scowling at the empty grate. Goodness, but he was a forbidding man. With that look on his face, he appeared ready to do murder.

"How old are you?"

"I'll be eighteen in two weeks," Grace said, too surprised to wonder at his question.

He made a low, angry sound and shook his head.

"Blackguard," he muttered under his breath. He shook his head, still scowling furiously. "You're younger than I would have liked, but I suppose it's of no matter."

"What isn't?" She frowned at him.

"We'll be married after your birthday then. Best not to leave it any longer, there's bound to be talk as it is."

"M-Married?" Grace repeated, stunned.

"Do you have any better ideas?"

Grace was too startled to understand what was going on, let alone think of better ideas. Had he... had he just proposed? No. No, he hadn't. He'd *told* her they were getting married.

"Mr Oak," Grace began, trying her best to sound like she wasn't about to have a hysterical fit, for she thought it all too possible. "I appreciate the offer, but—"

"Listen to me, child," he said, the words brooking no argument. "You're ruined. If you don't marry, you'll never be able to see your friends again. You'll shame your family. If they love you, they'll support you, but at what price? If they don't, you'll likely be thrown out. Either way, you have no option. That child needs a name, and I'm prepared to give it one."

Grace stared at him, fighting for breath, wishing she did not have to acknowledge the truth of his words. Her family would never disown her, but they would bear the shame of her mistake, and she could not bear that. Her child, too, would always bear the burden of illegitimacy when they had done nothing to deserve it. He was right. There was very little choice.

"Why?" she demanded, too choked with emotion to say more.

"My reasons are my own," he said gruffly. He seemed to stand taller as he carried on. "I know you likely expected to marry someone far above my station, but beggars can't be choosers. I'll not bring you shame. I've a fine house. I'm not as rich as your father, but you'll be well dressed, you'll have your own carriage, I'll see you and the child want for nothing."

Grace blinked up at him. "The child...."

Her throat closed up, and she swallowed hard, unable to express what she needed to ask him.

His dark eyes met hers, never wavering. "The child, girl or boy, will be treated as my own. No one will ever know otherwise. I'll never condemn it or treat it as anything but my own blood by word or deed. I give you my word."

She stared at him, stared into that strong, fierce face that made her want to shrink back in her chair and... and she believed him. Good Lord. What choice did she have? He was offering her a lifeline, her and her child. She had no other option. Somehow, she could not speak the words aloud, but gave him a sharp nod.

He let out a breath, something flickering in his eyes that she could not read.

"Good. That's good," he said. "I'll write to your father and ask to see him at his earliest convenience."

"No!"

He stiffened and Grace held out a hand as if to quiet his temper.

"It's only… not yet," she pleaded. "I had hoped to have these last weeks with my friends and—"

"One week." His voice was sharp, his expression daunting enough that she did not argue. "No longer. Then I will speak to your father. We must be married as soon as possible to avoid too much speculation."

Grace nodded.

"Very well," she said faintly, for she was hardly in a position to complain. "One week."

"Grace, are you quite well?" Florence asked. They were back at Holbrook, settled comfortably in the yellow parlour with books neither of them had read two words of. "I'd hoped luncheon might make you feel better. Should I ring for tea?"

Her friend had been quieter than usual, staring out of the window in a deep study. No wonder, with the challenges she faced. Florence's heart ached. At her words, Grace's lovely face turned towards her, eyes clearing slowly as though she was emerging from a dream.

"Pardon? Oh, I'm sorry, I was wool gathering. Yes, quite well. It did help, but tea would be nice, and cake, or biscuits. I am rather peckish." Grace gave a soft laugh and then returned to staring out of the window, as lost in thought as if Florence had never spoken.

Florence got to her feet to ring for tea, regarding her friend with concern.

"What was he like?"

"Who?" Grace turned back to her in confusion.

"The father."

The colour drained from the girl's face and Florence cursed herself for having mentioned it.

"He was a liar," Grace said, her voice harder and sharper than Florence had ever heard it. "He was wonderfully handsome, dreadfully charming, and he said a lot of pretty, meaningless things that I believed. Good heavens, but he could talk. He could speak of poetry and love and music, and he was always so witty and amiable, and yet now I wonder how I didn't see through it, for it was all so... so shallow. He wore this shiny golden veneer that hid a rotten soul, and I have never felt more foolish or stupid than the moment I saw the gold was nothing but tarnished brass, and I knew him for what he was."

"Oh, Grace," Florence said. She moved to sit beside her, taking her hand. "You were not foolish nor stupid. You were innocent and loving and everything that is good, and he took advantage of you. You have nothing to reproach yourself for."

Grace shook her head. "I have everything to reproach myself for, but I shall do better. I have been offered a chance and I shall take it and make something of it."

"What chance?"

Grace studied her, twisting her slender hands together in her lap, her grey eyes full of rain clouds. "Do you swear to keep this a secret if I tell you? No one can know. Not yet."

"Of course," Florence said, wondering what on earth had happened.

"I am going to be married."

Florence gaped at her. "The father…?"

Grace's delicate features twisted with revulsion at the idea. "Certainly not. No, someone else."

"Who?" Florence exclaimed, quite at a loss to imagine how she'd gained a proposal and from whom. "Does he know…?"

Grace's expression was appalled, her reply sharp with censure. "Of course! I would never trick a man in such a way. Marry him without him knowing my condition? Good heavens, Florence! What kind of wretched creature do you think I am?"

Florence shook her head, not having intended any insult.

"I beg your pardon, Grace. Indeed, I am not thinking at all. You are the very best, the kindest and truest of friends, and I spoke before I considered my words. I just… how did you manage it, and who?"

She looked up in frustration as the door opened and a servant appeared.

"You rang, Miss Knight?"

"Oh, yes, indeed. Might we have some tea and cakes, please?"

"Directly, miss."

The servant closed the door and Florence turned back to Grace.

"Mr Oak."

Florence's mouth fell open, shocked into silence, uncertain if she was outraged or grateful or just plain terrified.

Mr Oak?

"You told him… You told him you were…?" she began, not quite ready to make complete sentences yet.

Grace shook her head. "He knew."

Florence's expression must have been one of bewilderment, for Grace gave a little huff of laughter. "It's not terribly flattering, I grant you, but it seems I'm no different from a sheep, or a cow in calf. He could tell."

"And he simply offered for you, and you *agreed*?"

Florence was too stunned to keep the astonishment from her voice and was surprised at the way Grace bristled in response.

"He did, and I did. Yes."

"B-But, Grace…."

Her friend's posture was stiff and unyielding suddenly. "He's offering me a chance, Florence. A chance for respectability, a home for myself and my child. He'll give my baby a name so that it need never live in shame."

Florence nodded at once, knowing this was no small thing, only that she did not like nor trust Mr Oak and, as his wife, Grace would belong to him wholly. He would own her, body and soul, and her child. "I know, love, only… you know nothing about him. What if he's cruel? What if he mistreats you? The child won't be his. Perhaps he'll bear it ill will."

Grace shook her head. "He has promised me that the child will be treated as his own flesh and blood, no matter what. He swore he would never condemn it for…. He *swore*, Florence, and I believe him."

Florence frowned, uneasy and afraid for Grace, yet she knew how little choice her friend had. If this man would give her security, her child a name, Grace would be foolish not to accept, only….

"I don't like him, Grace."

Grace smiled a little. "Yes, I noticed. You're not exactly subtle, Flo."

"Well, I can't help it. He's so…."

Florence searched for a way to explain what it was about Mr Oak that unsettled her so. Mainly it was how he was so brusque, and his lack of tact or manners, but he… he just seemed so cold, so unfeeling. How would gentle, sweet-natured Grace cope with such a harsh, taciturn man for a husband?

"Yes, he is somewhat… difficult, but I must learn to manage him. I do not believe he is cruel."

"But you don't *know* that he isn't," Florence persisted. "You will be at his mercy."

Grace nodded.

"He will speak with your father? There's to be no elopement or anything of that nature?" Florence asked, suddenly struck by the dreadful idea.

"Of course," Grace said, squeezing Florence's hand. "Don't worry so. He wants to ensure there is as little gossip as possible. He means for everything to be done properly, if with as much haste as possible. A whirlwind romance," she added with a bitter laugh.

The laugh tore at Florence's heart but that Grace's father would be consulted was a great relief. The baron was a highly decorated soldier, a fierce man that even Mr Oak might quail before, if he had any sense. Baron Rothborn would never allow Grace to marry a man who would ill-treat her. If Mr Oak had nefarious intentions, her father would discover it and forbid the marriage to go ahead. Florence stared at Grace in wonder, in awe of how brave she was.

"Look at you. You appear as delicate as a snowflake, and yet you are so strong, so courageous."

Grace smiled, her expression full of warmth. "That is because I have such good friends. It's much easier to be brave when you know you are not alone, and you have someone you trust to confide in. At least as a married lady, I will not be denied the pleasure of your company. Speaking of which.... You have been keeping secrets, Florence Knight. So, confess all. I insist you tell me everything about Mr Henry Stanhope."

Chapter 12

Mister Knight,

*It greeves me to rite a letter of this nature,
but my Christian soul cant see wrong
done to an inosent child. Your dauter is in
mortal peril, sir and is in the hands of a
wicked bad man. Henry Stanhope is intent
on sedusing your pretty girl. Come kwick
and save her from damnation.*

**—Excerpt of a letter from an unknown
correspondent to Mr Gabriel Knight
(father of Florence and Evie Knight.)**

17th August 1839, Holbrook House, Sussex.

Henry stared down at the letter he'd been writing, muttered a
curse, and crumpled it into a ball.

"Hell!" he muttered, raking a hand through his hair. Try as he
might, he could not find the words to express to Gabriel why he
would be the best choice for Florence's husband. Tossing the letter
into the wastepaper basket he reached for a clean sheet and tried
again.

Dear Gabriel,

*I was hoping I might see you at Holbrook
with Helena. It has been too long since*

*we spoke. I understand business matters
have kept you in London and would not
presume upon your time if it were not
important. However, there is something
of the utmost importance that I wish to
discuss with you. If you have no plans to
visit Holbrook in the next few days but
can find time to meet with me, I should be
at your disposal and will happily journey
to London at a time and place of your
choosing.*

Yours etc,

Henry Stanhope.

It would have to do. Perhaps in person he could voice what seemed impossible to commit to paper. Of course, he risked Gabriel calling him out, but that was hardly out of the question by correspondence either. At least in person he could defend himself and offer answers and reassurances to any of Gabriel's reservations. Henry was under no illusion that there would not be reservations, if not an outraged denial. Henry and Gabriel had been friends, but they'd not seen each other in years, perhaps things would have changed.

Henry looked up at a knock on the study door.

"You have guests, sir. I took the liberty of showing them into the front parlour."

"Who?" Henry asked with a frown. He hadn't been expecting callers.

"The Marquess of Montagu, Mr Ashton Anson and Miss Vivien Anson and... guests," the footman said carefully.

Henry stood and reached for his coat, pulling it back on. "What the devil is Montagu doing here?" he wondered aloud. "Right, well, you'd best offer them some refreshments."

"I have done so already, sir. A tea tray is being prepared."

Henry nodded and hurried to the parlour.

"My Lord Montagu, this is an unexpected pleasure," Henry said, finding an assortment of guests in his front parlour of the kind that mystified him.

"I imagine it is," Montagu replied, his expression inscrutable, though something like amusement glittered in his eyes. "I'm afraid you will have the unenviable duty of advising me to mind my own business, but…."

At this point an elderly woman who had been installed in one of the comfiest chairs by the fireplace made a snorting sound.

Montagu paused for a second before continuing.

"But I was disturbed by the tales of corn dolls and witchcraft and more so by the attack upon your person. I am afraid I decided it was time you spoke to an expert and took it upon myself to provide one for you. As it happens, circumstances were… erm… fortuitous, and it seems I have provided two."

Henry blinked at the marquess, thoroughly bewildered.

"I'm sorry, my lord, I'm afraid—"

"Takes a poacher to catch a poacher, Mr Stanhope, is what Lord Montagu is trying to say," piped up the elderly lady by the fire. She had a plump, round face with wrinkled rosy cheeks that made her look like a well-preserved apple.

"And going around the houses to do it."

This came from her companion, a tiny Indian lady with skin the colour of well-polished mahogany and the longest, whitest hair he'd ever seen. She looked to be a thousand years old. Her eyes were bright and intelligent, and the intent way she was looking at him put him in mind of a blackbird listening for insects beneath the earth. She was dressed in the traditional manner of her country in a sari of stunning yellow, orange, and green silk.

"Allow me to make some introductions," Montagu continued smoothly. "I believe you know Mr Ashton Anson and his sister, Miss Vivien Anson, and this is their grandmother, Shrimati Dharani Das."

The old woman inclined her head, as regal as an empress. Henry bowed as deeply as if she were a duchess, some sixth sense he did not quite understand compelling him to treat her with the amount of respect she clearly felt her due.

Montagu continued with his introductions, "And this lady is—"

"I was his cook for most of his life," the old lady interrupted. "Mrs Bertha Appleton, though most call me Pippin. I'm too old to work now, of course, but he's not so cold and heartless as he looks, so he keeps me about."

Montagu made an impatient tsking sound and gave the old lady a reproachful glare. "Pippin, do you think you might let me finish my own sentences? I was going to introduce you as a dear friend of the family."

"I know, giving me airs I've no right to," Pippin replied, waving this away.

"Telling the truth," Montagu replied, his voice sharp enough to cut glass. "And giving you the respect you are due, you infuriating old woman, or do you not consider yourself our friend?"

Pippin folded her arms over her large bosom and looked somewhat mulish. "I've loved you like a son, and you know it, but I was your servant and there's no need pretending otherwise."

"I wasn't—" Montagu began and then threw up his hands. "Mr Stanhope, these two wicked old harridans have more than a passing knowledge of the... the *peculiar* problems you are dealing with. I suggest you confide in them, take their advice, and do so quickly. The urge to throw things increases with proximity and every passing moment, I assure you."

"If he wasn't so easy on the eye, I'd send him out of the room for that," Mrs Dharani murmured to her friend, staring at Montagu with undisguised admiration.

"*Nani Maa,* behave!" Ashton muttered, glaring at his grandmother with an anguished expression.

"Why?" Mrs Dharani demanded, looking genuinely perplexed. "I'm old, I'm entitled to be rude if I want to. I earned the right. Besides, it's fun. Behaving is dull."

Ashton groaned and rubbed his face with his hand while his sister looked at her grandmother with undisguised admiration. Going on the brightly coloured scarlet and yellow waistcoat Ashton was wearing, and what he'd heard about the rather forthright character of Miss Vivien Anson, Henry would wager the old lady had greatly influenced her grandchildren.

Henry decided he'd best intervene and quickly.

"I see. Well, I am delighted to make your acquaintance, ladies, but how do you think you can help me?"

"You'd best sit down, young man and tell us everything. And we'll need to see the dolls."

Rather to his amusement, Mrs Dharani waved at him to sit down as though he were the guest.

Henry did as he was told.

The two women studied him long and hard, making him want to tug at his cravat and fidget like a recalcitrant schoolboy about to receive a scolding.

"There's something here, something about this old house," Pippin said, and gave a shiver, though she didn't take her eyes from Henry.

Mrs Dharani made a soft clucking sound and nodded her agreement.

Henry frowned. "Well, it's very ancient, of course. Old houses often have a peculiar atmosphere and this one hasn't been a family home for a long time. It's been empty for years, so…."

"No, it's more than that. It's not a happy house," Pippin continued, as if he'd not spoken. "There's a dark presence, a sense of malcontent."

"My family were not exactly close," Henry admitted, frowning over her words, the certainty with which she spoke.

He'd often wondered at the different atmosphere between his home and Holbrook but had believed it was simply his perspective, the way he viewed both houses. He had been happy at Holbrook, but the coldness of his parents towards him and Harriet and how often he and his sister had been abandoned whilst their parents travelled the world must have coloured his attitude towards Saxenhurst. That others could sense something tangible was unsettling.

"We were not exactly a close family," Henry began, determined that they not make something out of nothing. "But—"

"Vengeance," Mrs Dharani whispered, closing her eyes.

"Aye," Pippin said. "Vengeance."

Henry turned to stare at Montagu, assuming the man would find this all as ridiculous as he did, though he could not deny the way the hairs on the back of his neck were standing on end. Montagu, though, was frowning at the old women. He turned towards Henry, perhaps sensing his gaze upon him.

"I know," Montagu said with obvious sympathy. "But you must hear them out. On the occasions I have failed to do so, I have regretted it. If nothing else, you must respect the opinions of these women who have seen much of life and are excellent judges of human nature. I trust their opinions, Mr Stanhope, whatever you think of their methods. I would strongly suggest you listen and pay attention."

Henry had been away from England for some time, but when he had left Montagu had been one of the most powerful, respected, and feared men in the country. He'd heard nothing to suggest that had changed or the man had lost his marbles, so... he supposed he'd best hear what the women had to say.

"In that case, I had better begin at the beginning," he said, and told them of everything that had happened since he returned.

They listened intently and with the utmost seriousness, making him feel increasingly foolish for not having taken the whole thing seriously from the outset. Florence had tried to warn him, but he'd been too pigheaded to listen, so certain of his own rightness he'd dismissed her concern. It seemed there was a good deal he'd been wrong about of late, though.

Once the ladies had heard Henry out, inspected the corn dolls, and consumed a quite astonishing amount of tea and cakes, everyone waited for their opinions. Henry took the opportunity to stretch his legs, walking about the room and giving the old women privacy in which to put their heads together whilst they murmured with low voices.

After what seemed an interminable wait, they gestured for him to come and sit down again.

"It's a strange thing to use these corn dolls, maidens and the like, in such a way. Almost against their will. They're positive symbols, used to bring luck," Pippin mused, turning the largest of the dolls in her hands. "This has been made with a great deal of skill and love, that much is clear, and I do not think it is anything to do with harvest. I think this represents a real person, a woman. Dharani?"

"Agreed."

The Indian lady gave him a sharp look, her dark eyes settling on him like a knife blade. "Have you wronged an innocent, Mr Stanhope?"

Henry was so taken aback by the accusation he could only stare, and then of course he thought of Florence, about the liberties he'd taken. Heat rushed up his neck and he cursed the old woman for he had the horrid suspicion he was blushing.

"No!" he said, a little too late and too vehemently. The old women exchanged glances. Henry cleared his throat. "That is… No, damn it. I'm… I'm courting a young woman, but I've just written to her father. I wish to marry her. There is no question of wrongdoing."

"*Nani Maa*," said Ashton. The young man was hiding a grin and Henry wondered if he was a close friend of Florence's. "I think you are barking up the wrong tree."

"Hmph," his grandmother said, still looking suspicious, an expression shared by Montagu whose piercing silver gaze was making Henry extremely uncomfortable. Montagu and Gabriel Knight were close friends and Henry did not need Montagu speaking out of turn before he'd had the chance to put his case to Gabriel himself.

"None of your business," he told Montagu defiantly, folding his arms.

The devil take it, must he explain his romantic affairs to everyone? His lordship quirked one blond eyebrow but said nothing.

"If not you, then your father, or even his father," Pippin murmured. "There is something here, an accusation of wrongdoing. I would say your accuser is certainly female, but it's tangled up with something else that muddies the water. For now, Mr Stanhope, you must discover who you or your kin has wronged."

"I've not even been in the country for years," Henry exclaimed, feeling like the women were ganging up on him.

Pippin nodded, sympathy in her eyes. "I'm not saying it is your fault, Mr Stanhope, but perhaps someone *believes* it is your fault, or perhaps you merely represent your bloodline, and this goes back years. Revenge is a strange thing. Resentments can smoulder for generations, and then something happens, a spark that sets a blaze. Perhaps your return was simply the spark required to set this in motion."

"I've been thinking."

"Oh, please don't start criticising Mr Oak again, Florence," Grace said with a sigh.

She knew full well why Florence feared for her; it was for all the same reasons Grace feared for herself. It was just such a lovely morning and she had so little time left before she must tell her parents and, heaven help her, marry Mr Oak.

Florence returned an indignant expression. "I wasn't going to even mention Mr Oak."

"Oh. I apologise then, do carry on."

They were meandering through the lovely gardens at Holbrook House after breakfast, before the sun got too high and it became unbearably hot again.

"I cannot help but think that this vendetta against Henry is something personal, yet he has not lived here for such a long time, and we know the only romance he had was when he himself was jilted."

Grace nodded, having heard everything now, both about Henry's past and Florence's campaign to win the man's heart. She could only smile. The poor fellow didn't stand a chance, for Florence was nothing if not single-minded.

"So what if it isn't Henry that is being targeted, but rather the Stanhope family? After all, Harriet is married now and Henry is the figurehead for the family, even if there are few of them left. Besides which, Harriet is too well guarded, being married to an earl. What if there is some old grudge, something that has been left to fester for years?"

Grace sighed and turned a suspicious glare upon her friend. "This *is* about Mr Oak."

"No!" Florence protested and then coloured. "Well, he is someone I suspect, I admit, but I'm not targeting him specifically, Grace, I swear. I only think we should make enquiries and see if we can uncover any old stories about the Stanhopes, and Mr Oak's family. You ought to know if he is involved, even if it his kin rather than he himself. Perhaps we might hear something that would shine some light upon it. I mean, we know Mr Oak's grandmother was a witch."

"He said a cunning woman, not a witch," Grace said firmly.

Florence raised a dark eyebrow. "For most people that's splitting hairs, or at least it would have been decades ago. Who else around here was known to have been, or still is a witch? People must know things like that. I think we ought to ask."

"Ask who?" Grace asked, not liking the sound of this one bit.

"Anyone who is from the area. Henry's estate begins only a few miles away, so I would think the servants at Holbrook would be a good place to start. I know some of them have followed in the footsteps of parents and grandparents, there are families that have worked for the St Clairs for generations. They'd know all the gossip and old stories from the area."

Grace frowned. "I don't know, Flo. I have a bad feeling about this. What if the person involved discovers you are digging for information?"

Florence shrugged. "Then perhaps they'll stop. Look, I'm not suggesting we snoop about people's houses or listen at keyholes. I only mean to ask a few questions about stories that must be common knowledge in the area. I can be subtle."

It was Grace's turn to raise an eyebrow at that. Florence huffed, putting up her chin.

"I can!" she insisted. "Just you wait and see."

"Henry!" Jasper greeted him with a warm grin and Henry experience a surge of relief. He felt as if he'd been wrung out and left to dry after his time with Pippin and Mrs Dharani. His utter disbelief in witchcraft had not been diminished, but some of the things they had said, things they had known about him, his family, and the house had unsettled him beyond bearing. "I see your time with Montagu, Pippin, and Mrs Dharani has left you a broken shell of a man. I'm hardly surprised. That combination is enough to destroy anyone's composure."

Jasper gave him a cheerful grin and steered him towards his study.

Henry allowed himself to be steered, giving a snort of laughter as he saw the full-sized stuffed grizzly bear was still in the same place it had always been. It wore a top hat at a rakish angle and a garish waistcoat Henry vaguely recognised.

"I can't believe you still have that thing," Henry said, shaking his head at the bear.

"What, George? Good Lord, yes. He's part of the family, couldn't part with him now."

Henry laughed and flopped down in the chair the earl indicated, silently accepting the drink Jasper poured for him.

"So, did they come up with anything?"

Henry shrugged, taking a swallow of brandy, and enjoying the warmth that bloomed as it slid down his throat. "Apparently, some female is set on vengeance, but whether against me specifically, the Stanhope men or the family at large is yet unknown."

Jasper pursed his lips. "Interesting."

"How so?"

"Well, it appears your Miss Knight has come to a similar conclusion."

"She's not *my* Miss Knight," Henry muttered, frowning into his drink, even though his guts strongly protested the lie. She was his, and he was going to do everything in his power to make it official.

"Oh, give over, Henry. Really, it's as clear as the nose on your face that you've feelings for her and she's hardly hidden her interest in you. Surely, you've arranged to speak to Gabriel by now, for if he finds out before you've...."

"I wrote to him this morning!" Henry interrupted, irritated at having his personal affairs discussed in this manner. "Not that it's any of your business."

Jasper's expression shuttered and Henry cursed, realising he'd offended his oldest friend.

"I beg your pardon," Jasper said, his tone cool.

"Hell!" Henry retorted. He downed the rest of the brandy in one large swallow and surged to his feet, intent on refilling the glass. "I'm sorry, Jasper. I just... I just hate being discussed."

Jasper's taut expression eased. "I'm your friend, Henry, or at least I thought I was. I'm not some malicious busybody picking over your affairs for fun."

"I know!" Henry took a breath and let it out slowly, trying to moderate his seething emotions. "I know," he said again, calmer now.

"Do you?"

Henry shrugged. "You do not know what it's like, Jasper, to see details of your life in the scandal sheets, to know everyone is discussing you over breakfast."

"Oh, ho, haven't I indeed!" Jasper retorted, snorting with amusement.

Henry sighed, remembering how notorious Jasper had been as a young man. He'd been happily married and respectable for so long it was easy to forget his rather colourful past. The earl had been one of the handsomest men of the *ton* and women had—and still did—throw themselves at him wherever he went. Jasper had quickly gained a reputation as a rake and had often been in the scandal sheets for some dreadful behaviour or other. In reality, his reputation had been exaggerated out of all proportion, but it hadn't stopped the gossips turning a little indiscretion into something dreadful and licentious.

"Perhaps, but the difference is, the stories never humiliated you and made you look a damned fool," Henry said wearily. "I just want to keep my private life private, is that too much to ask?"

"Of course not, but surely your friends and family don't count? We only want the best for you. You might remember I encouraged your suit with Miss Knight. I think she's perfect for you, and you for her, come to that."

"You truly don't think me too old?" Henry asked, sceptical and too aware of the anxiety in his question.

Jasper shrugged. "All I know is I've seen some of the men sniffing about her and I've been glad I never had a daughter. I'd have been hard pressed not to start killing people, and I know Gabriel feels the same."

"Is this supposed to be reassuring?" Henry demanded in outrage.

"Yes, if you'd let me finish! I only mean that I know you are a good man, you are honest and decent, and you would be the kind of husband I would wish for my daughter if I had one. I'd take the age difference over some of the fortune hunters and fools out there in a heartbeat."

"So basically, I'm better than the alternative," Henry said dryly.

Jasper rolled his eyes. "If you are determined to take offense, yes, you are."

"So you agree she could do better."

"Damn it! No, I don't agree, and stop putting words in my mouth. Obviously, in an ideal world you'd be closer in age, but the world is anything but ideal and nothing is perfect. We live with reality and finding happiness is a dashed hard business, so who gives a tinker's cuss if there's an age gap if you love each other? Life is too short, and I think Florence would be lucky to have you. There, you belligerent devil. Does that satisfy?"

Henry sat down again, nursing his brandy. "I suppose. I mean… yes, thank you, and I'm sorry. You're right, I am in the devil of a mood. All this nonsense about witchcraft and— Bloody hell, Jasper, I never expected to fall in love again. I didn't *want* to, but…."

"But there's not a lot of choice in the matter is there?" Jasper's expression was full of sympathy and understanding. He would understand too, knowing the merry dance Henry's sister had led him on.

Henry laughed and shook his head. "No. It would appear there isn't."

They drank in companionable silence for a while and a little of the tension singing across Henry's shoulders eased until he remembered what Jasper had said earlier.

"Wait, you said Florence had come to a similar conclusion. What do you mean by that?"

Jasper shrugged. "Only that she's been interrogating the staff all morning."

"What?" Henry sat up straight.

"I believe she is trying to discover any known witches or wise women in the area and any stories that might relate back to your family. She's very perspicacious," Jasper added with approval.

"And you let her?" Henry said, aggrieved. "What if she stumbled upon someone involved? She might put herself in danger."

Jasper frowned. "Calm down, old man. Aren't you getting a bit overwrought? She's only chatting to a few of the—"

But Henry was already on his feet.

"Where is she?" he asked, reaching for the door.

"The kitchens, last I heard," Jasper called after him as Henry did not stop to discuss the matter any longer. He was going to find Florence and put a stop to this at once.

Chapter 13

Dear Miss Weston,

I understand you do not wish to make our betrothal public yet, but I thought perhaps it would put your mind at rest to visit the place where you are soon to live.

I would be pleased to accommodate you if you wish me to invite Miss Florence and Miss Evie Knight, and whomever else you would want to accompany you for a visit under whatever pretext you prefer. Though it is not as grand as what you are used to, the farm is prosperous, and the house well maintained, but I thought perhaps you might wish to inspect it and see for yourself.

—Excerpt of a letter from Mr Sterling Oak to Miss Grace Weston (daughter of Baron and Baroness Rothborn).

17th August 1839, Bramble Cottage, Holbrook House estate, Sussex.

"Ah, well, there's always been talk of wise women and the like," said Mrs Simmons. The elderly woman had been nursemaid to both the earl and his son Cassius in her time and lived in a neat little cottage on the St Clairs' estate. "And there's plenty who kept their skills a secret too. There still are, I don't doubt. Folk can be suspicious of things they don't understand. As to who... let me see now."

Florence sat patiently beside Grace, sipping tea with every outward sign of calm, though she did not feel the least bit patient. Most people had been reluctant to speak to them, unsurprisingly. They were guests, and good staff knew they did not spread gossip, even if invited to do so, and the staff at Holbrook were both too well paid and well treated to disregard their duties. However, old Mrs Simmons was a kindly soul and clearly delighted to have a visit from two young ladies, so Florence hoped she might unbend enough to chat with them.

"Well, there was old Mrs Oak, she had a knack for medicine and the like, and she'd read your tea leaves. Cards, too. I know people respected her skills. Granny Merrick was another, mind she's long gone and never had no children. Mrs Hick... Ah, now some said she had the way, but she always swore she didn't. Mind, after what happened with her kin it's hardly surprising."

"Oh?" Florence asked, setting down her teacup.

"Oh, 'twas many years ago, sometime last century, but her great-great-grandmother was hanged for a witch. One of the last ever convicted, too."

"Good gracious," Grace exclaimed.

Florence swallowed, her hand going involuntarily to her throat. "On what evidence?"

Mrs Simmons frowned, considering this. "That I don't remember. I do remember she was with child at the time. They held her until the babe was born, and then hanged the poor woman."

Florence reached for Grace's hand as her friend made a sound of distress. "How horrid."

Mrs Simmons' expression was pinched. "Men interfering in women's business," she said tightly, shaking her head. "Always causes trouble. She was ill used. Her family struggled ever after that, what with the shame and trying to raise the babe. Her sister took the child on. If not for the St Clair family, I don't know what would have become of them."

"The family worked for the St Clairs," Florence said, perking up at this information.

"Yes. Still do, to my knowledge. I don't remember hearing that they'd moved on. Now the sister was a Harding, I'm sure, but didn't she have a daughter? My memory isn't what it was, sadly." Mrs Simmons closed her eyes, puzzling out the thread of the family tree. "Oh, it's on the tip of my tongue. Perhaps if you made another pot of tea, Miss Knight, while I think on it."

"Of course," Florence said, leaping up obligingly.

Anything if it helped the lady get her a name to question.

Henry strode down the path in the direction he'd been given for Mrs Simmons. Apparently, Florence had left the kitchens some time ago to speak to the St Clairs' old nanny. The path dipped and then rose again and, on reaching the top, Henry saw her walking back to the house with her friend Miss Weston. The two of them were chattering animatedly and Henry felt his heart give a most uncharacteristic lurch in the vicinity of his heart. How the devil had this happened, and with such ease. He had believed love was something that only his friends would live with, that he'd had his chance and lost it. How wrong he had been. It was hopeless to deny it any longer, he was in way over his head. So be it. If this was his last chance at happiness, and he very much suspected it was, then he was going to hold onto it until his last breath.

This time he would not let anything go wrong. Not that he regretted losing Lily, that had been for the best. He knew that now, even if it meant there were scars to bear. This time it was different.

He was not perfect, and he knew Florence could do better, but no one on earth would try harder than he would to be everything she needed, to make her happy. He knew how precious this feeling was, and how devastating it was to lose it.

He watched her as she followed the path towards him. Everything about Florence seemed to thrum with energy, she was so alive, so vital, and so very crucial to his future happiness. Henry could not lose her. He would not survive such a loss a second time. So, he must put a stop to this madness before she got herself into trouble.

"Henry!" she exclaimed, her expression one of such pleasure in seeing him, he felt quite winded.

"It's supposed to be Mr Stanhope," he said under his breath, hating that he sounded so old and fussy, but he didn't want gossip about them circulating before he'd spoken to Gabriel.

Florence rolled her eyes at him. "Grace is my friend, Henry, she knows about us."

Miss Weston blushed and avoided his eye. "Yes, well, I shall walk ahead. Good day, Mr Stanhope."

"Miss Weston," Henry said, giving her a polite bow before turning back to Florence. "Who else have you told?"

Florence shrugged, clearly unconcerned. "Not many people, but everyone seems to know, anyway. Apparently, I look at you like a lovesick puppy." She looked adorably disgruntled by this description and Henry was torn between pleasure at knowing she could not hide her feelings and wishing she'd try a bit harder to avoid getting him murdered.

"Yes," he murmured, unwinding a bit and unable to stop himself from teasing her. "I've noticed that too."

"Oh! You have not." She glared at him, looking so outraged Henry could not resist.

"There, you're doing it now."

She wrinkled her nose at him. "You, sir, are confused. That was most certainly not adoration."

Henry glanced around to see Grace was just about to walk around the corner and out of sight before grasping Florence's waist and pulling her into his arms. "And what about now?" he murmured.

Her lovely face coloured a little, her eyes growing dark as she slid her hands up over his shoulders. "Kiss me, and I'll show you just how much I love you," she dared him.

Desire hit Henry so hard it was difficult to breathe. He ought not, not out here in the open, but damnation…. She reached up, clasping his neck and tugging his head down to hers. It was madness, he ought not, not before he'd spoken to Gabriel.

"Kiss me, Henry," she murmured, brushing her lips over his.

"Not here," he managed, though it was hard to speak.

His heart was beating too hard, thundering in his ears. Had he ever felt like this before? Even with Lily, had there been this desperate, maddening desire? If there had, he could no longer remember it.

"Yes, here, now. I want you to kiss me. I think of you all the time, Henry, I cannot sleep for thinking of you."

"You think of me at night?" His voice was rough now, husky with need as he imagined her, alone in her bed, thinking of him. Oh, hell. *Henry. No. Behave.* This was bad. Very bad.

"Especially at night," the little wretch admitted, trailing her lips over the line of his jaw. "Alone in my bed, wishing you were with me, touching me…."

Henry, you dog. Wait. Think. You were coming here to stop her from… from… what the hell had he been coming to do? He couldn't think of anything but the fact she was near to him. Her lips were warm against his cheek, her breath fluttering over his skin, her body pressing closer to his….

"Florence, I've written to your father. Until then—"

"He's not here, Henry. I am, and I need you to kiss me. Just one little kiss. It's been forever."

"It was yesterday!"

"Forever and ever…" she murmured, tangling her fingers in his hair, staring at him with such adoration, such need….

"Hell!" Henry gave up. His self-control really was pitiful where this woman was concerned. He took her mouth, overwhelmed by the way she responded at once, opening to him, her desire as blatant as his own, holding nothing back. Her hands moved over him, exploring, enflaming him, and he drew back before things got out of hand. "Florence."

"Don't stop." She tugged his hand, pulling him towards a huge oak tree just off the path, hidden from view.

Florence ducked under the low branches, running to the trunk and leaning against it. She was breathing hard, her eyes alight with anticipation. Henry swallowed. God, she was lovely, and he'd wanted nothing in his whole life like he wanted her, but they must wait until they were married.

"Henry," she said, her voice low and breathless, full of wanting.

"You would tempt a saint, Miss Knight," he said, keeping a few feet of distance between them for he felt his sanity fraying at the edges. "I wrote to your father this morning and I mean to get his permission to court you. There will be no anticipating our vows in the meantime. Do you hear me?"

Florence pouted at him. "My, how cross and stern you are Mr Stanhope. Is this the kind of husband you will be?"

Henry's lips twitched, but he fought to keep his expression serious. "I don't believe I have actually asked you to marry me yet, Miss Knight. I cannot before I have your father's permission."

"Perhaps there is no need, perhaps I don't wish to marry a man who won't give me what I want?"

She sent him a coquettish glance from under her lashes, teasing him, the wretch.

"Ah, well. Then perhaps it is just as well we discover this now. I am too serious, too old, and you are too badly behaved, too flighty. A terrible match it would be. Better we forget the whole thing."

"Oh, Henry!" Florence exclaimed, looking genuinely cross now. "Just come and kiss me, you horrid man."

Henry laughed and moved towards her, leaning over her, one hand on the tree trunk on either side of her head. He stared down at her, smiling indulgently. "You are a spoilt child."

"I know, and you adore me anyway," she retorted. "Now kiss me, *please*."

"Just one kiss," he warned her, or perhaps it was himself he was reminding. It didn't matter, the moment their lips touched again he was engulfed in heat, in wanting so profound and overwhelming he did not know how to contain it. His kisses burned hotter, devouring her, his hands seeking skin, needing to touch, to possess. Henry could no longer think, driven by instinct, by the primitive need to take what was his. His hands grabbed at her skirts, finding his way beneath what seemed to be dozens of layers until his fingers felt the soft skin of her upper thigh.

Florence gasped against his mouth, and he realised he had surprised her, shocked her even. No. He must keep control, he must not take any more, but her skin was like silk, so warm and he wanted her so much.

"Tell me to stop," he begged her.

If she said the word, this would be over. She had the power he had let slip from his grasp.

Emma V Leech

Florence shook her head, staring up at him, her eyes glassy with desire. "Touch me."

Henry groaned and rested his head against the rough bark of the tree.

"Please," she pleaded. "Please."

She was trembling against him, aching with the need for his touch. Well, it would be cruel to leave her like this. Surely, he could give her this much and not go any further. He could. He must.

Henry turned his head into her hair, breathing in the intoxicating scent of her until he felt giddy with it. His fingers stroked up and her breath hitched.

"So soft, so lovely," he whispered, feeling the shiver that ran over her. "Are you mine, Florence?"

She nodded, her breathing becoming erratic as his fingers skimmed higher, finding the delicate crease between thigh and torso.

"Is this what you think about, at night, when you are alone in your bed?"

Florence nodded again but he would not let her get away with it a second time.

"Tell me," he insisted.

"Yes. Yes, I think about this."

"Then what should I do next? Where do you want me to touch you?"

A blush of such vibrant pink rose over her neck, colouring her cheeks, he could feel the heat of it.

"I... c-can't," she said.

Henry chuckled and nipped at her ear. "Oh, I think you can, but I'll be kind... this time."

171

He stroked through her curls and her hips canted towards his touch, eager for more. Henry's pulse was racing, hardly able to believe she would allow him this, never mind that he'd been devil enough to take it. He'd always considered himself a gentleman, had never dallied with innocent girls, not even as a young man, but Florence had a way of driving him on, of getting what she wanted that overrode all his hard-won control and made him act like a damned schoolboy. Well, this far and no farther. He would bring her pleasure, and then... and then he'd remember what the hell it was he'd wanted to talk to her about and take her back to the house.

"Henry." Her voice was full of anguish as he teased his fingers back and forth, so close to where she needed him but not close enough.

"I know, love," he murmured, dragging his mouth across her cheek to her lips.

He kissed her, deep and hard, their tongues tangling, stroking, and Florence gasped as he finally sought the little nub of flesh buried in that secret place and pressed. Her head fell back, and Henry kissed her neck as he caressed and toyed with her. His hand delved deeper between her thighs, one finger sliding inside her wet heat as she cried out, burying her face against his shoulder.

"Yes, like that, my beautiful Florence. God, you're lovely. I cannot wait to marry you."

She clutched at his shoulders, trembling, her eyes squeezed shut as he stroked and caressed her delicate flesh until he felt her the pleasure building, felt her muscles tense and quiver. He covered her mouth with his own, swallowing her moan of pleasure as she broke under his touch. She shuddered and jolted, with soft little sounds of surprised delight as he eased her through the final tremors.

He stared into eyes of green, thickly lashed and with that beguiling feline slant, utterly bewitched.

"I love you," he said, his voice hoarse, hardly believing he was uttering the words he'd sworn never to say again.

Florence blinked up at him, looking a little dazed, but her eyes filled with tears at his words, and she reached up and touched his face with her hand.

"Oh, Henry, I love you too."

"You bastard!"

Henry jolted, realising too late that he had failed to notice the sound of someone approaching, or that they were not quite so hidden as they'd believed.

Gabriel Knight looked about as angry as a man could look, and no wonder, considering Henry had his hands up his daughter's skirts.

Shit.

Gabriel lunged for him. Henry sidestepped, darting just out of reach, and ducking out from under the low branched.

"Papa! Papa, don't! *Don't!*" Florence shouted, to no avail.

Gabriel was far beyond listening in this moment. He wanted Henry's blood and nothing else would do. All Henry could do was try to stay alive until someone came and restrained him. The devil of it was Henry was ten years younger than Gabe and could hold his own in a fight, having done so often enough on his travels, but he could not fight back when he knew he was very much in the wrong, and that Florence would never forgive him if he hurt her father.

"Gabriel, we need to talk," he said, dodging a vicious upper cut that would have dislodge teeth and likely broken his bloody jaw if it had made contact. Gabriel clearly didn't spend all his days sitting on his backside either.

"I'll talk when you're dead," Gabriel growled, delivering a swift upper cut that Henry barely avoided the full force of, and which sent him stumbling backwards.

"Papa!" Florence yelled in fury. "I love him!"

"You'll get over it," Gabriel snarled, bearing down on Henry like one of the bloody trains he was so fond of.

"I will not fight you," Henry said, holding his hands up.

"Good. Makes it easier to rip your damned head off," Gabriel said, flashing the kind of grin any sane man would have nightmares about for years to come.

"Mama! Mama! Stop him!"

With one eye still on the raging bull that was his opponent, Henry noted the slight figure of Lady Helena hurrying towards them with a burst of relief, thank God… Ooof!

His attention divided, Henry was too slow to dodge the next blow and Gabriel's fist snapped his head back. He staggered and went down, and Gabriel followed. He took hold of Henry's cravat, keeping him in place and Henry watched with a sick sense of inevitability as his right fist drew back.

"Gabriel Knight, you will stop this nonsense at once, you great oaf!"

Gabriel stilled at once, breathing hard. With what appeared to be a herculean effort, he turned his head to stare at his wife. "He… He… with Florence…"

Gabriel bit the words out as if they tasted vile.

Helena however just threw up her hands and glared at her husband in exasperation. "Well, of course. The poor man is courting her. Did you think I didn't know? Did you not read the letter I sent you?"

"What letter?" Gabriel demanded, his expression creasing into one of confusion. "I got a letter telling me this bastard was seducing my daughter. And what the devil do you mean he's courting her? He's my age!"

"No, I'm not!" Henry retorted at once. Damned if he'd let the bastard age him by a decade.

"You shut up!" Gabriel growled.

Henry shut up, though the urge to break his future father-in-law's nose was beyond tempting. He supposed it wouldn't help matters, though.

"You mean to say you knew about this?" Gabriel asked his wife. "You... You let this depraved monster—"

"Well," Helena said, glancing from Henry to Florence, who was red-faced and mortified. "I'm not entirely certain what *this* is—though I could take a guess—but firstly, I doubt he's any more depraved than you were when we were courting and, secondly, I know Florence is in love with him. She has been pursuing poor Henry mercilessly from the moment we got here. Frankly, I'm surprised he held out this long. He didn't stand a chance, I'm afraid."

Gabriel gaped at his wife who gave a nonchalant shrug.

"What can I say, darling? She takes after me."

"Oh, Mama!" Florence ran to her mother who enveloped her in a hug.

"There, there, sweetheart. I ought to have known you would get poor Henry into dreadful trouble. I know I always did with your father. Didn't I, Gabriel?" she added, a note to her voice any sensible man would heed.

Gabriel's expression darkened, no doubt as he remembered all the trouble Helena had got him into. "I still want to kill him," he growled, his fist still tangled in Henry's cravat.

In fact, it was becoming a tad difficult to breathe.

"I know, darling," Helena said, her expression full of sympathy. "You may vent your feelings to my brother, I'm sure he'll sympathise."

Henry snorted, remembering all too well when Bedwin had discovered Gabriel had been courting his sister in secret. The duke had wanted nothing less than to castrate Gabriel Knight and hang his bollocks over the mantelpiece as a warning to others. The fist in his cravat tightened a bit more.

"I love her," he managed, though the pressure on his throat made the words somewhat strangled. "I wrote to you this morning, asking to speak with you. Want to marry her."

Gabriel lent down, getting up in Henry's face.

"You're too old," he said through gritted teeth.

"Gabe, my love, I know there is a significant age gap, but I ask you, how old was I when we eloped?" Helena asked him, and Henry noted she was tapping her foot impatiently now. Never a good sign.

Gabe stiffened. "That is neither—"

"I was barely nineteen," Helena supplied for him. "Florence is almost twenty-three."

"That doesn't change the fact—"

"And how old were you? Is the age difference so very much greater than ours?"

Gabriel's jaw was very tight.

Helena's expression softened, her voice full of understanding. "Let the poor man up, Gabe. I know she's your little girl, but she is no longer a child. She is a grown woman, and she loves him. She's made her choice, and I for one think it is a good one. Perhaps you would not have chosen him, but he is a good man and I believe he loves her. He'll take care of her, you know that."

Gabriel turned and glowered at Henry, the desire to sink his fist into Henry's face shining in his eyes all too clearly. He glared for a moment longer, and then let out an uneven breath and climbed off Henry, getting to his feet.

"Henry!" Florence cried, running to him. "Oh, darling, are you hurt?"

"Mostly my pride," Henry muttered, rubbing irritably at his jaw which was throbbing.

"You don't go near her again without a chaperone," Gabriel said, pointing a threatening finger at Henry who could do nothing else but nod in agreement.

"Probably best."

Gabriel looked like he wanted to murder him all over again.

"And it will be a *very* long engagement," he said through his teeth.

Henry had known this was coming and had enough sense to realise this was not the moment to argue. Sadly he was unable to communicate this to Florence.

"That's not fair! Papa, Henry did nothing wrong, and I want to marry him as soon as possible."

"Well, when I feel less like dismembering him and chopping the sections up into small pieces, and then the pieces into bite sized chunks, we'll talk about it," her father said, still vibrating with anger. "I had a brief spell working for a butcher in my youth," he added for Henry's benefit, and quite unnecessarily in his opinion.

Helena dragged her furious husband away by the arm. "Come along, we shall all return to the house and take tea like civilised people and discuss it properly," she said, her voice calm but firm.

Gabriel made a noise that sounded very much like a growl but allowed her to propel him back in the direction of the house.

Helena glanced over her shoulder to Florence and mouthed, *I'll talk to him,* before sending them both an encouraging smile.

Henry sighed, and they followed them back up the path. He turned to see Florence watching him anxiously.

"Are you cross with me?"

"With you?" Henry frowned in consternation.

"Yes, for getting you into trouble. It's just like Mama said, isn't it? It's all my fault. You didn't stand a chance. I've chased you and tormented you and forced you to kiss me. If I hadn't, you'd have never…"

She blushed then and Henry's heart felt as if it was being squeezed in his chest. She was utterly delicious, and he would marry her if it was the last thing he did. Even if Gabriel made him wait for years.

"Yes, indeed, it is undoubtedly all your fault, you wicked girl. You made me fall head over ears in love with you and tempted me beyond reason. I shall never be the same… and I've never been happier about anything, you little nitwit."

The look of relief in her eyes made Henry smile and he reached out, taking her hand.

"Keep your distance, Stanhope!" Gabriel yelled.

Henry sighed and let go of her hand.

"Oh, Gabe, leave them be," Helena scolded him.

The sound of husband and wife bickering as they returned to the house made Henry smile. "They are still as much in love as they were when they met."

"Yes," Florence said simply. "They don't always agree, and occasionally they have the most spectacular rows, but there's never any question that they adore each other. I think they work hard though, to keep understanding each other. They talk a lot."

Henry nodded. "I suppose I need some practise with that. It's only been me, Florence, for such a long time. I'm not used to discussing my thoughts or... sharing decisions, but I will try."

Florence glanced ahead to see her mother and father were still *discussing* things and slid her arm through his. "Oh, don't worry, darling, I shall remind you whenever the need arises."

Henry laughed.

Chapter 14

Dear diary,

At last! I thought the day would never come, but with a great deal of plotting, some spectacular intrigues, a little spying, and a soupçon of luck, I did it!

I finally got hold of a copy of The Ghosts of Castle Madruzzo!

And this time, no one is going to stop me reading it.

—Excerpt of an entry to the diary of Lady Catherine 'Cat' Barrington, (youngest daughter of the Marquess and Marchioness of Montagu).

Evening of the 17th of August 1839, Holbrook House, Sussex.

Florence retired to the library after dinner. She was not ready to go to sleep yet. The events of the day had been too exciting for her to think of closing her eyes.

Henry loved her. She had expected to need to fight harder for him, or at least to gain the declaration she had wanted. It was clear his all too public jilting had hurt him deeply and made him distrustful of women, even of his own heart. So for him to give her those words....

She gave a happy sigh.

The amount of trust he was putting in her was astonishing, humbling, and she only hoped she could live up to it. No doubt he'd had many sophisticated lovers in his years abroad, women with experience of life and love and *bedding,* that she did not have. Would he grow bored with her? No, she scolded herself. She was well educated, and she had opinions, too many opinions some would say. Not Henry, though, and if there was something she did not know or understand then she would learn. Henry would help her. She smiled at the idea. Henry would enjoy teaching her, like he had taught her this afternoon, under the oak tree. He had enjoyed that a good deal, so had she... until Papa had arrived and spoiled it.

Florence sighed. Poor Papa. He couldn't look at her this afternoon, or she at him if she were honest, and she had the rather lowering sensation that he was disappointed in her. Mama had assured her that wasn't true, just that he was struggling with the idea she was a grown woman and no longer his little girl. Though, really, she had been out in society since she was eighteen, surely it couldn't be that much of a surprise? She wondered who on earth had sent that odd letter to him. Her father had showed it to them, and the correspondent had been barely literate, the writing execrable. Was this the person who was making the corn dolls and causing Henry such strife? Surely, it must be connected.

She pondered this for a while before setting her book aside. She'd barely glanced at it, so there was no point in trying to read. The clock in the hallway struck ten and Florence sighed. It wasn't late but, if she was just going to sit and stare at the wall, she may as well go to bed and do it in comfort. She was just crossing the hall when a slender figure moved in the shadows, hurrying towards the servant's staircase.

"Susan? Susan Cooper?"

The girl stilled, staring at Florence as though she'd been caught out.

"It's all right," Florence assured her. "You're not in any trouble. I just wanted to speak to you. If you have a moment?"

The girl hesitated, clearly not wanting to be rude but needing to get about her business.

"I'm sorry, I know you've work to do, and I expect you want to get finished and go to bed. Do you think I might speak with you tomorrow morning?"

"I… I bring you hot water in the morning. Perhaps then, just for a moment… but why, miss? Are you sure I'm not in trouble?"

It was Florence's turn to hesitate, for in truth she did not know if the girl was involved with the trouble at the Hall after what Mrs Simmons had said. It seemed unlikely, though. This girl would have been a child when Henry left. She was younger than Florence, no more than sixteen or seventeen.

"I just want to speak with you about your grandmother, that's all," Florence said, realising she had not answered the question.

"Gran?" Susan stared at her, suddenly defensive. "What do you want to know about Gran?"

There was an edge to her voice which was hardly surprising. It must seem exceedingly odd that one of her employer's guests was asking after a lower servant's grandmother.

"I know it seems peculiar," Florence said with an apologetic smile. "Look, don't worry about it now. I just wish to ask you a few questions. I'll explain in the morning and then you can answer me—or not, as you choose—once you've heard me out."

"Very well, miss. Now, if you'll excuse me."

The girl dipped a curtsey and hurried away.

Florence watched her go, wondering if she was wasting her time, or if the girl's anxiety was not simply unease at the odd question, but guilt.

It was not until later that evening that Henry remembered why he'd been so intent on finding Florence earlier. The events of the afternoon had rather forced everything else from his mind. Helena had calmed her husband down sufficiently to talk him into receiving Henry tomorrow afternoon. The spectre of this daunting interview had been enough to fully occupy Henry's thoughts for the rest of the evening. So, it was not until after dinner when he remembered Florence's reckless scheme to interview the staff at Holbrook in search of a witch, of all things.

Still, she could hardly be interrogating anyone at this time of night. He must ask Helena if he could have a quiet word with Florence in the morning, before his interview with Gabriel. *Hell.* How did one go about persuading a young woman's father you were the best choice for her husband, when you didn't actually believe it yourself? He would simply have to be honest, which would likely mean Gabriel would agree he wasn't good enough and tell him to sling his hook.

Henry was considering this as he readied himself for bed when the sound of breaking china reached him.

"Damnation, not again."

It had been close this time. In fact, it sounded as if it had come from the room next door to Henry's, the one that had once belonged to his mother, and would one day belong to Florence. Not that he had any intention of allowing her to sleep there alone. Henry moved to the connecting door, listening for any sound of movement. He doubted the servants would have heard the crash, as their rooms were far from the master suites. There was no audible sound of a presence in the next room, and yet Henry's instincts prickled.

The fireplace poker was the best weapon he could lay hands on at short notice, but it would do. He reached for the door handle and eased it open a crack, listening. Still nothing. Henry waited, wondering what to do. He was bloody well not going to start believing in ghosts, but there was a menacing presence in the room, he'd swear it. The darkness seemed absolute, the light from his own room barely penetrating. His housekeeper kept the curtains drawn to protect the expensive carpets and bed hangings from the sun, and so no trace of moonlight outlined the shapes within. The looming canopy of the bed was there, but little else was discernible.

Henry stepped into the room, and pain exploded in his head as something stuck him hard. He went down, clutching at his head as someone kicked him in the stomach, winding him. The dim light from his room did not help illuminate the scene much, but it was just enough to glint off the edge of a knife blade.

It had been a while since he'd had to fight for his life, but Henry had survived a reckless few years when he'd first left England, not caring much what happened to him, and living dangerously. He'd learned a thing or two, once he'd realised he didn't actually want to die.

Though his head was exploding with pain, he rolled sideways and kicked out, striking at whoever had clobbered him before the knife struck. There was a grunt of pain, and he barely avoided another kick by shuffling back out of the way. In the dark he scrabbled on the ground for the poker he had dropped, and curled his fingers gratefully around the cold iron. He swung it, with more force than accuracy, but he hit something. There was a curse and the clatter of metal falling to the wooden floor. There was the muffled noise of someone searching the floor, then footsteps. Using the wall at his back, Henry pushed himself upright, fighting nausea as his head spun and his stomach roiled. A cool breeze washed over him and a strange musty smell, and then… nothing. No sound. No movement. Whoever it was had vanished.

There was the sound of feet again, but from the opposite direction—someone moving fast—and a light appeared in the doorway off the corridor.

"Sir?" came the familiar voice of one of his footmen. "Is everything well, sir? We heard—"

But Henry did not discover what it was they'd heard, as the darkness swallowed him up and he passed out.

18th August 1839, Holbrook House, Sussex.

"Henry!" Harriet exclaimed, on seeing him the next morning. "What on earth happened to you?"

Henry winced at his sister's shrill demand as the sound ricocheted through his head, scraping against the tender flesh like claws upon a wound.

"Attacked," he said succinctly. "Last night. Intruder. Must see Florence. Now."

Harriet stared at him for a long moment but thank God she was not one for hysterics or scenes.

"Come and sit down before you fall down. Temple, have someone ask Miss Knight to come to us as quickly as she is able," she instructed the butler calmly as she guided Henry through to the yellow parlour, which seemed far too sunny for his beleaguered senses.

Henry sat, trying to ignore the sickening thudding of his head. The doctor who had attended him had told him in no uncertain terms that he had a concussion, and he would not be responsible for the consequences if Henry did not do as he was told. Of course, the old quack had wanted to bleed him, too, an idea which Henry had rejected. He felt sore enough without someone cutting him up. Naturally, the doctor had washed his hands of him, which suited Henry fine.

"Good Lord, Henry, you've a lump on the back of your head as big as my fist," his sister exclaimed, on coming to examine him.

"Please, keep your voice down," he said through gritted teeth.

"What happened?" Harriet said, lowering her voice, though not enough in Henry's opinion.

"Someone in the room next to mine. No idea how they got in, or how they left. They just bloody vanished. The staff are all leaving in droves, they think it's a ghost of all things."

"How on earth did a ghost strike you hard enough to leave a lump like that?" Harriet demanded in disgust.

"Tell them that," Henry grumbled, having tried and failed to do so himself. Everyone was too terrified to spend another night in the house, and they'd begun looking at him like it was his fault.

"Tell me what happened when you were attacked," Harriet said, watching him with an expression that was full of concern. As clinical and precise as Harry could sometimes be, she was very caring.

"Get Florence first," he instructed. He was damned if he'd explain himself more than once and Florence would certainly want an explanation too.

Harriet sighed but must have recognised the stubborn note to his voice. She ought to; she sounded exactly the same when she'd made her mind up. It was a family trait.

They waited until Temple reappeared. "My lady, it appears Miss Knight has left the house. On enquiring about the staff, it appears she was seen a couple of hours ago, walking towards the village."

"A couple of hours ago? But it was only half-past six," Harriet said in astonishment. "Was she alone?"

Temple nodded. "Apparently so, my lady."

Something tense and agitated stirred in Henry's gut. "Where was she going? Does anyone know? I must go after her."

"I will ask the staff at once, sir."

"And Miss Weston," Henry added, pushing to his feet.

"Henry, what is this about?" his sister demanded. "You cannot go racing off in that state, you look ill."

Henry shook his head and then fervently wished he hadn't as his stomach roiled. "I don't know, not yet, but I intend to find out. I must go after her."

Harriet shook her head, trying to push him bodily back into the chair, which was not as difficult as it ought to have been. After fighting with Gabriel yesterday and then getting set upon in his own home, Henry was feeling more than a bit bruised and battered.

"Sit down, you great lummox! You're not going anywhere yet, not until we know more. I will send a couple of the grooms in the direction she was seen walking in the meantime, but you're not going haring off when you don't know where she's gone or for what purpose. You'll only go off on a wild goose chase. Let us have the facts first. What do you know?"

"I only know that Florence has been asking your staff about anyone in the area that might be a witch. Pippin and Mrs Dharani said it was a woman behind the corn dolls, someone I or the family had wronged. I need to know if Florence spoke to anyone last night."

"Before you were attacked, you mean? You think she's spooked someone?"

Thank God for Harry and her extraordinary brain, for Henry did not have the energy to explain what Harriet had grasped at once. He nodded.

Harry rushed to the door. "I'll fetch Helena and Gabriel."

Henry was never more grateful to his sister for explaining everything to everyone concerned with brevity and speed. By now Jasper, Gabriel and Helena, and Florence's sister Miss Evie, and their friend Miss Weston, had all gathered in the parlour.

Gabriel was pacing, glaring at Henry as though all of this was his fault. With a lurch, Henry realised he was right. If not for him, Florence would never have got mixed up in this. Oh, God, if she were hurt, he'd never forgive himself.

"Oh my." Miss Weston was pale, her wide grey eyes enormous as she realised her friend might be in real danger.

Henry could not think of that, he would find her, now, before any harm could befall her. For all he knew she had just gone for a walk.

"I think I know where she may have gone."

Henry's stomach knotted tighter and tighter as Miss Weston spoke, and his hopes that the events of last night were unconnected with Florence diminished.

"Yesterday, we visited Mrs Simmons. She was ever so nice and told us a lot about witches and wise women, but then she mentioned Mary Thompsett."

"Mary Thompsett? Good Lord, that must be over a hundred years ago," Jasper exclaimed.

"You know the story?" Henry asked, looking up at his friend.

Jasper frowned. "Somewhat. She was a local woman, and one of the last women in the country hanged as a witch. I remember my father speaking about it. He said it was a dreadful miscarriage of justice. In fact… I think the family still works for us. I'm sure he said…."

Henry went very still. "Who?"

Jasper frowned. "I don't know. I can't quite remember the story, the names changed as they married. All women in the line, as I remember. I know Mary had a daughter. I think her sister adopted her and they changed her name, not that it mattered. People have long memories. Well, people other than me," he added ruefully, frowning as he tried to remember. "Was it Hicks?"

"Yes, it was," Miss Weston said. She was clutching her arms about her middle and looked as if she might faint at any moment she was so pale. "Mrs Simmons said Miss Hicks was rumoured to be a witch but denied it. She married a Mr Cooper, her daughter Lucy died giving birth to an illegitimate child."

"Susan," Jasper said, nodding. His expression was grave. "Susan Cooper."

"Wait," Henry said, the name conjuring a memory of a young woman holding a posy of flowers. "I think I saw her. Was that the same Susan we saw that Sunday, outside the church?"

Jasper nodded. "Yes."

Harriet tugged at the bell pull and, a moment later, Temple appeared once more. "Bring Susan Cooper to us, please, Temple, but don't frighten her. She's not in any trouble."

Henry glowered at the door. "She damn well is in trouble if Florence is caught up in this."

"It's your bloody fault if she is," Gabriel growled.

The man had been pacing back and forth like a caged lion since he'd come in. Henry could say nothing; he felt just as Gabriel did and could not deny his accusation.

Temple returned moments later. "It appears Susan is not on the premises. Indeed, Nancy, with whom she shares a room, says she did not sleep in her bed last night, but that she returned here early this morning for work. She took hot water to Miss Knight, and no one has seen her since."

Henry's heart clenched. "Where?" he demanded of Temple. "Her parents, her kin, where would she go?"

Temple shook his head. "Her grandmother was her last living relative to my knowledge, and she died some weeks ago. As to where she might go, I am afraid I could not say."

"You wanted to see me, Mr Temple?"

A frightened looking maid whom Henry recognised as being Susan's friend from that day outside the church appeared at the door, having been escorted by a burly footman.

"Thank you, Stevens," Temple said, dismissing the footman. "Now, Rachel, don't look so frightened, the earl and Mr Stanhope just want to ask you some questions."

This didn't seem to reassure Rachel in the slightest.

"I don't know nuthin'," she said, a sullen look darkening her eyes, twisting her apron around in her fingers.

"Do you know why Miss Knight might have agreed to meet Susan, or where Susan might go if she were in trouble, or wanted to get away?" St Clair asked.

Rachel shook her head, her throat working. "No, but I bet it's that horrid Joe. I told her he was trouble. I don't like the way he looks at me, nor her neither."

"Joe?" Henry said, before Gabriel could open his mouth.

"Joe Foster, sir," Nancy said. "Him what digs the graves at the church."

Henry felt his stomach drop as he remembered the gravedigger that same day, the way he had watched the girls as they walked off, the way he had watched Florence, and then turned and looked at Henry.

"Oh, God," he said. "We need to get to the church. Now."

Louis César was halfway down the stairs when he saw the men racing out the front door. What the devil was going on? He turned as he reached the bottom of the stairs to find Evie watching them go. Her sweet face was pale and anxious.

"Evie, whatever is the matter?"

"Florence is missing," she said, her voice choked. "Henry is afraid she may have got mixed up in the business with the c-corn dolls." She covered her mouth with her hand to smother a sob.

"Chérie!" Louis exclaimed, his heart aching for her. Silently, he guided her back into the parlour before anyone saw her break down.

"Oh, Louis, I'm so frightened." She flung herself at him, burying her face in his chest and sobbing.

"Er…" For a moment Louis froze, uncertain what to do. He could not be caught alone with her in such a compromising position but… but damn it, the poor child was distraught. Louis put his arms about her, rubbing slow circles on her back. *"Voyons, Voyons, ma chérie.* Calm yourself. Tell me what has happened?"

Slowly Evie recovered her composure and Louis handed her his handkerchief.

"I'm s-sorry I cried all over your waistcoat," she said, diffident now, her cheeks pink with embarrassment and her nose red from blowing it with such vigour.

Louis smiled at her. "It's of no matter, I assure you." Still, he moved back to the door, opened it so no one could accuse them of impropriety, and gestured for Evie to sit down.

"Tell me," he said.

Haltingly at first, Evie told him of everything she had learned this morning.

Louis swallowed a curse, wishing he'd known this earlier. "What did the maid look like? Susan, was it?"

"Quite pretty, slender and blonde."

He nodded. "I believe I saw her."

Evie sat up straighter, her eyes growing wide. "Where?"

He hesitated, unwilling to tell the truth. "I could not sleep last night so I came down to… find a book," he improvised, deciding he'd rather not explain that he'd come down to find the brandy. "I must have fallen asleep—it was a dull book—and woke with a headache so I went for a walk to get some air. She was running. I thought at the time she looked rather upset, but she was too far ahead of me to call out to her, and it was none of my affair in any case."

She stared at him for a moment and then leapt to her feet and grasped hold of his hand.

"Show me," she demanded.

Louis frowned, uncertain if this was a good idea or not but… Oh, he could not deny her when she was so obviously frantic. "Very well," he said with a sigh, and led her out of the house.

Well, this was a pickle and no mistake.

You great ninny, Florence Knight! Florence cursed herself silently, though she might as well have shouted at the top of her lungs. No one would hear her. She muttered under her breath.

"Come and see my, grandmother, Miss Knight. She'll explain everything, Miss Knight."

Wherever the grandmother was, she was certainly not living in this hovel in the backend of beyond.

Idiot!

Though who would have thought such a slip of a girl as Susan Cooper could be so strong? Or perhaps so desperate. Florence had heard the alarm bells ringing with every step towards the dilapidated cottage, but she knew she was privileged beyond what most people could dream, and that others lived in conditions that she would never believe possible, so she'd said nothing, assuming the grandmother was dreadfully poor. She had not expected the push from behind, so forceful that she'd gone down without a struggle, hitting her head on the packed earth floor hard enough to make her ears ring. Too dazed and shocked to respond at once, it had been easy for Susan to overpower her and tie her hands behind her back. Her ankles were bound too, so tightly her feet were going numb.

Think, Florence, think, she instructed herself. Her heart was beating too fast, in sharp erratic thuds that were making her feel giddy and nauseated, but that would not help her. Her father and Henry would be looking for her by now. A wealthy heiress and granddaughter of a duke could not disappear without anyone noticing. Susan had been foolish indeed and soon she would realise how much of a fool. The girl had seemed terrified in any case, but of whom?

She had cried when she'd tied Florence up, apologising over and over and begging for forgiveness.

"Never meant this to happen, for things to go this far. It wasn't supposed to be like this," she'd sobbed. "He's evil... the devil, he is. Oh, Lord, whatever shall I do? I won't let him hurt you, though. I promise."

What it had supposed to have been like, Florence had no idea, but it was obvious that Susan had got in over her head. Hearing *him*—whoever he was—referred to as evil and *the devil* was far from reassuring, either. Susan's assurance that she wouldn't let him hurt her seemed a fragile hope too. The girl was clearly terrified. Now Susan had run off, which meant she'd left Florence in the hope her family would find her, or she'd gone to tell someone else about Florence... perhaps that evil someone who *had* meant things to go this far. All she knew was that she could not rely on Susan's reassurances.

She must escape.

Florence looked about the filthy space. It was a single room with a soot blackened fireplace; the tiny window was broken but too small to crawl through, and there was no furniture, just the packed dirt floor and the cold wall at her back. An odd white fur, like salt, grew over the damp stone, and the place smelled musty and forgotten. She wriggled her hands, trying to find some give in the rope but it was too tight. Perhaps if she could get her hands in front of her. Florence wriggled and strained but her huge skirts and layers of petticoats were in the way and her corset hardly allowed for much movement. It was impossible.

She muttered the rudest word she could think of, one that she'd overhead Papa say with some enthusiasm when he'd discovered his railway project would run thousands over budget. She said it again, louder, and then shouted it. For some reason it made her feel better, calmer, and so she took a deep breath and tried to think rationally. The cottage had not been that far from Holbrook, only a few miles, so it was likely still on the estate. This meant the earl probably knew about it, and they must be looking for her by now. All positive thoughts.

If Susan *had* gone to speak to whoever else was involved, Florence was very certain she did not wish to meet *the devil*, whoever he might be. Briefly, Mr Oak's stern countenance flickered into her mind, and she shivered. Could he be at the heart of this? His grandmother had been a witch by his own admission. Whoever he was, she needed to get out of here as soon as possible and for that she needed her hands free. If only there were something to cut the rope with. Florence stared around the barren room and sighed. She glanced up at the window, trying to judge what time it was by the sun, and cursed herself.

"You little fool!"

The window was *broken*.

It took a lot more cursing, and she scraped her elbow badly, but eventually Florence got herself to her feet by pushing against the wall and levering herself up. The window was thankfully low, but she still had to bend forwards to get her wrists high enough behind her back, not easy when her corset was so tight. She held her breath, struggling to get her hands elevated so she could press the rope against the broken glass.

It was impossible to see what she was doing, and Florence sucked in a breath as she cut her thumb. Her heart pounded in her ears as she felt the rope slide against the broken edge. Carefully she moved the cord up and down, her head spinning as the corset constricted her breathing. At last the rope frayed and broke and she gave a whimper of relief as she brought her arms forward. There was no time to celebrate her cleverness though and she sat down, working the knots that bound her ankles. It took too long, her fingers numb and her shoulders screaming with pain after being pulled back in such an awkward position, but finally she was free. Well, free of her bindings. She ran to the door and gave a frustrated shout as she discovered it wouldn't budge. There was no lock she could see, but somehow, she had been trapped in here.

She ran back to the window, wondering if there was any hope of squeezing through, but even if she stripped off her gown and petticoats her shoulders would never fit.

She was a prisoner still.

Chapter 15

Raphe,

What are you playing at, you pillock? You're all over the damned scandal sheets again. I think you'd best come and rusticate with me for a few weeks. At least give your liver a day or two to recover. It's really not so bad out here you know and the chances of being killed by falling plaster have significantly diminished of late. We even have a cook and a full staff, so you'll not starve like last time you were here.

Do come, old man. Bainbridge is just up the road. Perhaps we can pry August away from those dreadful females who claw at his peace of mind when he's home and it will be like old times?

What do you say?

—Excerpt of a letter from Daire 'Dare' Kelburn, Viscount Roxborough to Raphe Coote, Baron de Ligne.

18th August 1839, Holbrook House Estate, Sussex.

"You're certain she went this way?" Evie demanded for the fifth time.

Louis gave her a look which suggested she did not ask him again.

"Sorry," she muttered. "I'm just so afraid something has happened to her."

Silently he reached out and took her hand, curling his long, strong fingers about hers. Though she knew it was dreadfully inappropriate, she took it for the kind gesture it was. His touch gave her courage and they trudged on, following the path which was becoming muddy and overgrown.

"Look."

Louis' voice was pitched low, and she followed where he pointed to see footprints in the damp earth. They were indistinct, but it looked like two people had come this way. Going on the small size, they surely must be women or boys. Louis pressed a finger to his lips and Evie nodded.

"I ought not have brought you," he whispered as they moved forward. He turned back to her, and Evie knew he was going to send her back to the house. She gave a vigorous shake of her head, glaring at him.

"Evie," he began.

"She is my *sister*."

Louis stared at her, frowning, and then sighed. "You do as I say, and if I say run, you run."

She nodded, anything to keep going if there was a chance of finding Florence.

"Swear it," he demanded.

Evie rolled her eyes but made the sign of a cross over her heart. Louis' lips twitched but he seemed to accept that, and they carried on.

"The footsteps go that way now," he said, pointing into a thicket of scrubby trees after another ten minutes of stepping around muddy puddles and untangling Evie's skirts from brambles. Though the path carried on, there were no more footprints following it. Louis hesitated.

"Evie...."

"No!" Evie pushed past him before he could insist she go back.

She understood his concern, she felt it too, the sense there was something wrong, but if Florence was here there was no way on earth she was leaving without her. Brambles snagged at her skirts, but she did not stop to untangle herself now, forcing her way on, heedless of the rips and tears in the fine fabric of her gown.

"Wait," Louis hissed, moving past her. "You stay behind me or go home, your choice."

Evie gave him an exasperated glare but let him take the lead, and nearly ploughed into the back of him as he stopped in his tracks.

"Do you hear that?" he asked.

There was a dull thudding sound, like someone hitting something over and over. Evie's heart was crashing at twice the rate of whatever was making the ominous sound as they carried on, walking as silently as they could. Finally the path opened out and the remnants of what must once have been rather a sweet if tiny cottage came into view. The thatch was rotten and had collapsed in places, and the walls were thick with ivy. The banging stopped abruptly as something clattered to the floor and there was a muttered curse. Wait. Evie recognised that voice.

"Florence!"

She ran forward, cursing Louis as he grabbed hold of her waist, keeping her still.

"Evie?" replied the voice from inside the building, fear and hope and surprise all audible in that one word. "Evie, is that you?"

"Oh, Florence!" Evie ran forward with Louis at her heels. Whoever had trapped her inside had barred the door with a strong length of wood that Louis lifted free and tossed to one side. They pushed the door open, and Florence flew out, straight into Evie's arms.

"Oh, Evie, Evie! Thank God, I was so frightened I would never see you again."

Evie wept, too overcome to reply that she had feared the same thing. They held on to each other, crying and laughing with relief.

"You have Louis César to thank for bringing us here," Evie explained, once her tears had subsided enough to speak. "He saw Susan running in this direction early this morning and we found the stile that led to this path. We just kept walking until your footsteps ran out."

"I met her at the stile. She told me she was taking me to her grandmother," Florence said in disgust.

"Ladies, forgive me, but there is no time for this, we must get you back to the house. Your parents are worried sick."

Florence nodded, wiping her eyes on her sleeve. "I don't think Susan is working alone. She spoke about a man, an evil man who had gone too far. Oh, Evie, I'm very afraid it might be Mr Oak."

"Mr Oak?" Louis repeated, his scepticism obvious. Evie had to admit she hadn't warmed to Mr Oak either, but to think of him as *evil*?

Florence nodded, fear glittering in her eyes. "We must warn Henry. I don't know why Susan started this, or what she or Mr Oak believe him guilty of, but I think he's in real danger."

Louis and Evie exchanged a glance, but silently agreed not to tell Florence that Henry had already left in pursuit of her just yet. Evie did not know if Mr Oak or Joe Foster had been involved in this, but either or both of them could be on their way here now. They needed to leave.

The church was empty, as far as the men could tell, and there was no sign of anyone in the graveyard.

"Damnation." Gabriel ran a hand through his hair. The poor man was clearly on the edge, terror for his daughter making him sharp with everyone. "Where is she?"

"We'll try the vicarage," Jasper said. "Come on, Gabe. The vicar will know where Foster lives, or where his usual haunts are. We'll track him down, don't you fret."

Gabriel nodded, his expression grim. "The bastard will wish he was dead when I get my hands on him. Heaven help him if he's laid a finger on Florence."

Not if I get to him first, Henry swore silently. His body ached and his head was splitting and none of it registered. There was nothing else, no thought in his mind past finding Florence and getting her to safety. "I'll stay here and keep an eye out, just in case," he said.

Gabriel sent him a look of disgust but did not disagree. Henry wasn't about to make excuses or beg forgiveness. If anything happened to Florence, he would hate himself far more than Gabriel could ever manage. Damn it, but Florence had known, she had warned him from the very beginning that he was not taking the threat seriously enough and he'd dismissed her. Worse, he'd belittled her in front of everyone, and no matter that he'd apologised for it the knowledge made his throat ache with regret.

Please God, let her be safe.

He had been much struck by Helena too, who would be with them now if Gabriel hadn't put his foot down. It was clear to see where her daughters got their spirit from. She'd demanded the earl's duelling pistol and told them in no uncertain terms that Joe

Foster would speak to her if it was the last thing he did. Gabriel had not bothered to calm her down, but had sworn to her that Florence would be back safe and sound before lunchtime, and with such certainty even Henry had believed it. When Gabriel Knight said something was going to happen, it was impossible to believe it wouldn't be just as he said.

Henry walked the edges of the graveyard that surrounded the ancient church, keeping to the shadows as far as he could. The scent of freshly turned earth reached him and he paused as he looked past a large, crumbling statue of an angel to see a newly dug grave. The spade was stuck in the loose earth. So, Joe Foster had been here today, was still here, for a fellow didn't leave his tools lying about if he wasn't coming back. Henry darted behind the gnarled trunk of an ancient yew tree, watching for movement. Nothing moved. There was no sign of anyone, but there was something, a sound. It was distant, as if it were far off or... or below ground. Like someone pushing something heavy against a stone floor.

Henry crept forward.

"Oh, my darling, my darling, thank God!" Lady Helena cried, holding Florence tightly against her.

"Thank Louis... I mean Monsieur le Comte. He saw Susan running away from the house this morning and took us straight to where Florence was being held," Evie said, as their mother wept and covered Florence's face with kisses.

It made her feel as if she was six years old all over again and was very welcome. She hugged her mother tightly for a moment before pushing away.

"Mama, where is Henry?" she asked. For as much as she was relieved to be back to the safety of Holbrook House, this was not yet over. "I must speak to him."

"Oh, my word, Henry! Your father too, they went with St Clair to the church to look for you. Henry was attacked last night at his home… oh, he's well, darling," she added, as Florence made an exclamation of alarm. "Thankfully, he has a thick head, but he believes the gravedigger, Joe Foster, is somehow involved in all this."

Florence stared at her mother in shock. Joe Foster? Was that the unpleasant man she'd thought had been watching her in the churchyard?

"The devil," she whispered, a cold, sick sensation swirling in her guts. Perhaps it had not been Mr Oak after all, or perhaps… perhaps they were in it *together?*

"Whatever do you mean?" Mama said, one hand pressing to her heart.

"Oh, Mama, we must leave at once," Florence said, grasping her mother's hand. "I think Henry may be about to walk into a great deal of trouble."

It had to be a crypt. Of course, it had to be a crypt.

Henry stared at the steps that led down, and down, into utter darkness.

"Hell," he muttered.

The stench of things long dead wafted up, the air cold and unsettling, sliding over his warm skin as he descended towards the earthly remains of generations of Stanhopes. It reminded him of Egypt, of the tombs he'd visited. It had bothered him, the way the archaeologists had scrabbled in the sand, picking over the bones of the long dead and uncovering their treasures. Not that it hadn't been fascinating—the treasures had been marvellous things, glimpses of a world it was hard to comprehend—but for many of those adventurers and treasure seekers it had been all about the gold, and there had been little reverence for the dead. He almost felt like offering an apology now, as he saw the coffins of long-dead relatives arranged neatly on their stone shelves. An expression of regret was due for disturbing their slumber, was it not?

He bit back such foolish thoughts. No doubt Pippin and Mrs Dharani had got into his head with their talk of witches and revenge. There were no such things as ghosts, certainly no such things as witches. It was all nonsense. Yet the hair on the back of his neck was standing on end and he had the very strong sense that something was wrong. As he reached the bottom of the crypt he noticed the stink of scorched fat that mingled unpleasantly with the ancient dust of the decayed dead. Then he saw a small stack of tallow candles and a tinder box. Well, that was reassuringly substantial. Ghosts did not need to light a candle to see in the dark, of that much he was certain. He couldn't speak for witches, but he was content to assume whoever was down here was merely flesh and blood.

Human, he could deal with. Hopefully.

After a couple of attempts he got the tinder lit and, in turn, lit a candle. Ugh, he hated tallow candles, smoky, filthy things. It explained the greasy, burned meat smell though. The flame flickered wildly as a breeze fluttered through the shadowy confines of the crypt. Henry turned towards it, away from the entrance. There was another opening. Moving as silently as he could, he saw the small door. It was open now, but that must have been the sound he'd heard, of stone sliding against stone. It was a large plaque emblazoned with the family crest, and had been pushed to one side to reveal a rectangular opening, just large enough for a man to go through if he stooped low.

Bloody marvellous, a secret tunnel. As a boy, such a discovery would have delighted him. Right at this moment it was a little less appealing, especially as his head was still throbbing after his last encounter with whoever had clobbered him. It must be the same person, or people. Whoever it had been had vanished from the room before his servants had appeared, and not one of them had seen anyone else. This tunnel must somehow lead to the bedroom adjoining his own. Well, well, Great-great-grandfather Stanhope had been a canny old bastard and no mistake.

With deep misgivings, he ducked through the opening, discovering the tunnel had been worked through a large seam of chalk. He followed it as it went down and down and then levelled out. Much to his relief it was taller here and, though he still had to tilt his head, there was a bit more space. The revolting smoke from the candle was overwhelming in such a confined area, and Henry covered his nose with his lapel as the urge to cough became too strong. Suddenly the passage opened out into a wide area. The white walls gleamed a sickly yellow in the smoky candlelight, illuminating the pieces of broken barrels and opened boxes. The smell of brandy lingered, evident even over the stench of the tallow, and Henry could not help but imagine the smugglers here, toasting another successful run as they evaded the excise men. There was no time to linger, though, and Henry crossed the space to the where the tunnel carried on again. It seemed to go on forever, though it must only be the distance from Saxenhurst Hall to the church, which really wasn't that far.

At last the tunnel ended with a set of steep stairs cut into the chalk. Henry climbed, cautious now, aware that he was behind the walls of his own home. He stilled as he heard muffled voices, guessing he must be close to the kitchens. At least not all his staff had deserted him in terror... yet.

The passage ran until he reached another staircase, wooden this time and worn with age. The treads creaked and protested, and Henry held back a curse, praying they would not give way or make so much noise his arrival would be revealed. At the top of the staircase was another short passage. At the end, the panelling that hid the tunnel must have been left open, as daylight pierced through a narrow slit, illuminating the dim entryway.

Henry blew out the candle, set it down, and moved silently towards the light.

Chapter 16

Dear diary,

I'm so tired. I stayed up all night reading and did not sleep a wink. Truthfully, I am not certain I shall ever sleep again. The Ghosts of Castle Madruzzo was quite magnificent, though the villain was so much more interesting than the hero. How I wish he had not died horribly. He was so clever and wicked, funny too. I would far rather have run away with him than the hero who was something of a wet blanket and had no sense of humour. Bad men are always much more interesting for they need unravelling and I have always enjoyed puzzles. The descriptions of the ghosts and the villain's grisly demise was so vivid, though, and now I see it every time I close my eyes. Indeed it makes me feel a little queasy whenever I think on it.

I cannot tell Mama, or she will tell Papa and he'll be disappointed in me and that is worse than any other fate imaginable, even the villain's.

—Excerpt of an entry to the diary of Lady Catherine 'Cat' Barrington, (youngest

daughter of the Marquess and Marchioness of Montagu).

18th August 1839, Holbrook House, Sussex.

"Where is he, you villain?"

"Florence!" Mama scolded as Florence flew out of the carriage before the footman could even let down the step for her. They had not even reached Thistley Farm but had passed Mr Oak at the side of a narrow lane, mending fences.

Evie sent Louis César a pleading expression and he sighed, jumping down after her.

Mr Oak looked up in surprise as Florence ran up to him, with Louis close behind.

"Miss Knight?"

"Don't you, *Miss Knight* me! where is Henry?"

Mr Oak's expression darkened as he realised he was being accused of something and Louis stepped in hurriedly.

"Mr Oak, forgive us for interrupting your work, but we believe Mr Stanhope may be in danger."

"Oh, he knows," Florence said, vibrating with anger as Mama pulled her back and hushed her.

Mr Oak's anger seemed to evaporate to something closer to concern and, despite his brusque manner, Evie could not believe he would hurt Mr Stanhope. The two men had appeared to her to be friends.

"I told him not to meddle with things he didn't understand," Mr Oak muttered. "What's happened?"

As no one else seemed capable of speaking without accusing Mr Oak of wrongdoing, Louis ploughed on. "Miss Knight was attacked by Susan Cooper this morning. Miss Cooper tied Miss

Knight up and held her captive. Happily, we found her, as you see. Miss Cooper spoke of a man though, someone she referred to as the devil, and how he had gone too far. We know Henry suspected Joe Foster of involvement, but we have been to the church and there is no sign of Foster or Henry, nor Mr Knight and St Clair, who were with him."

"My father and St Clair went to the village to ask if anyone had seen my sister, or Mr Foster, but the vicar said Henry wasn't with them," Evie added desperately. She was horribly afraid someone was going to get hurt and, if they had to waste any more time driving about looking for people, she might run mad.

Mr Oak ran a hand through his unruly black hair. He had been hard at work mending a broken fence and had taken off his coat. His cravat had also been discarded, exposing a strong, tanned throat and the suggestion of wiry hair on his chest. His waistcoat hung open and his sleeves were rolled up to show powerful forearms also covered with dark hair. Despite her anxiety, Evie could not help but stare, fascinated by such a rare display of masculine virility. Most men would never be seen without their coat, let alone in such disarray. Evie had certainly never seen anyone dressed so. She wondered vaguely if Louis César was built in the same fashion beneath his elegant attire, but chased the thought away. There was no time for such frivolous meanderings. Though she doubted there was much that her father could not handle she still worried for him, and for Henry too, for Florence loved him and was clearly worried sick.

"Has anyone been back to the Hall?" Mr Oak asked, to which they all shook their heads. "Right. We'll start there. It's an ancient old place that hides secrets aplenty, by my reckoning. Just because Henry never found a tunnel doesn't mean no one else did. It would explain that corn doll on his pillow, assuming none of the staff are involved."

"Could they be?" Evie asked as they all hurried back to the carriage.

Mr Oak shrugged on his coat before climbing in after them. "I don't reckon so. I know everyone who works at the Hall, and they're all decent folk. I don't know of any grudges against Henry."

"And what about you, Mr Oak?" Florence asked, folding her arms and glaring at him.

The carriage fell silent, the sudden jerk and sway a little disconcerting as the horses moved forward, making the prickling atmosphere even more uncomfortable.

Mr Oak stared back at Florence unblinking. "I know you don't like me, Miss Knight, though I don't know what I've done to offend you. I've no pretty manners, I suppose, and I don't like to talk if I've naught to say, but I don't reckon that's an offense. All I can tell you is that Henry is my friend, and if he's got himself in bother, I mean to help him out of it. That's all."

"I'm sure my daughter meant no offense," Mama said and, from the way Florence jolted, Evie suspected she'd delivered a pinch to induce an apology.

Florence merely set her jaw.

"Aye, she did," Mr Oak said, though there was a glimmer of amusement in his dark eyes. "But she's worried for Henry, and I've a thick skin, so I'm told. Reckon I'll wear her dislike right enough."

Florence held her tongue, stubborn to the last, but Evie knew her sister and she saw the glimmer of doubt in her eyes. If she were wrong, which Evie fervently hoped she was, she would be quick to apologise to Mr Oak. One of the nicest things about Florence was that she never held a grudge. She would always acknowledge if she'd made a mistake and apologise. Evie could only hope that would be soon, preferably after they'd found Henry in one piece. Many girls longed for adventure and excitement, but Evie was not one of them. She much preferred the idea of everyone safe and sound, and thoroughly disliked the stress and anxiety that had made her heart thud in her chest all the time Florence had been missing. It was starting up again now as worry for Henry made her chest tight. She fisted her hands in her skirts and drew in a deep breath, trying to calm herself.

"*Courage, ma biche.*"

The murmured French was barely audible over the rumble of the carriage, but Evie turned to see Louis César's bright blue eyes watching her. They were an incredible shade, so vividly blue it was hard to look away from them. Evie had heard descriptions of the Mediterranean sea and hoped to see for herself one day. She wondered if the two colours were comparable. His gaze was placid, reassuring, and much of the tension left her shoulders. Louis did not appear worried, and he had led her straight to Florence this morning. If he was confident all would be well, then so was she. She let out a breath and put up her chin. Everything would be all right.

Something was very wrong. Someone had pulled the expensive bed hangings down in Henry's mother's old room. They had left them in a heap on the bed and, from the strong smell of alcohol permeating the room, doused them in brandy. Whoever it was clattering about in Henry's room was intending to set the place alight. Saxenhurst's ancient timber frame and extensive wood panelling would go up like dry tinder. Henry cursed under his breath, silently creeping to the window. It opened without so much as a squeak of protest and Henry could only be grateful the place had been well kept in his absence. He hurried to the bed and swept up the bed hangings, returning to dump the lot out of the window. The crashing about in his bedroom paused, and Henry held his breath until he heard it recommence. It sounded like someone was ransacking the drawers.

Henry moved as softly as he was able, trying to remember which floorboards creaked as he made his way to the door. It was not latched, and he pushed it open a crack. The man he remembered from the graveyard was inside. He had a large hessian sack, which he was busy filling with anything that looked valuable. The man's dirty hands reached for a cravat pin Henry had left on his dressing table. He turned it this way and that, watching the light glint on the emerald set in the golden mount. It had been a present from Henry's parents on his twenty-first birthday, one of the few gifts he'd ever received from their hands. Most had been posted from some foreign shore or other, usually arriving long after the big day. He wondered how many birthdays they'd missed, how many childish triumphs they'd never celebrated. Too many to count, for both him and Harriet. It was a melancholy thought, though not one that hurt as it once had. It had been their loss as much as his and his sister's, and at least they'd had each other, and the St Clair family. The old earl had been more a father to Henry than his own had ever been.

Though he ought to have more pressing matters on his mind, Henry made a vow to himself. If ever he should be fortunate enough to have a family with Florence, he would always be present in their lives. He would not keep distance between them, not even to protect himself. Loving her was a risk, a risk that made his heart tremble at the knowledge she could hurt him more than anyone he'd ever met, far more than Lily had managed. Lily had humiliated him and left a bruise that had lingered for too many years after. She had made him distrustful of women, even of himself, but that was over now. He could not protect his heart without becoming a lonely old man, and he could not bear that. Even knowing that a betrayal from Florence would destroy him, he would risk everything for her. With the benefit of maturity he could see now that Lily and Florence were nothing alike. Lily had been superficially beautiful, shallow, and ambitious. Florence's beauty was not all on the surface, it ran deep, down to a loving heart and a beautiful soul. He loved her to her bones, and no amount of denying it would save him now. So he may as well live it to the full, and he fully intended to. Just as soon as he'd dealt with the bastard robbing his house.

He was about to barrel through the door when a soft whimpering sound reached him. Henry turned to see Susan Cooper huddled in the corner, her arms covering her head. Her dress was torn, one sleeve hanging loose, and her forearms were bruised. Henry felt a swell of rage at the way the woman had been abused and… oh, God. If this man had touched Florence, he'd bloody kill him.

On the dressing table which Susan was cowering beside was a pistol. Clearly Foster had put it down and believed Susan so terrified she was no threat to him. Well, that may be true, but it did not apply to Henry. He crept into the room, edging towards the pistol, and Susan looked up with a gasp.

Foster turned around.

Florence was beside herself by the time the carriage drew up outside the Hall. Mr Oak and the comte climbed out before any of the ladies could reach the door.

"You should stay here," Mr Oak commanded, his expression fiercer even than usual.

Florence bristled. Mama glared at him, and even gentle Evie looked a little disgusted.

Ever the diplomat, Louis César qualified the brusque statement. "Until we ascertain all is as it should be."

"Run along, then," Mama said, waving them away with a dismissive little sniff.

"Mama!" Florence objected, stunned that her forthright mother would submit to sitting docilely whilst the men attended to business. Mama sent her a quelling look of such ferocity that Florence subsided, wondering what she meant by it.

As soon as the men were out of sight, her mother reached under the carriage seat and slid out a beautiful wooden box. She opened it to reveal two gleaming duelling pistols.

"Careful, it's loaded," she said, handing one to Florence.

Mama's green eyes glittered, and Florence let out a breath.

"I love you, Mama," she said.

"Of course you do," her mama replied nonchalantly. "And so you should for the effort I expended in persuading your father to teach you both how to shoot. Do try not to fire at anyone by accident."

"Don't I get a pistol?" Evie said indignantly.

"There's only two, darling, and it's Florence's beloved in danger. The next time I promise you may have one."

"The next time?" Evie squeaked, looking more than a little alarmed. "I am most certainly not marrying the kind of man who gets himself into such dangerous situations."

Mama's lips twitched, but she only patted Evie's knee.

"Of course you won't, dearest," she said, her voice soothing.

"The men went in through the front door," Florence said, as she climbed down from the carriage, hiding the pistol in the voluminous skirts of her gown in case anyone was looking.

"Yes. Round the back, I think," Mama said to her unspoken question before turning to John Coachman and the footmen who'd ridden with the carriage. "John, are you armed?"

"Yes, my lady."

"Good man. You watch the front, please, and make sure no one leaves. You two had best come with us and guard the back once we've entered. Well, come along, no dilly dallying."

The men leapt to do Lady Helena's bidding, as most men did when she issued a command, and they hurried around to the back of the house. They entered unhindered and made their way to the kitchen, where they found one of the footmen and the cook having a comfortable coze over a pot of tea.

"Are we interrupting something?" Mama asked politely, as the footman and cook sprang to their feet.

"My lady," the footman exclaimed, mortified. "Forgive us, we were just a little at a loss for what to do. The master left early this morning and we're all that's left of the staff. The ghost that attacked Mr Stanhope frightened everyone to death."

"Silly fools, ain't no such things as ghosts," said the cook calmly as she poured out another cup of tea.

The footman frowned, looking less convinced. "No, Mrs Taylor, right enough. I'd agree with you, only where did the devil go if he weren't no ghost? That's what I'd like to know."

"That is what we should all like to know, so why do we not go and find out?" Florence said in frustration. "Mr Stanhope has disappeared, and we fear he is in danger. I strongly suspect there is a secret passage into this house and—"

The sound of something heavy hitting the floor with a crash somewhere in the house interrupted her words.

"Oh, my stars," exclaimed the cook, clutching at her chest and looking a deal less sanguine than she had a moment earlier. "What was that?"

"It came from above us," the footman said.

"Well, come along then!" Florence exclaimed, pushing past them and hurrying up the stairs to the ground floor.

They all burst out into a back corridor and ran towards the entrance hall, where they almost collided with Mr Oak and Louis César.

"I told you to stay in the carriage!" Mr Oak said furiously.

"Oh, stow it," Florence yelled at him, having had quite enough of being told what to do for one day. She hiked up her skirts, taking the stairs two at a time, careful to keep the pistol pointing down.

"Florence, darling, do be careful," Mama called out from behind her, but another crash and a masculine grunt of pain echoed through the house and Florence ran, heedless of anything but the need to get to Henry.

"Henry!" she called and then screamed as Henry staggered out of an open doorway and hit the floor, cursing.

Another man fell upon him, fists flying like a madman as Henry defended himself. Florence cried out. Foster was in a frenzy of violence. She had never seen such hatred as she saw in the man's eyes, such... madness. Henry got in a blow that drove Foster's head back and used the moment to force the man onto his back. He tried to get to his feet, but Foster grabbed his ankle and pulled hard, tugging Henry back down. Henry's head smacked the hardwood panelling as he fell. He lay, unmoving.

Then things happened very fast, and yet so slowly that Florence was aware of every beat of her heart.

She screamed and raised the pistol as Foster pulled something from his pocket. There was a click, and a blade sprang free from the handle he held. He gave a laugh which made Florence's heart stutter; he sounded utterly unhinged. Mr Oak and Louis César surged past Florence, shouting, though she could not make out the words, too focused on Henry. Foster lunged towards Henry and Florence's finger tightened on the trigger as a shot ran out, a shot that wasn't hers.

Foster staggered and fell back against the wall, sliding to the floor and clutching at his right shoulder as blood welled between his fingers.

"Mama!" Florence gasped, as she saw her mother beside her.

A strong smell of gunpowder permeated the air. Her mother's face had blanched white, but her hands were steady, the pistol still raised.

"Give me the pistol, love, and go to Henry," she said calmly, not taking her eyes off Foster as she set the spent pistol on the floor and took the one from Florence's grasp. She levelled the loaded gun at the wounded man, who was shrieking loud enough to wake the dead.

Florence was only vaguely aware of the sounds around her, or of Mr Oak suggesting they lock Foster in the pantry for the time being. She ran to Henry's too still form.

"Henry, Henry," she sobbed, sinking to her knees beside him. "Oh, please wake up."

There was a pained moan and his eyelids fluttered open.

"Florence!" he exclaimed in alarm.

"It's all right. Mama shot him. It's all right, we're safe."

Henry subsided with relief. "Christ, my head," he muttered. "It's a wonder I've any brains left, they've taken such a battering of late."

"Oh!" Florence said, the terror of the past moments catching up with her. She drew in a breath of relief before she collapsed on his chest. "Oh, Henry, I was so frightened."

"Sorry, love," he murmured, a hand stroking her hair gently. "Come now, none of that. Wait, where is Foster now?"

"It's all right, Mr Oak is going to...." she began, and then her breath caught as she saw Susan Cooper standing in the doorway, holding a pistol. It was aimed at Joe Foster who was holding a wadded towel to his shoulder and staring at her, wide-eyed.

"You ought to have killed him, my lady," Susan said to Florence's mother, tears tracking down her cheeks. One eye was swelling, already almost swollen shut. Foster had beaten her, the vile brute.

"Perhaps," Mama said. She was still training a pistol on the man too. "But he will be punished for his crimes. I do not wish for a man's death on my conscience, and the burden of his death ought not rest with you."

"He tricked me, miss," the girl said, staring at Florence. She did not appear to have heard anything Florence's mother had said to her. "I only wanted Mr Stanhope to understand how his family had treated us, how much damage they'd caused, but I never meant to hurt him, nor no one else. Especially not you, miss. Truly. I only tied you up to keep you safe. I was afraid you'd interfere."

"And so I have," Florence said, trying to find a smile for the girl. "But it's all right, Susan. Put the gun down and—"

Foster lunged, grabbing Susan's ankle and pulling. She fell with a scream but still pointed the gun at Foster, who lurched sideways, out of the way. He must have seen her determination to finish him, seen the fear and anger in her eyes as she pulled the trigger.

Suddenly everyone was screaming, screaming Florence's name as Henry slammed her to the floor, covering her body with his own.

Florence stared up, into Henry's warm brown eyes. Her ears were ringing, and she couldn't breathe, though she wasn't yet sure if that was terror or the fact Henry was squashing the life out of her, his considerable weight pressing down on her. She was dimly conscious of commotion behind them, of someone hitting Foster and the man dropping like a stone, but all she could see was Henry.

"Florence, Florence, are you hurt?" he demanded, his hands moving over her in a way that made her blush, considering her mother was present, not to mention half a dozen other people, and was that her father's voice?

She shook her head, blinking at Henry, still a little dazed, until she saw the blood.

"Henry!" she whispered. "*Henry!* Henry, you're bleeding! Oh, help!"

Henry groaned and rolled off her to lay flat on his back. "Damnation, I need a rest."

"Florence!" Suddenly her father was kneeling beside her, his large hands cupping her face before he pulled her to him for a hug, holding her tightly. "Oh, my darling girl. I thought... I thought I'd lost you for a moment there."

"I'm fine, Papa, I'm fine, b-but Henry, he's hurt..." Florence sobbed, pushing her father's hands away and struggling to get to Henry.

Her father held her back whilst he inspected Henry himself, he turned to smile at her. "Just a flesh wound, love. He'll be fine."

Florence gave a strangled sob and Henry held out a hand to her. "Your father is right, Florence. I'm fine, love. Though I'd appreciate a few hours without someone trying to murder me. Ah, don't take on so. You're safe now."

"You c-could have been k-killed," she stammered through a storm of tears she did not seem able to check.

"She's right," her father said, staring at Henry intently. "You saved her life, you know. If you hadn't pushed her down...."

Florence stared at her father, hearing his voice quaver. He was white with shock. He rubbed his face with his hand and let out an uneven breath.

"Henry loves me, Papa," Florence said, meeting his eyes.

Her father stared at her and gave a soft huff of laughter. "Well, I suppose I can't ask much more proof of devotion from a husband than that he lay down his life for you, can I, love?"

"God Almighty, I hope not," Henry muttered. "Someone get me a drink."

Chapter 17

Bainbridge,

I need your help. I'm worried about Raphe. If he keeps up as he is, he'll be dead before the year is out. I want to get him to here at Rowsley, where I can keep an eye on him. Give me a hand, old man. I'll never get the devil on the train without someone to help me strongarm him.

I'm leaving for London Friday morning. I'll hope to see you at the station.

—Excerpt of a letter from Daire 'Dare' Kelburn, Viscount Roxborough to the Most Hon'ble, The Marquess of Bainbridge.

18th August 1839, Saxenhurst Hall, Sussex.

By the time the Foster had been given medical attention and been hauled off to the local magistrate, and the doctor had seen to everyone else, it was late in the afternoon. Mr Oak had made it his business to round up all of Henry's errant staff and send them back to work, each with a flea in their ear, so the house was being brought swiftly back to rights. By the time Henry made it down the stairs to his parlour, there seemed to be an informal tea party underway. Lady Helena, Gabriel Knight, and their daughter Miss Evie, the Comte de Villen, the Earl and Countess St Clair,

Montagu and Matilda, and even Pippin and Mrs Dharani were all squeezed into the front parlour. Tea, sandwiches, and a variety of cakes had been provided and everyone seemed to be speaking at once.

Florence leapt to her feet and ran to him.

"Henry, darling, should you be up and about? The doctor said you needed to rest."

"What I needed was to see you, love," Henry murmured, taking her hand, squeezing it, and wishing everyone else to the devil. He wanted to hold her close and never let her go but, as her parents were in the room, he supposed he'd best behave himself.

"Come and sit down before you fall down," Gabriel said gruffly, vacating a chair and steering Henry into it.

"Thank you," Henry said, sitting down with a sigh of relief.

"How's the shoulder?" Gabriel asked.

"Nothing compared to my head," Henry said with a short laugh. "Feel like I've been run down by the mail coach."

He looked up in surprise as Helena came over, leaned down, and kissed his cheek.

"I shall never, never forget what you did, Henry," she said, her green eyes shining with tears.

A blush stole up the back of his neck and he cleared his throat, feeling a little uncomfortable. "Oh, er… think nothing of it."

"Think nothing of it!" Evie exclaimed. "You saved my sister's life. I've never seen anything so heroic. Frankly, I hope I never do again, but it was dreadfully brave, Mr Stanhope, and we shall never be able to repay you."

Henry stared about him to discover everyone looking at him with admiration and warmth. He turned to Florence, who was smiling at him with such adoration his heart skipped about like a spring lamb. He was utterly sunk, and he didn't give a damn.

"Anything for you, love. You made me remember what it was to be alive. I couldn't lose you, Florence. I'd rather die."

There was a collective sigh from all the women present, though Henry barely noticed, too lost in Florence's green eyes. God, but he was in way over his head, and he'd never been so glad of anything in his life.

"Oh, Gabe. We must get them married. Just look, it would be cruel to keep them apart," Helena said, sniffling and dabbing at her cheeks with a lace handkerchief.

Florence turned to her mother with a little cry of delight and ran to her, hugging her tightly.

Helena laughed and hugged her back, and then they both stared at Gabriel, who scowled, folding his arms.

"Ugh. Oh, very well, but it's to be a proper ceremony, all the trimmings. No daughter of mine is to get married in some hole in the wall fashion."

"Well, if we work very hard, I think ten days should do it. Don't you, darling?" Helena asked Florence.

"Yes, please, Mama. Henry, what do you think?"

He laughed and held out his hand to her. "Whatever you want, darling. Absolutely anything you want."

Florence gave a delighted smile and then her expression faltered as Sterling Oak appeared in the doorway.

"Glad to see you well, Henry," he said, gruff as ever. "Susan wants to speak to you."

Henry looked up at Florence, who squeezed his hand and nodded. "Yes, of course. If you are up to it, Henry?"

"She almost killed Florence," Gabriel growled, not looking at all pleased by this turn of events.

"Oh, Papa," Florence said, her voice soft and so full of understanding for the young woman Henry felt a swell of pride for her. "She didn't mean to. She was aiming for Mr Foster, and I think we need to hear her out."

Henry nodded. "It sounds as if Pippin and Mrs Dharani were right, and my family has something to answer for. I'd rather know what it was and make amends if I can."

"It would be best, Mr Stanhope," Pippin said. "Time to lay old ghosts to rest."

"Karma," Mrs Dharani said, nodding.

"Right, I'll fetch her," Mr Oak said, turning away.

"Wait... Mr Oak," Florence said, hurrying after him. "I believe I owe you an apology. I am very sorry I accused you of hurting Henry and... and I'm sorry for being so rude. I know I was wrong, and I hope you can forgive me."

Mr Oak's expression did not change, but he gave the barest shrug of his shoulders.

"Least said, soonest mended," he said, and turned and walked off.

Florence sighed and turned back to Henry. "Honestly, I know he's your friend and I know I behaved badly, but really he's dreadfully hard work."

Henry grinned at her. "You'll get used to him, love. He's a good fellow beneath the surly exterior."

"A long way beneath," she grumbled.

A moment later Mr Oak escorted Susan into the parlour and they made room for her. She looked pale and wan, her bruises standing out in livid patches.

"I'm sorry, Mr Stanhope, Miss Knight, for all the trouble that's been caused," she said, looking utterly miserable. "It wasn't supposed to go like this, I swear. I had no intention of anyone getting hurt."

Florence nodded. "We believe you, Susan. Just tell us what happened."

Susan hesitated, looking around at all the grand people surrounding her. She seemed to shrink in on herself.

"Your grandmother was a wise woman, was she?" Pippin asked, her expression warm and full of compassion.

"Y-Yes, missus," Susan said, looking grateful there was someone less daunting to speak to. "Though she didn't like to practise no more. Didn't like teaching me neither, though I nagged her something fierce. Said it had brought us nowt but trouble. Which is certainly true."

"She told you a secret," Dharani said, her sloe dark eyes sharp as a blackthorn bush.

Susan swallowed and looked from her to Pippin. "Oh," she said. "You're—"

Dharani waved an impatient hand at her.

Susan took a deep breath. "Yes, she told me a secret when she was dying. She told me that my great-great-grandfather was the same as Mr Stanhope's. His blood."

Henry closed his eyes and damned his long dead ancestor, who seemed to still be causing trouble from the grave.

"He was a wicked man," Susan went on, giving Henry an anxious glance though her chin was up. "A smuggler, and he seduced my great-great-grandmother, even though he was a married man, and she was only seventeen. She worked here, in this house, and she even helped him on the runs sometimes, looking out for the Revenue. When she got with child he abandoned her, told her to get out of the house. So, she cursed him for his cruelty and said he'd suffer the consequences. She was angry, see, and afraid, but nothing went right for him after that, so he accused her of witchcraft. Everyone knew she was a healer like her ma before her. People always went to her for help, but they turned on her quick enough, accusing her of terrible things, of consorting with the devil."

Pippin nodded sadly. "I'm so sorry, Susan."

"Oh, God. She was Mary Thompsett," Henry said, putting his head in his hands, realising the story Mrs Simmons had told Grace and Florence was all too true.

"Who is Mary Thompsett, Henry?" his sister asked, her expression full of misgiving.

"You'd best listen, Harry," he said grimly. "I don't think our family is going to come out of this covered in glory, though."

Harriet swallowed but listened attentively as Susan carried on.

"They let Mary have her babe, then they hanged her. Her sister took the child, and eventually she married and had a daughter of her own—my grandma, that was—but the shame of it lingered. People can be nasty, saying things, you know. My ma hated it. It made her angry and Gran said she was a bit of a wild one. Anyways, she got herself in the family way, with me, and...."

The girl swallowed, her eyes filling with tears. Silently, Henry reached for his handkerchief and passed it to her.

"Tell me the rest, Susan," he said gently.

Susan wiped her eyes and gave a resolute nod, smoothing her rumpled skirts with shaking hands. "Ma worked here at the Hall too, though my gran didn't like it. Well, there's not much else roundabouts is there? It's here or the big house. Ma would never say who the father was, but Grandma thought it was one of the grooms. So she came here, to see him, to insist he do the honourable thing, but your father was here, sir, and he overheard them arguing. So he... he told Gran her daughter was a whore, and he'd not have her working here no more."

Harriet made a sound of distress and covered her mouth with her hand. Susan carried on, the revelations relentless, but Henry needed to know all of it, for how else could he make amends?

"Ma died when I was born and Gran couldn't work 'cause she had me to mind, so she couldn't pay the rent no more. So, your pa turned us out of our cottage. If it hadn't been for the kindness of the old earl, Gran said we'd have both starved. Lord St Clair let Gran do mending—she had a fine hand with a needle—and he gave us somewhere to live. When I was old enough, he gave me a job at Holbrook. I've always been very well treated, too. Your father was a very kind man, my lord. You're very like him, too," she said to Jasper, who smiled warmly at her.

Henry's throat tightened, his stomach twisting with revulsion. His father had been a cold man, more interested in things long dead than his family, but Henry had never realised how cruel he could be. Perhaps having their parents absent for most of their lives had been a blessing for both him and Harriet. The St Clairs had taken them in too, and the old earl had given Henry a better example of what a father ought to be. He met his sister's eyes, knowing she was realising the same thing.

"I only meant to frighten you a bit, Mr Stanhope," Susan said, weeping openly now. "But that Joe Foster, he caught me putting the corn dolls on the hedge and he... he said it weren't enough. He said you was a rich man, and you ought to pay for all the wrong done my family. I thought he was being kind, that he was on my side. But he wasn't on anyone's side. When I got frightened and wanted to stop, he hit me and said he'd tell you I'd done it all if I didn't behave. He made me write Mr Knight that letter, too. He was just plain wicked, and all he wanted was to steal from you. I couldn't do it no more, though. I told him I wouldn't hurt anyone else, and I wouldn't help him, and he went mad. He threatened me with all sorts if I didn't do as I was told, but... but I couldn't let him hurt Miss Knight, and I knew he was planning on robbing the house. I was frightened what he would do if she went poking about up at the Hall, so... so I panicked. I thought if I kept her out of the way until he was caught it would be all right, but then he discovered me coming to see you, Mr Stanhope, and....”

She broke down and Henry felt like an utter brute.

“Miss Cooper,” he said. “Susan.”

Susan looked up, sniffing and drying her eyes. “Yes, sir?”

“Susan, I don’t know what I can do to repay the wrong my family has done yours, but I should like to try. Especially as it seems you are our kin.”

Susan laughed, a rather bitter sound that sat ill against her youth and damaged beauty. “No, sir. I don’t want nothing from you but your forgiveness. Please... I know I’ve done very wrong, but please, don’t send me to the magistrate.”

“Send you to...?” Henry got up, appalled that she should think he would do such a thing, but why should she not. His kin had done nothing but use and abuse the women of her family, why should he be any different? “Susan, if my father or grandfather were alive, I would have something to say to them, but they are dead and so their shame is mine. Certainly, I won’t send you to the magistrate, but I must do something for you. I know you work at Holbrook now, but... but surely, there must be something I can do to help you?”

“Henry,” his sister said. “I think I have an idea.”

Henry could have kissed her. “I’m listening.”

“I’ve been teaching any of the staff who wish to learn, to read,” she said. “And Susan has been doing rather well.”

“My lady, that’s very kind, but you know my spelling is not very good,” Susan said, blushing a little.

His sister waved this comment away with her usual brisk impatience. “Susan, you’ve only been learning a short while. You have an aptitude for the work and, what’s more, I believe you enjoy it.”

"Oh, I do, very much," Susan said, her expression lighting up for the first time. "The best time of the week it is."

Harriet smiled at her. "And if you were properly taught, do you think you should like to take over the lessons?"

Susan gaped at her. "Like… Like a schoolteacher?"

"Exactly like a schoolteacher," Harriet said, nodding. "Of course, a schoolteacher would earn a proper wage, and they'd need a place to live, Henry."

Henry shot his sister a look of deep gratitude. Trust Harry to know how to fix this. Not that it changed the past, but perhaps they could do right by Susan, and any of her children that came after her.

"I can certainly provide a property on the estate, a cottage with a bit of land, so you can have a garden."

Pippin nodded at him approvingly. "That sounds just what's needed, Mr Stanhope, Lady St Clair. That should settle the past and give Susan a bright future, but I think she needs a bit of a rest first, and perhaps it is time she learned some other lessons, the things her grandma was too afraid to teach her. If you would like that, child?"

"You?" Susan asked Pippin, wide eyed. "You would teach me?"

"If you'd like to. You could come and stay with me. For a month, say. Let the dust settled here and the bruises heal."

Susan looked in astonishment from Pippin to Henry and then to Lord and Lady St Clair, all of whom smiled at her and nodded.

"My word," she said. "My word, I…. How did this happen?"

Dharani shrugged. "The Maiden takes care of her own."

Pippin chuckled and nodded her agreement. "The goddess will provide. She always does, doesn't she, my lord?" she said to Lord Montagu.

Montagu sighed and reached for his wife's hand, giving her the ghost of a smile. "I shall never contradict you on that point, Pippin, believe me. I know better."

Henry laughed, shaking his head. Montagu just shrugged.

"I told you to listen to them, didn't I?"

"So you did," Henry agreed. "So you did."

Chapter 18

Dearest Georgina,

It has been so long since we last saw you. I hope all your family are well and prospering in Scotland, though I do wish you would come and visit us more often.

I expect you have heard by now that Florence is to marry Henry Stanhope. It is a wonderful match and the two of them are so very happy together. I am so pleased for her. How lucky she is to marry a man she loves so well. If only we should all be so fortunate.

I wish I were with you now, Georgie. The wilds of Scotland are exactly where I would love to escape to, but we cannot always escape the future can we? No matter how far we run. Oh dear, all this wedding planning has made me sentimental and now I'm rambling and filling this letter with nonsense. Do write and tell me how you are, and your three brothers, of course. Are they still growing? I wonder the castle can accommodate such big men, and your father too. Are they still driving you to distraction?

—Excerpt of a letter from Miss Grace Weston (daughter of Jemima and Solo Weston, Baron and Baroness Rothborn) to Lady Georgina Anderson (daughter of Ruth and Gordon Anderson, Countess and Earl of Morven.)

26th August 1839, Holbrook House, Sussex.

Henry looked over his shoulder as they walked away from Holbrook House towards the lake.

"He isn't following us," Florence said, laughing at him.

Henry frowned. "I feel like I'm walking into a trap. Your father has been quite jovial all day, and now suggesting we might like to go for a walk as it's such a fine evening?" he added suspiciously.

"Mama spoke to him," Florence said, taking Henry's arm and leaning into him. "We are to be married in two days, after all, and he doesn't wish to trap you. He likes you. Besides, there's no need, I trapped you quite efficiently all by myself."

Henry looked down into her glorious green eyes. His heart did an odd somersault, as it always did when he looked at Florence, and as he suspected it always would.

"So you did," he replied, smiling at her smug expression. "Though I did help."

"Oh, you were a marvellous help," Florence added, and then blushed as she remembered just what he'd been helping her with when her father had interrupted them. She glanced up at him and smiled shyly. "I can't wait to be married, Henry."

"Nor I," he replied, meaning it with every fibre of his being.

He had given Gabriel his solemn vow to behave as the perfect gentleman and take no liberties before the wedding. This was no mean feat as he was discovering Florence was an impatient little devil. He'd spent the entirety of the past week like a cat on hot bricks, wanting to be alone with her whilst praying he could keep his vow. There was a wicked, dark desire in him to tell Gabriel to go to the devil and take what he wanted, but he knew why that was. Lily had jilted him just days before their wedding. Henry had been oblivious, full of excitement for the future, and suddenly his world had been turned on its head. There was an illogical part of him that was terrified history would repeat itself. The jittery, anxious place in his heart that was petrified something would go wrong made him want to claim Florence now, so there could be no backing out. He dreaded every night as much as he welcomed it, certain that he would wake to discover something had happened to stop the marriage, that she'd changed her mind, come to her senses. It was all nonsense. He *knew* it was all nonsense. At least, he knew it in the light of day when she was beside him. In the early hours of the morning, alone in his bed, then his imagination ran riot and his nerves jangled as he counted the hours to their wedding day.

"Let's walk down by the lake," she suggested.

Henry darted her a glance, finding his lips twitch as she smirked at him. No doubt the suspicion in his eyes amused her, the wicked girl. There was a summerhouse down by the lake, as she well knew.

"I'll behave, I promise," she said solemnly.

"Hmmm," Henry replied, uncertain she knew the meaning of the word.

"Well, you knew I was spoiled and wilful, Henry. I really don't see why you look at me so, it's not as though it should come as a shock to you."

He took her hand and drew her to a stop. She turned towards him, tilting her face up in enquiry.

"You're not spoiled in the least, Florence," he said, tracing the elegant line of her jaw with a finger. Every part of him ached for her, to love her as he wanted to, but it was only two more days, and he could be patient. He really could. His skittish heart had lasted this long, it could manage that. "You may have led a privileged life, but it's not spoiled you. You're kind and giving and everything that is good, and I love you."

Florence sighed, staring up at him, and then gave a huff of frustration and stamped her foot. "Two whole days, Henry! How shall I stand it?"

Henry snorted. "Did you really just stamp your foot?"

Florence pouted at him, staring up at him from under her lashes.

"Still think I'm not spoiled?" she whispered, her eyes glittering with mirth. "You will be forced to take me in hand, I'm afraid."

"Apparently so," he murmured, leaning down and nuzzling the sweet spot beneath her ear that he knew made her shiver. "I can't wait."

Florence sighed as his lips traced a path down her neck.

"But we must," she said, the regret in her voice audible.

"Two days," he murmured.

Florence gave a tragic sigh but nodded. "Two days," she agreed.

Henry smiled, gave her a chaste kiss, and promised himself a very large brandy when he got home. If he must be a blasted saint, there ought to be some reward on earth, because heaven seemed a jolly long way off.

29th August 1839, Saxenhurst Hall, Sussex.

Florence looked about the assembled company and felt quite thoroughly, blissfully happy. It had been the perfect day. Her family and some of their closest friends had gathered for the wedding, and the weather had been quite glorious. They had laid the wedding breakfast out beneath the shade of a large rose arbour and the heady scent was quite as intoxicating as the endless bottles of champagne with which Henry had supplied everyone. The company were relaxed and jovial and even her father looked pleased. They had been married in the church next to the Hall, though Florence was very relieved that Henry had overseen the sealing up of the tunnel that led to the house. Secret tunnels were all well and good in mystery stories; in real life they were a lot less welcome.

They realised now that the tunnel had been in his great-great-grandfather's room, but Henry's mother had preferred the view over the front of the house and had claimed it for herself when she'd married his father. Henry said it was likely the last time his mother had got her way about anything, but it explained why it was in the lady of the house's bedroom. It also explained why Henry had never found it, apart from the fact the secret opening was so well hidden in the panelling it was invisible unless you knew it was there. He'd not been so thorough in searching his mother's room as he'd not considered the fact his great-great-grandmother might be involved.

"Of course, if I'd thought for a moment she was as resourceful and determined as Florence, it would have been the first place I'd looked," he'd quipped, which Florence thought was quite the nicest thing he could have said to her.

They were going to spend their wedding night at Saxenhurst and decide later where they would like to go for their honeymoon. Henry had told her about so many fascinating places it would be difficult for her to choose, but there was no rush. Just being here, with him, was adventure enough for the moment though she'd prefer it if no one tried to kill or abduct either of them. Florence stared up at the handsome building that was to become her home. She was looking forward to changing just about everything at Saxenhurst.

"Making plans?" Henry teased her, sliding an arm about her waist.

Florence turned to study his face. "I am. Do you mind?"

"Not in the least. I've no fond memories of this building, I'm afraid. I should welcome a fresh start, with you."

She kissed his cheek. "I'm sorry it wasn't a happy place, but it will be, Henry. I promise. And it's such a lovely building."

"Is it?" Henry asked, frowning. "I suppose it is. On the outside, anyway. I haven't really looked at it objectively before. It's just always been here."

Florence huffed at him. "Then look harder. Saxenhurst has beautiful bones. The outside is perfection and the inside... the inside is like a lovely girl feeling uncomfortable because she's wearing a stupendously ugly dress. It will be unrecognisable by the time I'm done with it. I promise. I'll make it a home for us."

He laughed at her description. "I believe you."

She smiled and reached up to touch his cheek. "I'm so glad you married me, Henry, and you don't mind, do you?"

"Mind what?"

"That I rather pestered you into it."

He shook his head, his hazel eyes warm and full of adoration. "If that is what pestering looks like, I can only hope you keep doing it. I'm very happy, Florence. Happier than I ever dreamed possible, and that's all because of you."

Florence sighed and looked about at her friends and family. "It's been a lovely day, hasn't it? Utterly perfect, only...."

"Only?" Henry repeated, arching an eyebrow at her.

Florence leaned in and whispered in his ear. "When are they going home?"

"Ah." He grinned at her and winked before turning towards the Earl of St Clair.

"Er… Jasper," he said, before clearing his throat. "That thing we discussed…."

"Oh, absolutely!" Jasper sprang to his feet and clapped his hands together. "Ladies and gentlemen if I might have your attention, please. After this wonderful day, I think it only right that we raise one last toast to the bride and groom before we go on our way, and I do hope that you will all return to Holbrook with us where we have a celebration of our own devising so that we may leave the newlyweds in peace. Oh, and we have fireworks!"

There was a cheer and much laughter as everyone raised their glasses once again.

"Henry and Florence!" everyone said, and glasses chinked and there was yet another round of congratulations, but finally, the earl ushered everyone out to their carriages.

Florence bade her parents goodbye, managing not to sob at the bear hug her father gave her, nor blush too fiercely at her mother's whispered last-minute advice.

Finally only the earl remained as he handed his wife up into their carriage.

"Thank you, Jasper. You're a good friend," Henry said, shaking the earl's hand.

Jasper laughed and shook his head. "What are friends for, if not for clearing off unwanted guests on your wedding night? Congratulations, you lucky fellow. I'm looking forward to having you as a neighbour again. Don't let him go off gallivanting for too long, please, Florence. And you are always welcome at Holbrook."

"Thank you, my lord," she said, which Jasper scowled at.

"No, no, call me Jasper. We're practically family, you know. He's like a brother to me, so you must be a sister."

They laughed and waved the carriage off, and finally, blessedly, they were alone.

"Goodness," Florence said, feeling dazed and suddenly rather shy.

"Come along," Henry said, and towed her towards the house.

Florence hurried to keep up, inexplicably nervous. She wondered if she ought to have been in such a hurry to get rid of everyone.

"Must we run?" she panted, as they got to the top of the stairs.

"Yes," Henry replied. "I have a surprise for you, and I'll burst if you don't see it now."

Florence laughed at the obvious excitement in his voice; he seemed like a boy on Christmas morning. They entered his bedroom, and he went at once to a large, red leather box on his bedside table.

"I had it sent down from London. It's been there since I returned. It was being held by my bank for safekeeping, you see."

He gave her a rather sheepish smile and passed the box to her.

"For me?" she asked, wondering what on earth he had locked up so carefully.

He nodded. "It was hidden away safely, where no one could see it or touch it, and it couldn't come to any harm. Rather like my heart. But what is the point, Florence? Why have something so astonishingly beautiful, if you cannot see it and touch it and love it? It's a risk, having it here, but I'd rather know that seeing it makes you happy, even if we lose it, and I'd rather give my heart to you than anyone else, for I know you'll take care of it."

"I will, Henry, I promise," she said, her own heart beating very hard as she clutched the box to her chest. Suddenly it didn't matter a whit what was in the box, only that Henry had trusted her with it.

"Open it, then."

Florence unlatched the clasp of the box and lifted the lid. A gasp escaped her, the shock so profound she almost dropped it.

"Oh, my!"

Inside, nestled on a bed of white silk like blood upon snow, was the biggest gemstone she'd ever seen in her life.

Henry laughed, delighted by her reaction.

"A ruby, almost as big as a hen's egg," she said, remembering the description he'd given when they'd gone for the ill-fated picnic where he'd berated her for worrying about him. "The Indian prince gave it to *you*?"

Henry nodded. "We were friends and, like I said, to him it was a mere trifle."

"Oh, my word, Henry, and you said you'd not be able to buy me jewels!"

"Well, strictly speaking, I didn't buy it. It was given to me."

Florence stared at it, awestruck.

"I'm too terrified to touch it," she admitted. "I don't want to damage it."

"It's not so fragile as all that, love. But it is yours, all yours."

She looked up at Henry, knowing he was not merely speaking of the ruby. "You have my heart too, Henry. You know that, don't you? I knew the moment I saw you that you were the one, though I couldn't have told you why at the time. I can now. You are everything I want, everything I have ever wanted, because you see me, Henry. You love me, even when I'm being irrational or difficult, or behaving badly. You're kind and honest, and I know I can always depend on you, and that you will never belittle me or dismiss my opinions."

He frowned at that and shook his head. "I never will again. I was the biggest fool alive not to listen to you. The stupid thing was... I wanted to."

"You did?" she smiled at him, wondering what he meant by that.

"I was terrified of you, of how you made me feel. I couldn't take my eyes off you, wanted to be near you constantly, and... I rather hated you for making me want you so badly. That's why I was so abominably rude. I'm sorry."

"I'm not," Florence said, setting the box aside. She moved closer to him and slid her arms about his waist. "I'm glad I had to chase you down, Henry Stanhope, for you know I do love a challenge."

He smiled at her words, but there was a look in his eyes that made her breath come faster.

"Um..." she began, racking her brain for something to say.

"Florence, I'd like to take you to bed now."

Oh. It was finally happening. She couldn't breathe. This was ridiculous. Why was she so nervous? She'd been pursuing this man for weeks, desperate for his touch, and now she had it... Lud, but her wretched corset was tight.

"Florence?"

"Um... bed. Yes. Yes, we should certainly, definitely... g-go to bed." She nodded, her head bobbing up and down too fast, staring at the object in question as her pulse thundered in her ears. "Because that's what people do, w-when they're married. They go to bed. Together. It's nighttime, after all, and—"

"Florence?"

"Yes?"

"You're babbling, love."

"I know. I can't make it stop."

"Don't worry. I can."

Henry kissed her, pulling her into his arms and slanting his mouth over hers. For a moment she stood rigid in his embrace, and then all at once the tension drained out of her body as the rightness of the moment wrapped about her as firmly as Henry had. There was no need to be nervous, no need for anxiety. Henry was with her, and that was all that mattered. She was safe, he always made her feel safe. He pulled back, staring down into her eyes for a long moment, searching her expression.

"Better?" he asked.

Florence sighed. "Much. Thank you."

The grin he returned was boyish and pleased and quite irresistible.

"Right, let's get this dress off you," he said, standing back to consider her beautiful gown as though it were one of the labours of Hercules.

It was lovely and delicate, the silk a very pale shade of silver and trimmed with large swathes of Honiton lace. It had also been the very devil to get into.

"Perhaps I should ask Maisie—"

"No." Henry's dark brows drew together, and he shook his head, a look of fierce determination in his eyes. "I learned to sail, I can manage rigging, I can even tie a gunner's knot, so this... this is... I can do this. Turn around."

Florence bit back a smile and turned, waiting as her husband patiently undid buttons and hooks.

"I'm thinking of going into dress design," he muttered. "Because whoever is currently responsible for this mode of fashion is a damned sadist. A woman designed this, surely? No man in their right mind would make it so damned difficult to undress his wife. Not a sane one, anyway."

He chuntered on, grumbling under his breath a bit longer until the dress was completely undone. Florence stepped out of it.

"Now the corset," she said brightly.

Henry groaned.

Florence laughed as he tugged and cursed at the strings of her corset. Perhaps it was nerves, but the situation tickled her immensely and the harder she tried not to laugh the worse it got. He was kneeling behind her now, wrestling with a knot.

"A fine thing, laughing at your husband on your wedding day, tormenting him with this confounded contraption. A plague on all modistes the world over, I hope their whale bones splinter and their strings snap."

Florence slapped a hand over her mouth, hysteria bubbling inside of her. Goodness, but he was funny.

"There!"

Henry's exclamation of triumph was so full of pride that it was the last straw. It was no good, she turned to look at his jubilant expression and laughed until tears ran down her cheeks and she was gasping for breath. And then his hand slid up the back of her knee, her thigh, his finger tracing a delicate line under the curve of her bottom. She made a hiccoughing sound and stopped abruptly.

Henry sent her a devilish look, his eyes glittering with mirth. "Ah, now I have your attention, do I, wife?"

Florence swallowed as he leaned in and nuzzled his face against her stomach. Her chemise was very fine, almost transparent, and his warm breath reached her skin, sending little shivers fluttering over her belly. Both hands were beneath her chemise now, stroking her bottom as Henry kissed his way across to her hip bone.

"Take it off," he commanded.

With hands that were not entirely steady, Florence reached for the hem and pulled it off over her head, leaving her in only her stockings. Henry stared up at her, his gaze raking over her with such heat and admiration it felt like a caress.

"I can't believe you are real," he said, his voice low and rough. "My word, Florence, I don't know what the devil I did to deserve you, or to make you believe that I do at any rate, but... thank you. Thank you for choosing me."

Florence's vision became a little blurry, but she smiled at him.

"You've too many clothes on, Henry," she said. Her voice was a tad wobbly, but she was determined not to be shy and missish. "Do get a move on."

He gave a bark of laughter and got to his feet, shedding clothes at a quite astonishing rate. She had always admired Henry for being so elegantly dressed, never a crease or a hair out of place. The way he discarded his clothes now, flinging them hither and yon with abandon, it was hard to believe it was the same fellow, but she appeared to have motivated him to hurry up with no trouble.

Florence stared as he tugged off his shirt, watching the play of muscle as he moved. She had known he was an athletic sort, but she had not been prepared for the strength of him. He had broad shoulders and powerful arms, and his chest was lightly covered with dark hair that led off in a thin trail which disappeared beneath the waistband of his trousers. His upper body was as tanned as his face, and she wondered where on earth he'd been to wander about with no shirt on under the sun. Her question must have been evident in her eyes, for he smirked at her.

"I did a lot of sailing. There's no one to see if you're hot and take your shirt off when you are miles from shore."

"Oh," she said, at a loss for anything more sensible to say except, "You are very fine, Henry."

"I'm relieved you think so," he said, and her breath caught as he shucked his small clothes and kicked them aside.

Florence stared. Mama hated that girls were not educated as their brothers were and had always been very frank about explaining things most people thought young ladies ought know absolutely nothing about. Sex was no exception and she had prepared Florence for her wedding night with quiet, no-nonsense explanations, and a few medical drawings which she said would make seeing her husband for the first time less of a shock. Well, it had worked… up to a point. That point being that Henry was rather magnificent and looked nothing like a dusty medical drawing.

Good heavens.

Something hot and impatient uncoiled in her belly and Florence swallowed, her mouth suddenly dry.

"Are you going to start babbling again?" he asked her, a mischievous glint in his hazel eyes.

It took a moment for her to unglue her tongue from the roof of her mouth, but she managed a taut nod. "It is a distinct possibility, once I remember… er… words."

He laughed and strode to her, sweeping her up in his arms. "Well, that's the biggest boost to my ego since you kissed me in the shepherd's hut."

Florence squealed at the sensation of being lifted in his arms, his naked body against hers.

"Well, someone had to do *something*," she said, striving for dignity, which became impossible as he dropped her onto the mattress and she bounced, much to her husband's approval from the look in his eyes. "Because it was clear you would never kiss me, no matter how I encouraged you. You were so troublesome, Henry. I thought you would never touch me."

"I didn't dare," he said, climbing—no, *prowling*—across the mattress as he crawled over her.

"Whyever not?" she asked, her breath catching at the look in his eyes.

"Because I knew it would end like this," he murmured, and then his mouth was on hers, his body flush against her body, and the shock of his skin, so hot and hard, pressed against hers, was a delirious pleasure. He lifted his head to gaze at her. "You bewitched me from the first, you little she-devil, but I had to make a show of putting up a fight, at least."

"Utterly pointless," she said, gasping as he trailed hot kisses down her neck, across her collar bone, and made his way to her breast.

"It *was* utterly pointless," he agreed amiably, and then his mouth closed over her breast and any further conversation became impossible. He teased and tortured the tightly furled bud of her nipple before trailing his mouth across the valley between her breasts and starting all over again. When he finally raised his head, Florence was breathing hard.

"Fair warning, I am going to kiss you everywhere," he said, watching her expression intently.

Florence nodded, quite happy with this plan.

His lips quirked. "My, my, not even a little scandalised?"

She shook her head. "Mama warned me," she said, somewhat smug though the words were too breathless to sound sanguine.

"I see," he murmured against her skin. "I shall have to try harder, then."

Privately, Florence thought he did not need to try at all, for it was one thing to be told your husband would likely enjoy kissing you in all sorts of extraordinary places, and quite another to be on the receiving end of those kisses. His hot mouth and silky tongue descended along her body, leaving a cool trail of damp skin. Florence shivered, even though she was burning up, and knowing his destination did not diminish the shock of his mouth upon her, the sensation of his hot tongue swiping over her most private flesh. She cried out, that wanton sound also a revelation, but it was impossible to keep quiet when he did such wicked things.

"The walls are thick, love, don't fret," he said, and she heard the amusement in his voice as he correctly interpreted her concern. "No one will hear, I promise."

She prayed he was right as he returned to his work and any vestige of sanity melted like butter on hot toast. Her concentration diminished, nothing outside of the feel of his mouth upon her registering as he licked and suckled. She grew dizzy with the decadent pleasure of it, her blood somehow effervescent in her veins as the sensation built and built and....

Her hips bucked so hard Henry held her down, his strong hands keeping her in place as she writhed beneath him, waves of such intoxicating joys rolling over her that she could do nothing but submit to it until she was a whimpering puddle of liquid honey, utterly spent.

"Oh my," were the only coherent words she could manage. "Oh... Oh *my*."

Henry crawled back up her body, staring down at her and looking vastly pleased with himself. Well, she could hardly blame him. It had been rather magnificent. She giggled at his expression.

"Stop looking so smug," she murmured, though speaking seemed a great effort.

He shook his head. "You'd best get used to this expression, for I shall be wearing it often."

Florence quirked an eyebrow at him, and he gave a low laugh, moving to lie alongside her.

"Oh, not just for this," he assured her. "But whenever I go anywhere with you, and all the fellows look at me and think *you lucky dog. How the devil did you manage it?*"

He turned her pliant body so that her back was to his chest and nuzzled her neck as his large hand caressed her, cupping her breast before sliding back down her belly between her legs.

Florence gasped as he gently touched her oversensitive skin, sliding into the damp heat and stroking again.

"Henry," she said, a hint of uncertainty in the tone of her voice.

"Shhh," he crooned. "Trust me."

She did, so she subsided, rather astonished as her insides quickened and tightened all over again. Florence gave a soft sob as an ache began deep within her, pleasure and pain and longing. All at once she felt so empty it was unbearable and she pressed back against him, seeking his body, the part of him that would make it right. The hot slide of his arousal against her was only another torment, teasing her as it glided over her needy flesh in languid strokes designed to make her wild.

"*Henry*," she said, his name a definite complaint now, but he only gave a low chuckle and nipped at her ear.

"Not yet, love. It will be easier for you the longer you wait. I don't want to hurt you."

"No, you want to drive me insane," she whined, which only made him bury his face against her neck to hide his laughter.

"Poor darling," he crooned, his voice unsteady.

Perhaps taking pity on her, he turned her onto her back, settling between her thighs.

"Oh, yes, yes, Henry, please…." she begged, beyond shyness or shame or anything but the need to have him inside her.

"Raise your legs," he commanded, groaning as his cock nestled snugly against her. His gaze settled upon hers, his eyes so very dark now. "Kiss me."

Florence did, hungry for his mouth, but he gentled her, slowing everything down again, his hands sliding over her with calm, lazy strokes until she thought she'd run mad. His strong fingers tweaked at her nipple, and she gave a startled cry, the sensation arrowing straight between her legs. That heated place was throbbing now, the gentle caress of his flesh over hers delicious, maddening and inciting but not quite enough.

She stared up at her husband, seeing now that he was not unaffected either. His breathing was laboured, his skin passion-flushed and, as she stared at him, he moved, thrusting inside her. She gasped. Suddenly he was sheathed within her, filling her, and the sensation was overwhelming. Florence gasped and clung to him, disorientated.

"Darling?" he said, and she knew it was a question, but she couldn't find an answer, so she only nodded and held on tight.

He let out a breath of relief and retreated, sliding back inside her and... oh. Oh, that was....

Henry watched her face and whatever he saw must have reassured him, for his mouth quirked up a little. Florence let out a breath of laughter too and then he was kissing her again and it was all a delicious tangle of limbs and emotion and such intimacy that it hardly seemed possible.

"Henry," she said, his name now the extent of her vocabulary. It could be translated to mean, *yes,* and, *oh, yes,* and *I love you,* and *don't stop*, and, *please, please, yes!*

The only thing in the world was the race to the finish, chasing that glittering explosion of joy together, and the only thing more marvellous than how it felt being flung into the darkness as the pleasure overwhelmed her was knowing that Henry was with her. She heard the primitive cry he made, felt his body quake as the climax took him and he spilled inside her, collapsing at last with his chest heaving and his arms still tight about her.

Florence stared up at the ceiling, dazed and giddy with wonder, stroking her hands up and down his sweat-damp back, a ridiculous smile curving over her mouth which she suspected she'd wear for days, perhaps weeks to come. Henry gave a weak laugh and rolled to lie at her side, pulling her into his arms.

"Well," he said, still breathless. "That was worth waiting for, though I'm not certain I could have lasted another day."

Florence gave a helpless snort of amusement and covered her mouth with her hand. It was hardly very ladylike. But Henry only gazed at her, looking as besotted as she felt, and she knew it didn't matter. She could always be herself with this man. She would never need to mind her tongue or worry about being ladylike, because he loved her.

"It certainly was worth waiting for, Henry."

He reached out and stroked her cheek with a finger. "You were worth waiting for too, love. I'm so glad I did, so glad I didn't just marry the next girl who came along but waited for you to come and unearth my poor discarded heart."

"You are a very patient man, Mr Stanhope," she agreed, her chest too full of everything she felt to express it with such pretty words. So instead she kissed him, speaking softly between each tender press of her lips. "I love you. I have loved you. I will always love you."

Florence laid her head on his chest, listening to the strong beat of his heart and thinking about the rather eventful few weeks they'd lived through. An awful lot had happened in a short time.

"No regrets?" he asked, stroking her hair.

"Only one," she said with a sigh.

She looked up to see his quizzical expression.

"I failed my dare," she explained.

"Ah, yes. A pity that, but you set out to accomplish it, and you *did* get me to the altar, which I believe was your intention."

She brightened at that. "Yes. Yes, it was, so... so perhaps it worked, even if I didn't keep to the letter of it."

"I should say it did," he remarked gravely.

"Oh, good." Florence laid her head back down again with a contented sigh as a rumble of laughter vibrated through his chest. "You saved my life," she said quietly.

His arms tightened about her. "You came to save mine. I was rather occupied with fighting that brute off as I fell into the hallway, but I shall never forget the sight of you standing on the landing, the sun slanting across your beautiful face and the pistol glinting in your hand."

Florence made a disgruntled sound. "For all the good it did you. Mama shot him, not me."

"She was protecting you, as you would protect our daughter if it were necessary, and I know if she had not, you would have. You've never needed a dare to get what you wanted, my love. You would dare anything for anyone you cared for. I admire your spirit and your bravery, Florence. I love how bold you are."

Florence sat up and stared down at her husband, a strange sensation in her chest of hope and optimism and excitement for everything to come. "We are going to be disgustingly happy, you do know that?"

He nodded, his expression grave but his eyes alight with pleasure. "I do. Though I insist we intersperse the happiness with the occasional passionate row, for I suspect making up afterwards will be extremely satisfying."

"A deal, Mr Stanhope," she said, sitting up and offering her his hand as if to seal a bargain.

Henry took her hand and shook it. "A deal, Mrs Stanhope."

"Oh," she said, delighted by the sound of that. "Mrs Stanhope. I like that."

Henry's fingers tightened around hers and he tugged her back down until she sprawled across his chest.

"So do I, love," he said with a wicked smile. "So do I."

Epilogue

Dearest Greer,

Of course I want you to come and stay. I miss you dreadfully, though I admit it surprises me to say so, and don't make faces – which I know full well you are doing – because we drive each other to distraction, and you cannot deny it. I am afraid I simply cannot let you come at the moment, though. I am so sorry.

Daire's friends are here, Baron de Ligne and Mr Lane Fox. I'm afraid the baron is rather out of sorts and, much as it pains me, I do not believe it is a suitable household for an unmarried lady. Yes, darling, I know that makes me sound like great Aunt Maud, but truly, I don't mean to be a bore. It's just <u>not</u> a good time. I swear I will send for you the moment they are gone.

Please forgive me.

—Excerpt of a letter from Elspeth Kelburn, Viscountess Roxborough to her sister Miss Greer Cadogan

(daughters of Mrs Bonnie and Mr Jerome Cadogan).

30ᵗʰ August 1839, Holbrook House, Sussex.

"Did anyone see you?" Grace asked nervously as she saw Mr Oak appear from out of the tree line. He was sure of foot, moving so silently through the woodland that she had not heard him approach. Though he was expected, she still experienced a start at the sight of him, her heart giving an anxious jolt, like jumping at a lightning strike in the middle of a storm.

He had got a message to her via one of the laundry maids, demanding she meet him by the stile that followed the path from Holbrook to the village. It was a suitable meeting place as, if anyone saw them, she could say she had just been going to the village on some errand and had run into him by accident.

She felt a little sick and exceedingly nervous at being alone with him. He was just so dreadfully big and fierce and intimidating. Did the man never smile or take a frivolous thought into his head? That she would be bound in wedlock to him soon was so disorientating and bizarre she could hardly take it seriously. It *was* serious, though. The most serious decision of her life. This gruff, unsmiling man would share her life, her bed, her body.

He gave her an impatient glance in answer to her demand. That look spoke volumes about bolting horses and stable doors without him ever opening his mouth, but Grace just put up her chin. The wretched fellow might put her in a quake, but she refused to let him cow her. If she was going to go through with this insane notion of marrying a man she didn't know, she had best learn to stand up to him.

"No," he said with his usual brevity.

Mr Oak would never use a full sentence if one word would do. If possible, he'd just nod or grunt and never open his mouth at all.

She'd been in his company for perhaps a few hours and yet she had gathered this much. He would never be a conversationalist. Any fond imaginings she'd had of cosy winter evenings by the fire, talking to her husband, went up in a proverbial puff of smoke. Well, it was her own fault. She'd been an utter fool and fallen for a pretty face and a man who wielded words like confetti, showering pretty nothings upon her with abandon and then leaving them in the dirt like so much refuse. At least Mr Oak's words seemed sincere, no matter how sparse they were. He had offered her refuge, after all, though she still did not know why.

She stared up at him expectantly. After all, he had summoned her. He frowned down at her, and she fidgeted under the weight of his scrutiny. Somehow, she kept forgetting how large he was and, each time she saw him, it shocked her all over again.

"Well?" she demanded, a little exasperated.

"I gave you one week to speak to your parents. It's been two. I said we would marry after your birthday."

Grace drew in a breath. Well, really, what had she expected?

"That is true, though things have been a little complicated, what with murder and mayhem, and then of course there was Florence's wedding. I didn't want anything to overshadow her happiness."

"And her hearing that you were marrying me would be a big black cloud," he remarked, dry as dust.

She sent him a sharp glance. For a moment it occurred to her to wonder if she'd hurt his feelings with her offhand remark, but he appeared so remote and unreachable it seemed unlikely such a thing were possible. Still, she did not wish to offend him. "I did not mean that. Besides, she already knows I am to marry you. I told her the day you asked me. I just…."

Grace let out a breath and closed her eyes. There was no point in delaying. Indeed, every day she prevaricated was another that would make people question the paternity of her child, and she could not have her baby bear her shame. Everyone must believe she had given herself to this stern, intimidating man. That they had been walking out together and had simply anticipated their vows and nothing more shocking. She was struggling to see how anyone could believe it at all, so delaying would only make matters worse.

"It is my birthday tomorrow. My parents arrive this evening. I will speak to them the day after tomorrow. I will tell them you will call on my father in the afternoon. You have my word."

He gave a taut nod and turned away, obviously intending to walk off without uttering another syllable, the beast.

"Wait."

He stopped at once, turning back to her, his dark gaze unreadable.

"Why are you marrying me?" she asked, hearing the desperate note to her voice. "And don't say your reasons are your own, for that is not the least bit reassuring."

"You want reassurance?" he asked, and she wished there was some way of knowing what the devil he was thinking, for his face was expressionless, neither compassionate nor judgemental.

"It would be nice, yes," she said tartly. "I mean, for all I know, your reasons are so you may lock me in an attic or chop me into bite-sized pieces and feed me to your pigs!"

He reared back at that, and at least this time she could read his thoughts with ease. He looked utterly horrified.

"Christ, you've an imagination. Is this what you think of me?" he demanded.

Grace threw up her hands, exasperated. "No! Well, maybe… but what am I supposed to think? You tell me I *must* marry you when we've barely spoken two words to each other. I want to feel grateful to you for rescuing me, I wish to know the man I am to be bound to for the rest of my life, but you've given me nothing."

He frowned at her, which seemed to be his habitual expression, but she got the impression he was thinking very hard. She watched as he thrust his hands into his pockets, looking strangely peeved.

"Do you have a looking glass?"

"What? Well, yes, of course—"

"There you are, then," he answered, as if that was all the explanation she could possibly desire and turned as though to leave.

"Wait!"

He muttered something under his breath and stared up at the heavens.

"Miss Weston?" he said, or rather growled.

Grace ignored his tone.

"You think me pretty, then?" she asked warily, somehow doubtful that a man like him noticed such things. He seemed far too practical, the sort who would judge a wife by the breadth of her hips and her ability to birth fine, healthy sons. Grace's slight frame would hardly accommodate that kind of thinking.

"Is there a man alive who doesn't?" he asked tersely, kicking at a stone on the path and sending it skittering down the lane.

Grace felt her eyebrows go up, a little taken aback by the irritated demand. "I... I don't know."

He made a sound of such mocking disbelief she did not know what to make of him. She stared at her feet, somehow disheartened to know that was the only thing he found appealing about her. Though what had she expected from him? Some declaration about how the sound of her voice made his heart glad, or her smile lit the room, or that he had heard her laughter and known it was the only sound that had ever made him feel truly happy? She had heard such sweet nonsense before. At least he was honest. He desired her. That was the long and the short of it, and he was prepared to take on another man's bastard to have her. Well, so be it.

She nodded her understanding, but perhaps he saw something resembling hurt or disappointment in her gaze as he spoke again.

"I won't ever hurt you," he said, his voice still gruff but sincere. "I won't berate you with harsh words or lay a hand on you in anger so long as I live. I'll keep you safe, the baby too. I certainly will never lock you up *nor* feed you to my pigs," he added with a curl of his lip.

"Well, that is reassuring," she said with a sigh, grateful for his words.

He shrugged. "There's barely a scrap of meat on you. Hardly a meal for a hungry sow."

Grace bristled. Was he serious, or was that amusement glinting in the depths of his dark eyes? It was impossible to tell.

"Thank you so much for your candour, Mr Oak. I feel *so* much happier about marrying a complete stranger. Good day to you."

She doubted he missed the sarcasm dripping from the words, but she did not care. The unfeeling beast! It was very hard to be grateful to your knight in shining armour when the fellow was great, lumbering oaf.

"Wait."

Grace was so surprised at being called back she almost stumbled. Mr Oak's hand shot out, curving around her upper arm and keeping her upright.

"Steady," he said.

"Thank you," she said, relieved when his large hand released her. The heat of his touch had burned through the fine muslin of her gown, and she felt disconcertingly as if she'd been branded by it.

"Here," he said, appearing oddly uncomfortable as he handed her a small parcel.

It was no bigger than her palm and wrapped in tissue paper. Grace stared it, perplexed for a moment, but accepted it from him. He didn't look at her as she took it, but then glanced sideways at her, jerking his head at the offering.

"For your birthday."

He walked off then, without another word. Grace watched him go, his long strides taking him swiftly out of sight. He was built like his name suggested, strong and of the land, like there was nothing that would bend him. He would stand tall and proud against whatever was thrown at him and never give an inch to anything or anyone, certainly not a wife. Grace sighed wearily and stared down at the parcel. It was carefully wrapped, now she came to look at it, though tied with string not ribbon. She tugged at the neat bow, curious.

Grace made a little sound of surprise as she pulled the paper free. A tiny wooden fox filled the palm of her hand. It was beautifully carved, giving the impression of a sleeping animal that was perhaps still alert, listening out for danger from the way its ears pricked up. Its nose was hidden beneath the elegant curve of its tail, and it was so very lovely that Grace felt tears prick at her eyes and suddenly she was crying. Oh, she had become so ridiculously emotional of late. The slightest thing had her weeping, but this…. Had he made this? Had he made it for *her?*

She stroked a delicate finger over the creature's back, astonished by the delicacy and beauty of the piece. Grace looked up, staring blindly through her tears at the field through which Mr Oak had disappeared, back into the woods and out of sight.

"We did not see that." Florence's voice was firm as Henry turned to look at her. She dragged him out of sight before Grace turned and saw them.

"You might not have, but I did!" Henry protested. "Is that… was that… was that a… *a secret assignation?* Are they…?"

Florence sighed and shook her head. "I swore I wouldn't tell anyone, Henry."

"I'm not anyone, love. I'm your husband. What's more, you've told me nothing that I've not seen with my own eyes. Sterling is my friend, but if he's messing around with Miss Weston—"

"Oh! They're going to be married," Florence said impatiently. "But if you breathe a word of that to another living soul, I shall never forgive you."

Henry gaped at her, so obviously astonished she might have laughed if she didn't feel so wretched for Grace. She wanted her friend to be as happy as she was, but that was not to be.

"Sterling Oak and Miss Grace Weston?" Henry repeated doubtfully, as if trying to make the two names fit in the same sentence and failing.

She could hardly blame him. Grace was as fine, fair, and delicate as a snowdrop, and Sterling Oak… well, he wasn't.

"But when? How? I didn't think they even knew each other past a 'good day,' and 'how do you do?'"

Florence sighed and took her husband's hand.

"I can't tell you. I'm sorry. I want to, but it is not my secret to tell. I can only tell you that Mr Oak's intentions seem to be honourable. I hope they are at any rate," she added under her breath. "You said he's a good fellow beneath that stern exterior, Henry. Tell me it's true. Will he look after Grace?"

To her relief, he did not just give her a glib answer but considered the question in earnest.

"I've been away a long time, love. He was a boy when I left and I cannot yet say we are close friends, though I can say I like and respect him. To answer your question, from what I know of him I would say yes. If Sterling takes a wife, she'll be well cared for. From seeing him at work, I'd say anything he does he does seriously and with attention to detail, with the utmost care." He shrugged. "Does that help?"

Florence leaned into him, smiling up into his handsome face. "Yes, it does. Thank you."

Henry leaned down and kissed her. Florence wrapped her arms about his neck, opening her mouth to him and inviting him in. He gave a low groan as he pulled her closer.

"Oh, lord! Don't, love. We're supposed to be at Holbrook by noon."

Florence shrugged, feeling devilish. As much as she loved seeing her friends and family, she was in no hurry to relinquish her husband's undivided attention. Perhaps that was why she'd insisted they walk.

"So, we'll be a little late," she murmured. She pulled at his hand, dragging him off the path and into the darkness of the woods.

"Here," Henry muttered, guiding her to a secluded place, screened from view by a thicket of blackthorn. He backed her up against a tree and pressed closer.

"Mr Stanhope, you are a very bad man," she whispered, sounding far too pleased for that to be a complaint.

He snorted, cupping her face with his hands. "No, Mrs Stanhope, it's all you. You're a very wicked woman and you've led me off the path, quite literally."

"I know," she said with a heavy sigh, gazing up at him from under thick lashes. "Can you ever forgive me?"

"On one condition," Henry said gravely as his hands dropped to her bottom.

His arousal was obvious, making desire swell inside her in hot, rippling waves.

"What's that, Henry?" she asked breathlessly.

"Don't ever stop."

Next in the Daring Daughters Series....

Their mothers dared all for love.
Just imagine what their daughters will do...

The Trouble with a Dare
Daring Daughters Book 6

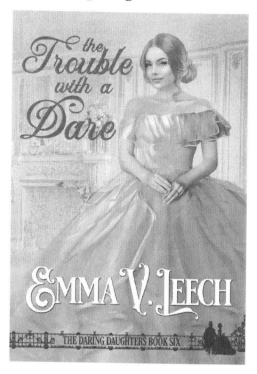

A Desperate Young Lady...

Miss Grace Weston is in trouble. In fact, Miss Weston is in about the worst trouble a young unmarried lady can get herself into. No amount of regretting will change the fact that she was nitwit enough to be seduced by a handsome face and a lot of romantic nonsense. No amount of weeping will change the fact that she will have a child out of wedlock. She will break her parents' hearts and taint the whole family with her shame.

Her folly will forever exclude her from the society to which she belongs...

Unless something extraordinary happens.

A Quiet Man...

Mr Sterling Oak is a man of few words. Raised by his ambitious father to be a gentleman, he treads a line between his family's lowly past and the society that scorns him. An educated farmer with a fine house and dirt beneath his nails, he hides behind silence rather than reveal the man he really is.

When Sterling's keen eye detects that which no one else has yet noticed, something moves him to make the delicately lovely Miss Weston an offer of marriage.

A Devil's Bargain...

Grace does not know what to make of Mr Oak. He appears little more than a big, mannerless brute with a scowl, a man who would rather grunt a reply than endure a conversation. Yet what choice has she? Her husband to be is fierce and intimidating, but Grace is desperate, and not as fragile as her fair beauty may suggest.

Accepting the devil's bargain is probably the second worst mistake of her life...

Unless it turns out to be the beginning of something wonderful.

Keep reading for a sneak peek

Chapter 1

Dear Elspeth,

You do indeed sound like Great Aunt Maud, and I have heard too much from her of late. How unfair that you let your husband's friends come and stay and not your own sister. Your twin, no less! I think you are very unkind to me. You know how tiresome it is when we must visit fusty old relations like Maud. She'll spend the entire time furious because Mother makes her wild, and she'll disapprove of me merely for breathing the same air. I shall go mad, and it's all your fault!

—Excerpt of a letter from Miss Greer Cadogan to her sister Elspeth Kelburn, Viscountess Roxborough (daughters of Mrs Bonnie and Mr Jerome Cadogan).

1st of September 1839, Holbrook House, Sussex.

Grace took a deep breath. This time, she would say the words. She would. She had been trying all morning and now it was growing late. Mr Oak would be here soon to ask her father for her hand in marriage, and she must tell them before he arrived. It was just so... so dreadfully difficult. Her heart was thudding in her chest, so fast she felt giddy and disorientated. She curled her fingers into the silk-covered arm of the sofa, the edge of which she perched upon as if ready to flee. Her mother and father were standing together by the window, admiring the view as they always did when they visited Holbrook. Well, it was a very fine view, and worth admiring.

Oh, get on with it, you coward!

"Mama? P-Papa? There's s-something I need to tell you."

Her parents turned towards her. Her father was still an imposing man, an old soldier with a heroic army record. Baron Rothborn's bearing was as upright and proud as ever, despite the cane he walked with to bolster his injured leg. His arm was about Mama's still slender waist, and she stared up at Papa as if she were a new bride, still besotted after all these years. Grace had wanted that, to look at her husband with such adoration, but she had thrown her chance away on a man who had turned out to be shallow and faithless. Her own fault. She had no one else to blame, therefore she would not complain or make a fuss.

"Yes, love?"

Her father smiled at her, his expression so full of warmth that she faltered, her eyes burning. Grace swallowed as her throat closed and she blinked to hold back the tears, but it was impossible. Her father's smile dimmed, and Mama hurried to sit beside her.

"Grace, what is it? Are you unwell?"

"Oh, Mama, I-I...." The tears fell, a hot slide of shame and regret pouring down her cheeks. "I c-cannot...."

How could she tell them, how could she admit to her stupidity, her reckless idiocy?

"Grace."

She looked up at once, hearing the tone of her father's voice and reacting to it.

"Tell us," he commanded.

"Papa," she said, her throat thick with anxiety. "I am so very s-sorry. You will be so disappointed in me."

"Never," her father said, a thread of anger behind the word. "Never that. Now tell us and we will make it better, whatever it is."

She looked up into the stern face of the man who had always made it better. Whenever she had fallen and grazed her knee, whenever some fair-weather friend had hurt her feelings, or her brother had finally had enough of her and retaliated until she cried... even when *she* had been the naughty one, Papa had always picked her up, always made it better, never mind whether she deserved it. *Not this time,* whispered a voice in her head. *Not this time.*

"I'm g-going to have a baby."

"Oh no," her mother whispered. "Oh... Oh, my love, my Grace."

Her mother pulled her into her arms and held her tight. Grace clung to her, but could not tear her eyes from her father. He was pale, his stance rigid, as though he'd been carved from stone. Grace waited for his reaction.

"Are you certain?" her mother asked, a desperate note to the question. "Perhaps you are mistaken—"

"There's no mistake, Mama," Grace replied dully, wishing with her whole heart it was only that.

"Who?" Papa asked, sounding far too calm.

Grace shook her head. "It does not matter now. He will not marry me and... and I would not have him if he offered."

"Grace," he began, his voice thick with concern.

"No. I'm so sorry, Papa."

Her father closed his eyes, but not before she'd seen the anguish there. He took a deep breath and then held out his arms to her. Grace gave a sob and got to her feet, running into them as she had done as a little girl. She buried her face against his chest and wept as her father's powerful arms closed about her.

"We'll protect you," he promised her, his voice unsteady. "We'll go away. No one will know—"

"No," Grace said, pulling back to look up into his familiar face, seeing his determination to do whatever it took to protect her. "No, Papa. It's…. It is all arranged. I am going to be married."

Grace felt a gentle hand on her cheek and turned to see her mother standing beside them.

"You said the father would not…."

Grace's smile was uncertain. "He won't, but… but someone else will."

It took some time to explain everything, mostly because Grace found it so hard not to cry, but her parents were as patient and understanding as she had known they would be. It had never been fear of retribution or their anger that had stopped her from confessing, but that they would be so upset for her. They would worry for her and, if she were not perfectly happy, it would break their hearts and that would make her utterly wretched. Papa tried to persuade her to confess who the father was, but Grace refused. Why, she was not entirely sure. Not to protect him, for she certainly had no feelings for him now and would rather the world see him for the devil he was. Perhaps it was to protect her parents from having to see the man in society and know there was nothing they could do. Perhaps it was for her own pride, so they would never know she'd been shallow enough to be dazzled by a handsome face and figure.

"But what do you know of this Oak fellow, Grace?" her father asked, bringing her back to the conversation.

She turned to look at him, seeing his brow creased with worry.

"I know he has offered me a lifeline, Papa," she said simply. "He will give me a future, a home, a name for my baby. He has promised he will accept it as his own child, and that he will never hurt either of us."

"What is he *like,* though?" Mama asked. Grace looked down to where her mother's hands clasped one of hers, holding it protectively, as if she could shield her daughter from pain, if she only held on tight enough. "What kind of man is he?"

Grace gave a little laugh. "I… I hardly know. He dresses and sounds like a gentleman—well, most of the time—but he does not have an easy manner. He looks rather fierce and does not seem comfortable in company. Mr Oak is not wealthy, but I believe he is comfortably off and has a fine house, and a prosperous farm. Mr Stanhope regards him well, I believe. They are friends as well as neighbours."

Neither of her parents seemed greatly reassured by this explanation.

"He has been very kind to me," Grace ventured, which was true. For, though his manner was brusque, and he was brutally forthright, he had been kind in his way.

Her father responded to a knock at the door and the butler appeared.

"There is a Mr Oak here to see you, Lord Rothborn."

"Show him in, please," Mama said, before her father could respond.

The butler looked at her father, who nodded in agreement.

"I'd make no decision without you, Jem, love," Papa said, once the butler had closed the door. "Surely you know that."

"Of course I do," Mama replied, looking a little indignant. "I just wanted to save you the trouble of thinking about it."

A look of such understanding passed between them that Grace felt her heart ache, but then there was another knock at the door and her heart was pounding for quite a different reason. Mr Oak strode in, and Grace felt her breath catch. As ever his expression was fierce, his bearing that of a man who would take his leave the moment it was possible. He put her in mind of an untamed horse, ready to bolt at a moment's notice. A stallion, she corrected herself as she took in the sight of him, remembering all over again how large he was, a lifetime of working the farm having built powerful shoulders and strong limbs.

"My Lord Rothborn, Lady Rothborn," he said, giving a stiff bow. "I don't doubt you're not best pleased to see me, but I mean to do right by Miss Weston. I know I'm not what you'd look for in a son-in-law, but—"

"Why would we not be pleased to see you, Mr Oak?" her mother asked, her grey eyes watchful.

Mr Oak faltered and Grace had the distinct impression that he had rehearsed his part carefully and her mother's question had thrown him off balance. He stared, his dark brows knit.

"She's with child," he said, blunt as ever.

Grace winced.

He noticed her reaction and his face darkened further. "I'm sorry for it, but we must marry at once."

"Yes, but… the child is not yours," her mother persisted, staring at him with interest.

Mr Oak's gaze flew to Grace, full of accusation.

"What did you tell them?" he demanded.

Grace gazed at him in shock, so surprised by his obvious annoyance that for a moment she did not respond. "The truth, of course. Surely you did not think I would let them believe the worst of you?"

His face darkened. "Better that," he said, his voice terse as he turned on her father. "She was taken advantage of and if I ever discover who the bas—*blackguard* was, he'll wish he'd never been born. Miss Weston had no defence against such a man, no experience to—"

"I know that," her father cut in sharply, his expression rapt as he stared at Mr Oak. "And if there is any retribution to be meted out, I shall be first in line, but you... you would have had us think *you* responsible, perhaps even suspect you of being a fortune hunter?"

Grace watched, startled to see colour flare high on Mr Oak's cheeks.

"I'm hardly penniless," he said, his jaw tight.

Interest flickered in her father's eyes and his voice was apologetic when he spoke. "I meant no disrespect, I assure you. I only wish to understand why you would do so."

"None taken," Mr Oak replied gruffly. "And because Miss Weston needs protecting."

To her surprise, a look of mingled pain and regret settled upon her father's strong features. "I am culpable, and I know it."

"No!" Grace exclaimed in horror.

"I did not mean to imply...." Mr Oak said, both he and Grace speaking at once.

Her father held up his hand. "You did not need to imply, Mr Oak, and Grace, darling, if I had guarded you closer—"

"You ought not need to keep watch on me every hour of the day, Papa! I am young, perhaps, but not a child. You both taught me right from wrong, and I knew I was doing wrong and I... I am ashamed. I regret it very, very deeply, but the deed was mine, the decision was mine, and I kept the truth from you. I sneaked out of the house at night. What were you to do? Lock me in my room?"

Her father sat heavily, one hand going to his thigh and the war wound that still caused him such pain. He massaged the muscle, his expression taut.

"Why did you seek to protect our daughter in such a way?" her mother asked him. She sat with her hands clasped in her lap, self-contained and calm although her eyes were still red from weeping. Her voice was gentle, as though soothing a fractious child. "Why not just tell us the truth? Grace has a significant dowry. Surely you knew we'd think the worst of you, believe that you had seduced her on purpose?"

"I didn't know about the dowry, and I don't care either way. I'll not have you treat her as though she's done wrong when she knew no better," Mr Oak said, folding his arms.

He looked belligerent and unhappy, and Grace fidgeted on the sofa, uncomfortable in the unsettling atmosphere, quite at a loss for what to think of her husband–to–be. It touched her that he would defend her so fiercely, but she found herself irritated that he believed her so witless. With a rueful sigh, she had to admit that she had hardly given him reason to think anything else.

Her parents studied Mr Oak with open curiosity, clearly as baffled by him as Grace.

"I assure you, we know where the blame lies, and we would never punish Grace for it," her father said, his gaze never leaving Mr Oak.

Grace frowned at that. Much as she wished to believe she was blameless, she knew that was not true. Yes, she had been naïve and foolish, but she had known it was reckless. At the time, she hadn't cared. She'd been idiotic enough to believe herself in love and that it was all terribly romantic, when it had been nothing but childish infatuation. It was astonishing how quickly one grew up and saw the world in a new light when calamity struck.

"She's almost three months gone. We'd best marry as soon as possible. There'll be talk either way, but it won't do to linger," Mr Oak said.

Grace jolted in shock, and her mother gave a little gasp at his bald statement.

Mr Oak heard her intake of breath and frowned. "It's best we speak plainly, my lady, but I am sorry if I offend you."

"I am not offended," her mother said softly, turning to stare at Grace. "Why? Why did you not tell me at once, darling? Did you not feel you could confide in me? Did you think I would not understand?"

"No!" Grace said, helpless as her eyes burned, and the tears began all over again. "I knew I could confide in you, but I knew I would break your hearts, and I... I could not bear it."

She blinked as a handkerchief came into view. Mr Oak held it out to her, his expression as dark and forbidding as always, despite the kind gesture.

"Well then," her mother said, forcing a tremulous smile. "I think we had best get to know our new son-in-law. I, for one, believe I am going to like him very much."

Despite everything, Grace almost laughed at the sceptical look in Mr Oak's eyes. He looked quite horrified by that statement. No doubt because it appeared to mean he must endure a conversation, of all things. Grace bit her lip and sent him an apologetic glance. He held her gaze, but his expression was as unreadable as always.

"Grace, darling, why don't you run upstairs and freshen up? I shall ring for tea, and Papa and I shall have a quiet chat with Mr Oak."

Grace looked to Mr Oak, wondering if it was safe to leave him alone with them or if the prospect would have him changing his mind and running for the hills. He gave a brief nod and some of the tension left her shoulders. Of course he wouldn't back out. Mr Oak might be an odd duck, but he was an honourable man. Of that much, she was certain.

Chapter 2

Dear Arabella,

*I am to be married to Mr Oak. He is a
stranger to me, and I am sick with nerves.
I have not the slightest right to repine, for
this situation is entirely of my own
making, but I am afraid all the same. He is
so very stern and unsmiling and though I
wish to be a good wife to him, I do not
know what he will expect from me.*

*I know Bainbridge was quite a stranger to
you too, Arabella, and that your marriage
is wonderfully happy, so if you have any
advice for me, I beg you will be frank and
tell me how I ought to go on.*

**Excerpt of a letter from Miss Grace
Weston (daughter of Solo and Jemima
Weston, Baron and Baroness
Rothborn) to Arabella Grenville, The
Most Hon'ble, The Marchioness of
Bainbridge (daughter of Mrs Alice and
Mr Nathanial Hunt).**

1st of September 1839, Holbrook House Estate, Sussex.

Sterling took his time walking back to the farm, watching his feet move across the ground rather than looking ahead. The distance between him and his home did not seem far enough, and he concentrated on his boots as they took him closer, sometimes through meadow grass that swished and whispered against his legs, sometimes upon the dirt road, moving around puddles from last night's shower of rain.

His mind was as tangled as a bramble bush, catching momentarily on something before breaking free with a painful wrench. Hopes and fears and a dozen or more questions tumbled through his mind. Each one clamoured for his attention, but he seemed unable to concentrate on any one of them. All he could see was Miss Weston's wide, grey eyes when he had first told her he would marry her. It had been the way she had looked at him when he had promised to treat her baby as his own child. She had been so terribly afraid—terrified—but then she had stared at him, stared at him as if she could see into his heart, into the farthest corners of his soul, and she had believed him.

Grace Weston had put her trust in him.

Of course, she had come back days later and asked if he meant to lock her in an attic or feed her to his pigs, but still. He snorted at the memory. Good Lord, but she had an imagination. His mother would not like that. His mother would not like any of this one bit, for anything resembling a creative spirit would be ruthlessly crushed. In her eyes, imagination was fatal flaw, one that Sterling had learned to keep hidden since he'd realised how she feared it, and Grace....

He sucked in a breath. No. Grace would not be crushed, Grace would not have her love of beautiful things and her flights of fancy chased from her. He would protect her from that.

The knowledge that he must face his mother now, tell her he was getting married, and that she must move out of his home and into the cottage he had prepared for her was not pleasant. There would be a scene. Sterling hated scenes. Especially *her* scenes. Her spiteful fury rubbed against his skin like nettle rash, making him all on edge. It made him want to lash out, but he'd never lose his temper with a woman, not even one who provoked him beyond bearing. There was no escaping it, though. Things were going to be hard enough for Grace without having in his mother living in the same house as her.

Grace.

The name suited to perfection. She was slim and elegant as a reed, her features so delicate they might have been painted on porcelain. Sterling had ventured to consider what it might be like to take her in his arms and found the idea so audacious he wondered if he would ever dare, or if he'd be able to do it without bruising her. She seemed too delicate for such earthly pleasures.

Without really considering where he was going, he found himself in the churchyard next to Saxenhurst Hall, standing by his father's headstone. He laid a hand on the thick engraved stone, warm from the afternoon sun.

"You'd like her," he said. "But Mother is going to pitch a fit the likes of which we've not seen since you sent me to university."

Sterling smiled and let out a slow breath before giving the headstone a fond pat.

"Ah, well. Worrying is for the living. You rest easy, Pa."

Though he knew he was killing time, putting off the inevitable, he took the long way around. He checked fences as he went, spoke a few words to some of his men and bided for a time at the hogpound talking to the duchess. She was a fine fat pig, a Gloucestershire Old Spot, and Sterling enjoyed conversing with her, reckoning her the most intelligent creature on the entire farm. The duchess huffed out a sigh, her vast belly quivering and one large ear twitching as she reclined in all her porcine majesty on a bed of clean straw.

"I know, I know," Sterling grumbled. "There's no need to nag me. I'm going."

He took off his hat, tapping it against his thigh as he turned to look at the farm. It was a handsome building, very ancient in places, though his father had modernised it a good deal, extending it and making it grander. It had belonged to his mother's family. Her father had been the local squire and father had courted her with high hopes, his ambitious eye on moving up in the world. Sterling laughed softly. *The best laid schemes of mice and men.*

He walked to the front door and pushed it open, setting his hat aside and ensuring his best boots weren't mucky after his excursion through the yard. He made his way to the kitchen, knowing this was where he'd find his mother. His housekeeper and cook, Mrs Gladwish, looked up as he walked in, her pinched expression telling him that his mother had been there for some time.

"Ma, you've staff for that," Sterling said, though he knew he was wasting his breath.

His mother looked up from the pot she was stirring, one chapped, work-worn hand fisted on her hip. "I can't stop you wasting good money on help we don't need, but I'll earn my keep."

Sterling bit back the words brewing on his tongue. It was as well to pick his battles, and there was a fine war to wage before dinnertime. He'd do well not to get distracted by the same old skirmishes.

"A word," he said shortly, jerking his head towards the door.

His mother's pale blue eyes narrowed upon him. "Out with it, then."

Sterling sighed. She had to make every blasted conversation a battle of wills.

"In private," he said, and walked out before she could find something else to say.

She made him wait, but Sterling had grown too used to having his patience tested to allow that to set up his bristles. Instead, he considered the parlour, with its large inglenook fireplace and low, timbered ceiling. This was the oldest part of the house and, even though they'd lowered the floor, Sterling could not stand without crooking his neck. He liked it all the same. It was familiar and cosy.

He tried to imagine Grace here. Grace, with her slender white hands and eyes full of clouds. Would she despise him? Gratitude could fester into loathing, and resentment for all she had lost might make her bitter. He'd been to university, been educated like a gentleman, and could pass in that world if he must, but he always felt an imposter, as if at any moment someone would point at him and turn him out for aping his betters. Not that he thought them his betters. He counted Henry Stanhope and Cassius Cadogan, Viscount Oakley, as friends. Sterling had been at Oxford with Cassius, and he'd never felt himself anything but his equal, but a woman might not look at him that way. Ladies—that fine breed of creature that his father had wished him to marry—did *not* look at him that way. If they looked hard, they saw his rough edges and heard the slight burr to his accent that crept in now and then, the words and phrases his father told him to forget, but that slipped out when he was either fully at ease or all on edge.

The door opened and his mother came in, still wiping her hands on a cloth she tucked under her apron strings. She folded her arms. It was all nicely calculated to remind him of what they were and their place in the pecking order. Once upon a time, his mother had been a handsome woman and might have married up. It had been her father's ambition, but the old squire's extravagance and folly had given her a disgust of anything she deemed unnecessary or frivolous. So here she was, in a gown that was years old and faded, still working in the kitchens, and wearing an apron as though Sterling needed her to work her fingers to the bone to keep bread on the table. *Not now,* he told himself.

"I'm to be married."

Sterling did not consider himself a spiteful man, but there was a small part of him that enjoyed the jolt of shock that made her eyes grow wide and her mouth drop open. She had not expected that.

"Who?" she demanded.

"No one you know."

"No. You've not thought to bring her to meet your mother. Ashamed, are you?"

There was a glint of satisfaction in her eyes at that.

Sterling sighed. "No. If I'd thought the meeting would bring either of you pleasure, I would have introduced her, but it won't. Truth is, I did not expect to be marrying yet, but she's breeding, so it's sooner rather than later."

His mother looked truly shocked now, and no wonder. Sterling had always despised men who took advantage, sowing their seed with neither care nor judgment. That his mother would believe him such a man rankled, but he was damned if she would judge Grace for her predicament. Things would be hard enough for his wife as it was.

His wife.

The word warmed him, steeling him against his mother's disapproval, a fierce desire to protect Grace from her situation, from the world, motivating him to stand firm, as it had from the first.

His mother strode towards him, eyes flashing with anger, and raised her hand to strike him. Sterling caught her wrist, holding her off with ease. It was the first time she'd tried that in a long time. He'd not allowed her to strike him since he'd returned from university for the first time. His father had been so proud, glowing with it, and she had done her utmost to take the shine from the day.

"Stupid," she spat at him. "What kind of slattern are you taking to wife?"

He tamped down the spark of anger at hearing Grace spoken of so. It was hardly a surprise that she would do her best to rile him.

"She's no slattern, and I'll not hear you speak of her so. You'll treat her kindly, Ma, or else."

"Or else," she sneered, her colour high as she wrenched her wrist free of his grasp and turned away from him. "I'd thought you'd more sense but no, for all your fancy education and fine talk, you've been caught by the oldest trick in the book."

Sterling snorted at that, unable to help the faint smile that tugged at his lips. "I doubt anyone else will see it that way. They'd believe it was me did the catching. Took some persuading before her father saw me as anything but a fortune hunter."

She spun around at that, eyebrows tugging down, deep furrows in her brow.

He paused, drawing the moment out, uncertain if he was enjoying tormenting her for once or just delaying the inevitable explosion. "She's a lady, with a generous dowry. Daughter of Baron Rothborn."

His mother's breath caught, her hand pressing flat against her heart, and for an awful moment Sterling wondered if he'd gone too far, if the shock was too much for her and she'd drop dead with outrage. Instead, she closed her eyes, and then she laughed.

It was not a pleasant sound. Sterling bore it, though he longed to run from the room, to leave her and her spite and her need to drain everything of colour and pleasure and reduce it to bread and water and some puritanical desire for the ordinary.

"Well, you've done your father proud," she said, and he heard the mockery in the words. "You've married above yourself. You'll have a bride who's too fine to lift a finger, who'll want more than you can give, and you'll make yourself a laughingstock. She'll despise you and make a fool of you, and that's all that will come of this fine day's work. Your children will be just as your father made you, neither fish nor fowl, never satisfied with a good day's work and a warm hearth, always wanting more."

Sterling snapped, the fear that there was truth in what she said making the words explode from him with more force than he'd intended.

"Better that than being too afraid to want anything at all!"

She just snorted, shaking her head at him in disgust. "I know what happens when people get greedy, when they want more. My father ruined us, and forced me to marry your father, but I was glad of it. I thought he was a sensible man, thought he had a prosperous farm and a good living, and we'd be content. But no, just another dreamer, like my own father. Your pa thought he was marrying into a fine family, more fool him. My father left us nothing but this house and tricked your pa out of my dowry. Reckon he hated me for that. I thought he'd put his dreams aside after, but he was more determined than ever, determined you'd be a gentleman, putting ideas in your head. What nonsense! You can't make a silk purse out of a sow's ear. 'Tis better to be satisfied with your place, with what you've got, but you'll learn…. You'll see. You'll see, when I'm right."

Sterling let her rant, let the words wash over him as he always did. He was stone, impermeable, and nothing she said could touch him. It had taken years to build the walls about himself, to shut off his feelings and keep his hopes and dreams hidden away. It didn't always work. She knew just where he was most vulnerable and always struck with precision, but he never gave her the satisfaction of knowing she'd hurt him. His face was a mask, and he knew it made her wild that he would not argue with her like his father had done. He could not deny a moment of satisfaction once she'd finally run out of breath, and he said his own piece.

"I've readied the cottage. You can borrow Annie and Jeb to help you move out. A house can't have two mistresses, and my wife will have the running of this one. It's no longer your affair. Tell Mrs Gladwish I'll eat at The Lamb tonight."

Sterling walked out and closed the door on her before she recovered from the shock of his words. He wished he could take more pleasure in her obvious disbelief, but he was not a vindictive man, despite so many years of provocation. This had been his mother's home all her life, and he knew it was a hard thing he did, but she had made her choices. If he let her remain in the house, she would make Grace's life a living hell, and that he would not allow.

Pre-Order your copy here: The Trouble with a Dare

The Peculiar Ladies who started it all…

Girls Who Dare – The exciting series from Emma V Leech, the multi-award-winning, Amazon Top 10 romance writer behind the Rogues & Gentlemen series.

Inside every wallflower is the beating heart of a lioness, a passionate individual willing to risk all for their dream, if only they can find the courage to begin. When these overlooked girls make a pact to change their lives, anything can happen.

Eleven girls – Eleven dares in a hat. Twelves stories of passion. Who will dare to risk it all?

To Dare a Duke
Girls Who Dare Book 1

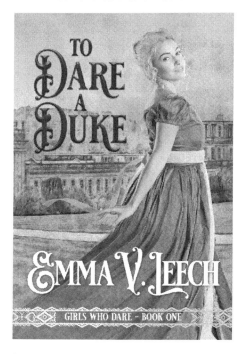

Dreams of true love and happy ever afters

Dreams of love are all well and good, but all Prunella Chuffington-Smythe wants is to publish her novel. Marriage at the price of her independence is something she will not consider. Having tasted success writing under a false name in The Lady's Weekly Review, her alter ego is attaining notoriety and fame and Prue rather likes it.

A Duty that must be endured

Robert Adolphus, The Duke of Bedwin, is in no hurry to marry, he's done it once and repeating that disaster is the last thing he desires. Yet, an heir is a necessary evil for a duke and one he cannot shirk. A dark reputation precedes him though, his first wife may have died young, but the scandals the beautiful, vivacious and spiteful creature supplied the ton have not. A wife must be found. A wife who is neither beautiful nor vivacious but sweet and dull, and certain to stay out of trouble.

Dared to do something drastic

The sudden interest of a certain dastardly duke is as bewildering as it is unwelcome. She'll not throw her ambitions aside to marry a scoundrel just as her plans for self-sufficiency and freedom are coming to fruition. Surely showing the man she's not actually the meek little wallflower he is looking for should be enough to put paid to his intentions? When Prue is dared by her friends to do something drastic, it seems the perfect opportunity to kill two birds.

However, Prue cannot help being intrigued by the rogue who has inspired so many of her romances. Ordinarily, he plays the part of handsome rake, set on destroying her plucky heroine. But is he really the villain of the piece this time, or could he be the hero?

Finding out will be dangerous, but it just might inspire her greatest story yet.

To Dare a Duke

Also check out Emma's regency romance series, Rogues & Gentlemen. Available now!

The Rogue
Rogues & Gentlemen Book 1

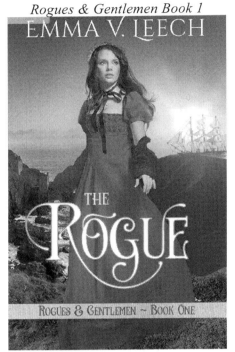

The notorious Rogue that began it all.

Set in Cornwall, 1815. Wild, untamed and isolated.

Lawlessness is the order of the day and smuggling is rife.

Henrietta always felt most at home in the wilds of the outdoors but even she had no idea how the mysterious and untamed would sweep her away in a moment.

Bewitched by his wicked blue eyes

Henrietta Morton knows to look the other way when the free trading 'gentlemen' are at work.
Yet when a notorious pirate bursts into her local village shop, she

can avert her eyes no more. Bewitched by his wicked blue eyes, a moment of insanity follows as Henrietta hides the handsome fugitive from the Militia.

Her reward is a kiss, lingering and unforgettable.

In his haste to flee, the handsome pirate drops a letter, a letter that lays bare a tale of betrayal. When Henrietta's father gives her hand in marriage to a wealthy and villainous nobleman in return for the payment of his debts, she becomes desperate.

Blackmailing a pirate may be her only hope for freedom.

**** Warning: This book contains the most notorious rogue of all of Cornwall and, on occasion, is highly likely to include some mild sweating or descriptive sex scenes. ****

Free to read on *Kindle Unlimited*: The Rogue

Interested in a Regency Romance with a twist?

A Dog in a Doublet
The Regency Romance Mysteries Book 2

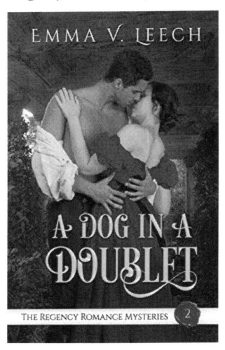

A man with a past

Harry Browning was a motherless guttersnipe, and the morning he came across the elderly Alexander Preston, The Viscount Stamford, clinging to a sheer rock face, he didn't believe in fate. But the fates have plans for Harry whether he believes or not, and he's not entirely sure he likes them.

As a reward for his bravery, and in an unusual moment of charity, miserly Lord Stamford takes him on. He is taught to read, to manage the vast and crumbling estate, and to behave like a gentleman, but Harry knows that this is something he will never truly be.

Already running from a dark past, his future is becoming increasingly complex as he finds himself caught in a tangled web of jealousy and revenge.

A feisty young maiden

Temptation, in the form of the lovely Lady Clarinda Bow, is a constant threat to his peace of mind, enticing him to be something he isn't. But when the old man dies, his will makes a surprising demand, and the fates might just give Harry the chance to have everything he ever desired, including Clara, if only he dares.

And as those close to the Preston family begin to die, Harry may not have any choice.

A Dog in a Doublet

Lose yourself in Emma's paranormal world with The French Vampire Legend series…..

The Key to Erebus
The French Vampire Legend Book 1

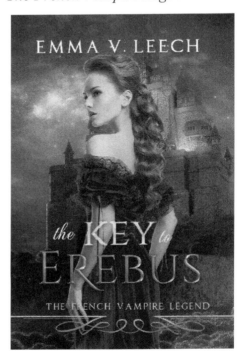

The truth can kill you.

Taken away as a small child, from a life where vampires, the Fae, and other mythical creatures are real and treacherous, the beautiful young witch, Jéhenne Corbeaux is totally unprepared when she returns to rural France to live with her eccentric Grandmother.

Thrown headlong into a world she knows nothing about she seeks to learn the truth about herself, uncovering secrets more shocking than anything she could ever have imagined and finding that she is by no means powerless to protect the ones she loves.

Despite her Gran's dire warnings, she is inexorably drawn to the dark and terrifying figure of Corvus, an ancient vampire and master of the vast Albinus family.

Jéhenne is about to find her answers and discover that, not only is Corvus far more dangerous than she could ever imagine, but that he holds much more than the key to her heart …

Now available at your favourite retailer.

The Key to Erebus

Check out Emma's exciting fantasy series with hailed by Kirkus Reviews as "An enchanting fantasy with a likable heroine, romantic intrigue, and clever narrative flourishes."

The Dark Prince
The French Fae Legend Book 1

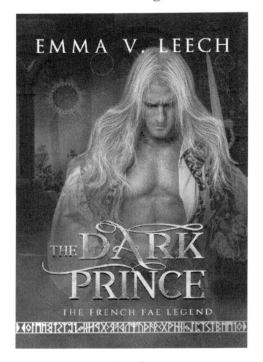

Two Fae Princes
One Human Woman
And a world ready to tear them all apart

Laen Braed is Prince of the Dark fae, with a temper and reputation to match his black eyes, and a heart that despises the human race. When he is sent back through the forbidden gates between realms to retrieve an ancient fae artifact, he returns home with far more than he bargained for.

Corin Albrecht, the most powerful Elven Prince ever born. His golden eyes are rumoured to be a gift from the gods, and destiny is calling him. With a love for the human world that runs deep, his friendship with Laen is being torn apart by his prejudices.

Océane DeBeauvoir is an artist and bookbinder who has always relied on her lively imagination to get her through an unhappy and uneventful life. A jewelled dagger put on display at a nearby museum hits the headlines with speculation of another race, the Fae. But the discovery also inspires Océane to create an extraordinary piece of art that cannot be confined to the pages of a book.

With two powerful men vying for her attention and their friendship stretched to the breaking point, the only question that remains...who is truly The Dark Prince.

The man of your dreams is coming...or is it your nightmares he visits? Find out in Book One of The French Fae Legend.

Available now to read at your favourite retailer

The Dark Prince

Want more Emma?

If you enjoyed this book, please support this indie author and take a moment to leave a few words in a review. *Thank you!*

To be kept informed of special offers and free deals (which I do regularly) follow me on
https://www.bookbub.com/authors/emma-v-leech

To find out more and to get news and sneak peeks of the first chapter of upcoming works, go to my website and sign up for the newsletter.

http://www.emmavleech.com/

Come and join the fans in my Facebook group for news, info and exciting discussion...

Emma's Book Club

Emma V Leech

Or Follow me here......

http://viewauthor.at/EmmaVLeechAmazon

Emma's Twitter page

Can't get your fill of Historical Romance? Do you crave stories with passion and red hot chemistry?

If the answer is yes, have I got the group for you!

Come join myself and other awesome authors in our Facebook group

Historical Harlots

Be the first to know about exclusive giveaways, chat with amazing HistRom authors, lots of raunchy shenanigans and more!

Historical Harlots Facebook Group

Made in the USA
Las Vegas, NV
13 July 2024

92218296R20178